THE TELS ...

WINNER for genre fiction in the
Writer's Digest's International Book Awards.

Second place for science fiction,
ForeWord Magazine's Book of the Year.

"Dallas writer Paul Black makes his first foray into the world of science fiction with *The Tels*. It's a HIGHLY ORIGINAL novel set in the near future and IT MOVES AT LIGHTNING SPEED. Mr. Black has quite an imagination and puts it to good use. The MIND-BENDING PLOT centers on Jonathan Kortel, who is approached by a shadowy group called the Tels, who covet his telekinetic gifts. The ENSUING ACTION IS BIZARRE enough to read like something straight out of *The X-Files*."

~ *Steve Powers, Dallas Morning News*

"(*The Tels*) is WRITTEN SO SPLENDIDLY, at times I forgot I was reading science fiction – with the emphasis on fiction. The characters are realistic, and the hero is someone you relate to, worry about and wonder if he's going to be able to cope with the reality that is set before him. This is definitely ONE OF THE BEST SCIENCE FICTION NOVELS I've ever read...the BOOK IS REMARKABLE."

~ *Marilyn Meredith, Writer's Digest's 11th Annual Book Awards*

"...*Soulware* was a BRILLIANTLY EMBROIDERED STORY, mixing science and fiction in a plausible and entertaining way...I absolutely LOVED THIS BOOK!"

~ *Ismael Manzano, G-POP.net*

"...it moves at lightning speed.
Mr. Black has quite an imagination
and puts it to good use."

"I agreed to review the science fiction novel, *The Tels*, by Paul Black as a favor to my coworkers.... I had expected the handoff to come attached with a few snickers...I was truly amazed by how wrong I was. Not only did I enjoy the book, I almost feel guilty that I got to review it...The book is the kind of science fiction that I like to read, not weighed down with technical jargon that the average person cannot understand....The prose is light and catchy, but did not fail to bring the emotional hammer down when necessary. It's a character-driven piece that was WORTH EVERY SECOND I'D SPENT ON IT...get your hands on a copy of *The Tels*."

~ *Ismael Manzano, G-POP.net*

"The biggest complaint about science fiction is that there is always too much science and not enough fiction. In *The Tels* Paul Black brilliantly combines the two in a novel that is almost too plausible...Blending sex, government intrigue and a new reality aren't easy tasks but Black is up to it. Taking us for a ride through a world totally different from our own and yet with the emotions that aren't going to change between now and 2109...*The Tels* DOESN'T LET GO AND STAYS WITH YOU AFTER THE LAST PAGE."

~ *Leslie Rigoulot, Continental Features Syndicate*

"...I was totally hooked...*The Tels* is for anyone who loves a good story, with LOTS OF ACTION AND GREAT CHARACTERS."

~ *Jo Ann Holt, OC Tribune*

"A riveting science fiction novel...an imaginatively skilled storyteller."

"This story by Paul Black is as STRONG AND WELL WRITTEN as any of the stories of my heroes: Robert Heinlein, Isaac Asimov, Andre Norton, or Anne McCaffrey. He is one of those writers that we who worship this genre look for every time we pick up the novel of an author who is new to us...The CHARACTERS COME ALIVE for you. You feel right along with them. You can believe the decisions they make. And best of all, nothing is clear-cut and simple. The story brings us to a strong ending while leaving us with the desire for more...I recommend *The Tels* to every lover of sci-fi. Good work, Paul! Welcome to my bookshelves!"

~ *John Strange, thecityweb.com*

"Paul Black's ENGAGING PROSE promises big things for the future...."

~ *Writer's Notes Magazine*

"...a GREAT READ, full of suspense and action...."

~ *Dallas Entertainment Guide*

"A RIVETING science fiction novel by a gifted author...*The Tels* would prove a popular addition to any community library Science Fiction collection and documents Paul Black as an IMAGINATIVELY SKILLED STORYTELLER of the first order. Also very highly recommended is the newly published second volume in the *Tels* series, *Soulware*, which continues the adventures of Jonathan Kortel in the world of tomorrow."

~ *Midwest Book Review*

"*The Tels* is an addictive read...
manages to capture the reader in the first
ten pages...*The Tels* has it all."

"Black rises above the Trekkie laser tag spastics found in your typical sci-fi novels resting on the grocery store racks. His sensibilities broaden from machine gun testosterone to discreet fatherhood, from errant sexuality to wry humor. HE DELIVERS A CHARGE OF VENTURE RARELY FOUND IN FIRST-TIME WRITERS. And *THE TELS* HITS THE MARK as a solid adventure serial, leaving you hanging for the next publication."

~ *Brian Adams, Collegian*

"*The Tels* is an ADDICTIVE READ from first-time novelist Paul Black, a promising new storyteller on the sci-fi scene. He manages to capture the reader in the first ten pages. He introduces us to a set of intriguing characters in a totally believable possible future. There is a grittiness and sensuality to his writing that pours out of every word in the book. Whether it's his description of the preparation of a good meal, the seduction of a beautiful woman, or a fight to the death, *THE TELS* HAS IT ALL. Even people who don't read sci-fi will want to read this book. The action is great and would make one hell of a movie. Is Hollywood listening? Paul Black has a winner on his hands. I can hardly wait for the next installment."

~ *Cynthia A., About Towne, ITCN*

"*Soulware* doesn't miss a beat as it continues Jonathan's story, the story of his quest to find out exactly who he really is and why the Tels are so interested in him. The ending makes it clear that there's more to come, and readers who crave their science-fiction with a hint of weirdness can look forward to the next book in the series."

~ *Steve Powers, Dallas Morning News*

Other books by Paul Black

THE TELS

SOULWARE

Aimee
Thanks for all
your support!

nexus point

PAUL BLACK

NOVEL INSTINCTS

This book is a work of fiction. Names, characters, places and incidents either are products of the author's imagination or are used fictitiously. Any resemblance to actual events or locations or persons, living or dead, is entirely coincidental.

NOVEL INSTINCTS PUBLISHING
1400 Turtle Creek Blvd. Suite 140
Dallas, Texas 75207
www.novelinstincts.com

This book can be ordered on the web at most major retail sites including www.barnesandnoble.com and www.amazon.com.

ISBN: 978-0-9726007-3-6
Library of Congress Control Number: 2007921887
Printed in the United States of America.
10 9 8 7 6 5 4 3 2 1

Cover photo: PhotoDisc /GettyOne.
Author photo by Michael Barley.

AUTHOR'S NOTE The Tels series is a trilogy. *Nexus Point* is the third and final book, and the reader should know that it is the continuation of Jonathan Kortel's struggle as he continues his quest to discover his power and destiny. Even though *Nexus Point* can stand alone as an independent novel, I would highly recommend that you read books one and two (*The Tels* and *Soulware*) so as to fully enjoy the story from its beginning. If you're a fan of the first books, thanks for coming back and please enjoy the read. But if you are new to the Tels, get ready to enter a fascinating world that could be just around the corner.

FOR MOM AND DAD

~

I think about you everyday.

BOOK THREE

NEXUS POINT

WASHINGTON, D.C., 2113

How 'bout that beer? 1

THE Elbow Room was the kind of bar that accepted its clientele like an old whore: as long as your credit was clean, you were welcomed. Bixx usually liked being at the Room, but right now there were a billion other places she'd rather be.

Rocket folded his arms angrily across his chest. "The guy is not coming."

"He is," Kreet said, "trust me. And if you say that again–"

"Will you two *please* shut up!" Bixx slammed her beer onto the table and a dollop of its head backflipped onto Rocket's fries.

"So much for my genetically tailored taste." Rocket watched the foam spread over the remnants of his "Mico's Special."

"If you believe all that biofood crap," Kreet said. "Besides, you're almost done with these." He reached over with his fork and harpooned the largest fry in the basket. "I don't taste anything different," he mumbled between chews.

"God, Kreet, how old are you?" Sanjiv asked.

"He's 22, though you'd never know it," Bixx said dryly. "And Kreet, you couldn't tell anyway. Those French fries have been prepared to Rocket's genetic profile.... Only he can taste the difference. The resequencing protocols they use today are light years past what they had five years ago."

"Thank you, Miss Genius, for enlightening us." Kreet kicked back the last of his beer.

Rocket took Bixx's hand and his forefinger stroked her knuckles. It was his special sign of affection, reserved for moments when he felt her feelings might have been bruised. She had come to appreciate its meaning, but more often than not it was unwarranted.

"Don't let Kreet bust you," Rocket said. He squeezed her hand. "You're smarter than all of us combined.... You can't help it that your pretty little head is so full of data."

Besides being overly protective, Rocket could say things that didn't come out quite the way he wanted. This was an aspect of his personality that Bixx didn't appreciate. She shot him a harsh look.

"So, Kreet," Sanjiv said, "tell me again: how did you make the connection with Kortel?"

Kreet smiled over the rim of his beer and placed the glass on the table. "I didn't," he answered. He wiped his mouth with the back of his hand.

Sanjiv blinked. "Then how did you?–"

"Kortel was brought to me...sort of. I had this guy approach me last month. He said he'd heard of my concept and could help me deliver it." Suddenly Kreet's glass slid toward the half-filled pitcher, ran around the bowl of mixed nuts and parked itself between two empty glasses.

The others stared at Kreet.

"What?" he asked.

"Man, are you that stupid?" Rocket said. "We're in public."

"Fuck the normals," Kreet replied. "What's the sense of having this power if I can't use it now and then? Nobody saw it anyway."

"You've got a lot to learn, Kreet," Sanjiv said. "Our gift isn't something to take for granted."

"Thanks *dad*, I'll remember that when I get to be your age."

Sanjiv scanned the table for sympathetic eyes. "You see, everybody? This is the reason I moved out."

"Kreet, give it a rest," Bixx said. "Now tell us, who was this guy who contacted you?" She was always skeptical of Kreet's schemes. They were notorious for being void of detail and full of shit.

"He wouldn't say. Said it would expose him too much."

"So, you just went along with whatever he said?"

Kreet leveled a cold glare. "He had incept points...with the matching responder data."

"Did Kortel answer?" Sanjiv asked.

Kreet swung his attitude around. "No. But do you really think a guy like him would leave an answer?"

"So basically you have no idea if he's going to show or not?" Bixx asked.

Kreet hesitated. "If you're wanting some kind of confirmation, I don't have one. So, no, I don't know for sure if he's showing. But this guy had *Russian* responder data. Do you know how hard that is to get?"

"Of course I do," Bixx said. "Remember, I'm from Moscow?" Even though she hadn't been back to Russia for over two years, Bixx knew that Kreet's contact had to be very jacked to have that kind of information. At least, she'd never known anyone like this. Sure, you could get most anything on the Russian black net, but nothing approaching what this guy was offering. Kreet could be a real asshole sometimes, but she had to admit that the little shit could always find an angle. Still, she was tired of his constant dissing, and was seriously thinking about breaching Tel protocol and giving Kreet a headache he wouldn't forget.

"Funny thing about this guy," Kreet said. "He didn't look well. I mean, it wasn't like he was sick or something – more like he had been through some kind of brain trauma."

"Why do you say that?" Sanjiv asked.

"Because he had this face twitch, and sometimes he'd lose his focus. Said he'd been in an accident. And I could tell that part of his hair and scalp had been regen'd."

"How could you tell that?" Rocket asked.

"Because he had red hair like yours, and a small part of it didn't match perfectly. It was right here." Kreet pointed to the top right side of his head, just past his hairline.

"Prefrontal cortex," Bixx said.

"So?" Kreet asked.

"Memory, dumbass."

Sanjiv whistled.

"He was a Tel, right?" Rocket asked.

"No, he was a normal," Kreet said sarcastically. "And he knew right where Jonathan Kortel was, imagine that."

"Fuck off you little–"

"Enough!" Bixx yelled. Her glass of beer exploded. It radiated outward to a 2-foot diameter, then froze in midspray before it collapsed to half its size. The sphere of beer and glass shards moved slowly around Bixx's arm and past the edge of the table, where it fell and splattered across the the Elbow's scarred wooden floor.

They held their positions, as if all their atoms had locked down.

"Ah, sorry guys," Bixx said.

Rocket leaned into her ear. "Easy, baby," he whispered. "Let's get it under control, okay?" He squeezed her hand, this time to the point of pain.

"I'm not going to say this again," Sanjiv said sternly. "All of you have to get control of your displacement fields...especially in public. I can't always be here to stop things from getting out of control." A small drop of blood was hanging from Sanjiv's nostril. He quickly wiped it away with a napkin.

"I'm sorry," Bixx said, "but you two" – she motioned to Kreet and Rocket – "have got to cool this bullshit between you.... It just pisses me off."

Rocket began to protest, but Bixx raised her hand and silenced him.

"Look, don't you guys get it?" she said. "I'll bet this guy who approached Kreet has been erased before, and he's had restoration surgery to the area of the brain that controls recent memory. The Agency doesn't do that for just anyone. This guy is, or was, a major player."

"Well," Sanjiv said, "whoever he is, he gave Kreet the right incepts." He pointed past the table to the front of the bar. "Look who just walked in."

Bixx turned and watched Jonathan Kortel walk through the crowded bar with the ease of a man who knew his power. It wasn't an arrogant swagger, just a gait that had a strength to it she couldn't define. It was like he knew fate had dealt him a strong hand, but he hadn't made peace with it yet. To look at him now, dressed in a simple black T-shirt, jeans and a pair of work boots – Russian-made by the looks of them – she would have never guessed that he was the most powerful telekinetic in their culture. The rumor was that he was faster than the speed of light. Since their gift was based on the mind's ability to manipulate gravity, that meant Jonathan Kortel, in theory, could bend time.

Even though she and the others had worked with him before, Bixx was still struck at how unassuming he appeared. He was basically average in height, build and looks, although there was a kind of gritty handsomeness about him that came more from the way he carried himself than his physical features. His calm expression didn't waver as he approached their table.

"Jonathan," Kreet said as he stood, which was odd to Bixx, since Kreet rarely showed respect to anyone. By default, Kreet had always been their group's leader, but Bixx figured he must still be gun-shy because of Kortel's "lesson" two years prior. Kreet had challenged Kortel, and had ended up on the losing end of his anger. Everyone at the table followed Kreet's lead.

Kortel, mindful of his unusual discharge effect, didn't offer his hand. He acknowledged Kreet with a nod, then met everyone's face with a slight smile. He stopped at Bixx. Rocket nudged her foot under the table.

"Hello, Bixx," he said.

Bixx choked a little on her spit. Her hello came out more like, *hell no*, colored by more of her Russian accent than she liked. It always surfaced when she was nervous.

Kreet rolled his eyes.

"You've cut your hair since the last time I saw you," Kortel noted. "It looks good on you."

"Thank you," Bixx said. "You look, ah...good too."

Kortel smiled past the moment's awkwardness and gestured for everyone to sit.

Bixx took her seat, mentally chastising herself for being so nervous. Rocket affectionately patted her knee under the table, but the gesture didn't help much.

Kreet had gone to some lengths to assemble the old group. Bixx and Rocket still lived in the warehouse space they had once all shared, but Kreet and Sanjiv had moved out, complaining they couldn't take the other anymore. The only one missing from the gang that had helped Kortel seek his revenge on their Agency's leadership was Sasha. The scuttle Bixx had heard was that Sasha and Kortel had had a baby, but she never put much credence in that story. Kortel didn't seem the type who would have allowed something like that to happen. Besides, Kortel had been a fugitive for the last two years, moving from safe house to safe house throughout the Russian Tel network. He had taken a big risk coming back to New America, and an even bigger one to meet with them. Kreet must have laid down some good bullshit to get him to the table. Or maybe it had been something more important, because in truth, nothing Kreet could have said would have brought Kortel out of hiding. As Kortel took his seat, Bixx wondered what that might have been.

Kreet gestured to the pitcher in front of him. "Would you like a beer?"

"No, thanks." Kortel shot a quick glance over his shoulder, and Bixx got the sense that he was checking his surroundings. His view wasn't spooked – just a cool, professional assessment that appeared ingrained, almost instinctive. He brought his attention around and planted it on Kreet, who flinched reflexively.

"Thanks for entertaining my request, Jonathan," Kreet said. "I hope you like this bar. When you said you wanted to meet in public, I figured this place was as good as any."

"That's okay, Kreet. I owe you guys my life." He smiled at Sanjiv when he said this. "The bar's fine. I don't like meeting in private....You never know what to expect, and things can get *difficult* sometimes." He glanced about again. "So," he said, relaxing somewhat and eyeing the set-up of beers, "what's on your mind?"

"It's like I said in my message. We have an idea that we think demands your attention. Oh, and thanks for clearing that channel. You were hard enough to find without the Russians running interference."

Kortel's eyes narrowed, and the worry lines at the sides of his temples deepened.

Kreet continued. "There are a lot of us who think it's time for a...a change."

"A change?" Kortel repeated.

"Yeah, you know. A change...in leadership."

"I think we just had one a few years ago, didn't we?" He laughed slightly, but instantly quelled it. His lean face hardened, and his attention focused on Kreet again.

"No doubt. The Agency is still trying to put the pieces together after your, ah, adjusting of its structure."

Bixx reflected on the events of two years ago. She couldn't really blame Kortel for seeking revenge on their Agency's leadership. In their quest to create a supertel, Jeffrey Trumble and Cyril Takeda had conducted covert experiments on Kortel that could have disabled or even killed him. It wasn't a secret that the two leaders had become dangerous with their judgments; yet in spite of the evidence that showed Kortel had acted in self-defense, most of the Tel world believed he had gone too far. The deaths of Trumble and Takeda had sent the New American Agency into a freefall, and Kortel into exile. He was still considered unstable and dangerous, although looking at him across the table, Bixx thought that the man who many felt was the next step in evolution was beginning to look older than his years.

"Well, Kreet, lay it out...what's this shift you want?"

Kreet searched his friends' faces. "We're sick of our existence," he said flatly.

Kortel's face didn't register the statement. He casually folded his arms.

"And there's a lot of us throughout the culture that feel the same way," Kreet said.

Kortel sniffed slightly, like he was fighting back the start of a summer cold.

"Look, we don't mind being Tels. What we mind is the secrecy." Kreet leaned forward. "We want to come out."

Kortel cleared his throat. "Impossible. We've been under since the 1950s. You can't just spring the knowledge of our existence on the outer world. For one, you'd never get all the other Agencies to go along. Hell, good luck finding the Pac Rim guys. And the Arabs? After Hawaii, they're so buried, they'll never come out of the desert."

"Not with the right advance team."

Kortel shook his head. "Kreet, this idea of yours is too dangerous. You know the score. If the Tel culture came out of hiding, the normals would hunt us down...and I'd bet the general public would probably never hear about it." He pushed back from the table, clearly done with the meeting.

"There is a way," Kreet declared.

"Look, I've seen the data. If we came out, the world would freak, and we'd either be hunted or worshipped. In either case, the model's conclusions always end up the same: a tougher life than we have now. And you know something? What we have isn't really that bad. We already have influence over most of the world. If we came out, we'd lose all of that. No, your idea is flat-out stupid."

Bixx's heart sank. She looked at Rocket and could tell he was crushed, too. When this was over, she was going to personally kick Kreet's ass. He should have explained the concept further instead of jumping right to the end.

"It's not my idea," Kreet said.

Kortel eyed him. "It's still too dangerous." There was a sharp edge of frustration in his voice, and Bixx was beginning to wonder if those bulletins about Kortel were true.

"What if I said the leader of the advance team would be someone as powerful as you?"

Kortel quickly stood, his anger now on full display. "Kreet, you're really trying my patience. I took a big gamble meeting with you. Who is this person?"

Kreet met Kortel's glare. "Zvara."

The anger in Kortel's face fell away. Bixx could tell Kreet's declaration had hit him like a Light-Force weapon. He slowly sank into his chair.

The bar was filled with the usual noise of the end of a work week, but around their table, a silence had descended that seemed custom-made for the moment. A cold shiver spiked through Bixx's nerves.

"Now," Kreet said, as the pitcher of beer and a fresh glass floated into his hands. "How 'bout that beer?"

Summertime. 2

JONATHAN Kortel awoke to the muffled turbine blast of a police gunship executing a vertical liftoff. As it slowly rose past his hotel window, it filled the bedroom with a chaotic strobe of red and blue lights. Thank God D.C. still prohibited the cops from turning on their sirens before they reached a thousand feet. The room fell back into a patchwork of deep shadows, and an odious tinge of spent fuel flooded his nostrils. Kortel could hear the transition blast as the craft cleared the roofline, followed by its sirens Dopplering away as it turned north and headed toward the main part of the city. When his eyes adjusted, he found himself on the bed, still dressed. He couldn't remember coming back to the room, but there was much he couldn't remember lately...this being one of the minor items.

He walked into the bathroom. Its lights greeted him, slowly intensifying like he had taken the stage for an audience of one.

"Water, please. Cool."

Clean water had become such a commodity in the D.C. Zone that even the cheapest hotels had regulator chips built into their faucets.

"Cooler, please." The flow chilled slightly, and Kortel splashed two cupped handfuls against his face. He filled for a third but stopped when he again noted a tremor in his left hand. He grabbed a towel and patted his face dry. Checking the mirror, he picked at the white flecks of cotton stuck in his stubble. No micro-dryers. "Cheap fucking hotel."

Then he remembered. Zvara. Sitting at the desk, he asked for the windows to lighten. It took a moment, but eventually they did, and as he gazed at the backside of his nation's co-capital, he thought about Kreet's idea. Or was it Zvara's? Did it matter? Hell yes.

Kreet, who was basically a kid, was dumb like a fox. But he could never pull off something as bold as coming out. There had been others who had tried, but they never got further than the back page of the tabloids. The Agency's disinformation machine made sure of that. And Kreet's source for the incepts sure sounded like James McCarris. The red hair, the tall build. But it was the regen'd scalp that nailed it for Kortel. He thought he had erased McCarris two years ago, but leave it to the Agency and their army of biosurgeons to put McCarris's memory back together again. At least some of it. Kortel seriously doubted that the Agency's biolab boys could have actually restored all of his memory (though it depended how much McCarris had backed up), but it didn't matter now. If McCarris had wanted to kill Kortel, he would have already done it. But why help Kreet? Maybe the biolab boys hadn't restored McCarris's memory.... Maybe they had just given him something new altogether.

He glanced at his watch. *1:32 a.m.*

Kreet's plan seemed too clean to have been conceived alone. The more Kortel thought about it, the more the Zvara connection made sense. Maybe Zvara had made contact with Kreet. Or at least someone close to Zvara had. Like an associate or a relative. Shit, of course.

Kortel reached across the table and grabbed his netpad. He tapped in coordinate numbers he hadn't thought of for a long time. The pad's tiny screen flared, and the NetTel logo faded in, danced out of view, and the word CONNECTED appeared in a trendy typeface Kortel had never seen. A young woman's dark face pixeled up. Her cropped tangle of thick ebony curls framed lustrous green eyes that blinked back at Kortel. Her full lips parted into a wary smile.

"Jonathan Kortel, we were wondering when you'd surface. I assume this is a secure transmission?"

"Hello, Sasha. It's been a long time. And yes, we're tight as tight can get." He passed the tip of his finger across her image, and the screen's organics quivered.

"You're looking good, at least what I can see of you."

Kortel placed the netpad on the desk. "Is that better?"

"A little. But nothing beats being there in person." Her smile widened.

"You've cut your hair. Seems it's the trend these days."

"Pardon, you broke up a little?"

"Your hair...it looks nice short."

"Yeah, it was time to cut it. My summer 'do, you know." She tentatively looked off camera, then back. "So, Jonathan, how have you been?" Her voice had shifted to a quieter tone, and the smile had contorted into a mask of tight concern.

"All right, considering my situation."

"We heard that you had reentered the country, direct from Moscow into Chicago?"

"Yeah, I had some unfinished business to take care of."

"That was very risky."

"It was worth it."

"And did you take care of your business?"

"You could say that."

An awkward silence fell between them, and Sasha glanced away again.

"Why are you in Washington?" she asked. "It's still not safe for you to be back in the country."

"You tell me."

Sasha's face screwed into a question. "I only know you're there, not why. Look, Jonathan, we keep tabs on you, but we're not going to interfere. It's your choice if you want to take risks or not."

"That's comforting."

"You didn't answer my question."

"I met with your old gang."

"You mean Kreet and Rocket and everyone?"

"Just like old times. I think Kreet still holds a torch for you."

"Please, I just had dinner. Why were you meeting with them?"

"Kreet has a new plan for our culture to come out. Says he's assembling a front team that should be able to convince the other agencies. He wants me to be its number-two man."

Sasha shook her head; her curls fell across her face. She brushed them back with a swipe of her hand. "He's been dreaming this ever since I met him. Who does he have as the leader for this team?"

Kortel smiled for the first time. "Your father."

Sasha laughed nervously and folded her arms. "That's rich. How can he get a hold of him when I can't?"

Kortel shrugged. "Hard to say. I was kind of hoping you'd know something about all this."

Sasha shook her head again. "I wish I did. Believe me, I'd warn Dad about Kreet."

"Kreet says it was all your father's idea."

This statement seemed to make Sasha's face pale slightly, edging her already beautiful dark skin to a lighter shade of coffee. She bit her lip and looked off camera again.

"Oh, yeah, there's something else," Kortel said.

Sasha looked back, and there was tightness at the corners of her eyes.

"Seems I didn't erase James McCarris all that well."

"How do you know that?" she asked, her voice cracking a bit.

"'Cause I think he's the one working for your father. He gave Kreet my incept points. You and your father are the only two people who had them."

"Jonathan, I...I don't know what to say. Could your Russian contact have?–"

"No! There's no way Dmitri would have known. And even if he did, he would have never told anyone."

Silence settled over them again.

"Jonathan," Sasha said finally, "what can I do to help?"

Kortel sighed. "Find your dad for me, before Kreet takes this plan any further."

Sasha's image stared out from the screen, and Kortel flashed back to the first time he had met her father. Armando Zvara had ascended through the ranks of the Agency, attaining the head role at the unprecedented age of 34. His power level was legendary, speculated to be near 8 on a scale of 10. The leadership then, as they had with Kortel, tried to enhance Zvara's power level with bioaugmentation, but the experiments had failed. It had been rumored that he had requested a change of identity and appearance, and that he had assumed the role of a Recruiter. He was living a simpler life, until a file caught his attention and sent him on a trip to Chicago, where he discovered a young man whose telekinetic power surpassed even his.

"Jonathan?"

"Hmm?"

Sasha's eyes were staring from the screen. "Where did you go?"

"Oh, I was just remembering the first time I met your father...back when I ran my old restaurant."

Sasha smiled. "You know he thinks of you like a son."

Kortel thought for a moment. "Sasha, my mother and

father disappeared with Hawaii." He rubbed his temple. "Still, it's a nice thought."

"So what are you going to do next? Go back to Russia?"

"No," he said, stretching, "I think I'm here for a while."

"That's a dangerous choice. You're not seriously considering Kreet's proposal are you?"

"That all depends."

"On what?"

"If your father's involved or not."

"Look, let me find my dad. You, on the other hand, should keep your head low. There're still those who were loyal to Trumble and Takeda who would like to see you erased...permanently." Sasha hesitated. "I was wondering..." she looked down, as if her next question caused her pain. She raised her eyes. "How are you feeling? Have the side effects gotten any better?"

Kortel glanced at his left hand. "Some days are worse than others. But overall it's not bad."

"That's not what I asked–"

"Sasha...concentrate on finding your dad, okay?"

She nodded, then asked, "And you, what are you going to do?"

Kortel hesitated. "Go find an old friend."

Sasha's face filled with worry. "You're not going to–"

"Sasha! This is my life, remember? I'm sick of hiding. Besides, maybe it's time we did come out."

Sasha sighed heavily. She stared for a second. "Promise me you'll be careful?"

Kortel grinned. "It's good to see you again, Sasha."

She smiled hesitantly, and the connection ended.

The lights of the D.C. Zone wavered in the thermals of the torrid summer night. In the distance, dark smoke rose like a nebula between two office towers, the latest gang act that made up the background for local news. Kortel looked down at his left hand. It had begun to spasm again. He was getting used to different parts of his body acting of their own volition. This month, it had been his left hand. Six months ago, his right thigh, which had a bad tendency to twitch violently when he had made love to Reza. Probably why she never returned his messages. He reached for his jacket draped over the back of the chair. Digging through its inside breast pocket, he fished out the pneumatic infuser. He turned the tiny device over in his hand and clicked it on. A barely audible hum reflected off the window's ballistic plexi as it sequenced through its presets. He raised the infuser to his neck and released 10 ccs of justification.

And exhaled.

The sound of the device hitting the parquet echoed somewhere at the edge of his hearing. He rubbed at the injection point, feeling for the welt that always came.

"Music, please. Low volume. Jazz. Smooth. Miles Davis if you have it." He coughed slightly and tasted the metallic bitterness that had become his friend.

The room obeyed with Davis's rendition of *Summertime* from *Porgy and Bess*– one of his favorites from the mid 20th century. The weight behind his eyes grew, and the lights of the Zone blurred even more.

To old friends. 3

THE instrument panel of Kortel's rental chattered as it dialogued with the vast Interway network of the Southwest. Kortel had given up trying to figure out how to turn off the audio feature. The vehicle exited the four-lane grid and slipped onto a feeder road that paralleled the artery for roughly a mile. The panel chattered again, and the system disengaged from the Interway link.

"You are leaving the Interway; manual control has been engaged," a silky female voice declared. Probably created from some bioengineer's wet dream and selected by the previous user. Salesman.

Kortel drove the rental down the feeder and into the parking area of a store that had seen better centuries. It looked like the TP Mart Corporation had barely retrofitted the place to modern standards. A vestige of prehistoric corporate culture still hung from a pole near the road. The sign was riddled with rusted dents that Kortel concluded had come from a time when people could actually carry a projectile-firing weapon. The image of a winged horse was still visible in its center, and the word MOBIL hung below on its own appendage. Kortel parked in the first available space, slipping between a classic ethanol burner and one of the new Familiagons advertised on the Net. *Big Enough for Everyone Important to You* was its tagline. Kortel thought it didn't look any bigger than his rental, but what did he know? He didn't have kids or a family.

An old man sat on the store's front porch next to a big white metal box with two chrome doors on the front. He was leaning against the wall, balancing in an oddly constructed canvas chair. His work shirt looked as if it hadn't seen a hydromat for a decade, and his sleeves were rolled tight above the elbows. Dust was caked like icing over the bottoms of his khaki pants and boots. Through the filtered lens of Kortel's optics, the guy could have been right out of a Dorothea Lang photo. Kortel glanced over his shoulder at the small island of sage and rusting metal columns near the feeder road. The geezer laughed.

"Pumps," he said. He cleared his throat and spat.

"Excuse me?" Kortel asked.

The old man laughed again. "Pumps. Gas pumps."

"Yeah, I know."

"Before the damn Biolution." He spat again.

Kortel shut the door to his rental, and its organics hissed into their dormant settings. He walked over to the old man, who was eyeing him from under the tattered rim of a long-billed cap. The same winged horse logo was stitched in faded pink on its brim. Kortel figured it had been bright red once.

"If you're thirsty," he said, "we got sodas, beer, even Hydrolike. We ain't got much biofood, if you're into that." He gave Kortel the once-over. "You look like you would be."

"Thanks," Kortel said. "But what I really need are some directions."

"Nice glasses. Those Sori Wear?"

"Yeah."

"They dialogue with your netpad?"

"Of course."

"Then why don't they tell you where to go?"

"Because..." Kortel said. He removed the optics and slipped them into the breast pocket of his shirt. "Where I'm going is a little out of the way." He had to squint now to see the old man.

"New Mexico isn't out of the way *enough*?"

"It is, but I'm going somewhere pretty remote."

"Where you're standing is about as remote as it gets."

"Right." Kortel was growing impatient.

"Where're you headed?" the old man asked.

"Chaco Canyon."

"Bitch to get to."

"I'm actually going to a place near there, by the north side of the park."

Another spit, deep and full of mucus. "Nothin' there except rattlers and jackrabbits, and not much of either."

Kortel nodded. "My pad says to take 509 north from San Mateo, then west on 9. But that's where it gets confusing."

"You'll need to take 57 up through the park. After that, you're on your own."

"Thanks." Kortel started walking toward the store's entrance.

"What's out there?"

"A friend, I hope." Kortel pulled the screen door open.

"You serious?"

"He's a bit of a loner." An elderly Native American woman shuffled out of the store. She was wrapped in a brightly colored shawl, even though the store's thermometer registered nearly 90 degrees. Kortel held the door for her.

"You'll need more than that rental."

Kortel sighed and walked back. The screen door shut with a crack. "Let me guess," he said, shielding his eyes from the bright New Mexico sun. "You've got the perfect car for the trip, right?"

The old man hocked another loogie, then grinned with all the teeth he had left.

* * *

Kortel glanced at the clock in the dash. *7:57 p.m.* Its dial was cracked and faded to the point that if the sun hit it just right, Kortel had to practically lean out the window to read it. He hadn't driven a pre-Interway truck since his uncle's back in Carbondale. That was 17 years ago. What the old man had rented him had probably been top of the line in the middle of the previous century. It was a Ford Super Duty supposedly retrofitted to run on ethanol, but it didn't smell like it. With the windows down, it smelled faintly like driving through a giant fart. Maybe it ran on methanol. The geezer had given him four extra cans full of whatever it used and said he might need them "just in case." In case of what, Kortel wondered. They rattled together, bungeed as tight as he could get them against the back of the cab.

* * *

It had been 20 minutes since Kortel had exited the boundary of the national park, and he was still headed north, sort of. He had left Highway 57 two cigarettes back and was now on the remains of a dirt road that reminded him of the paths his uncle had driven when he was checking natural gas wells for the government. Since Kortel hadn't driven a manual much, he found it hard to keep the wheels in line with the ruts. He glanced at his netpad, but it had gone off-line an hour ago after it bounced against the dash when the Super Duty hit a large hole.

Kortel was driving on instinct. The land looked familiar, but he had only been here once, and that was years ago when his friend had moved to New Mexico to "concentrate on his priorities." The turnoff still had the little sign with the carved marijuana leaves, but time had weathered it so that they could barely be made out. The ruts emptied onto another two-lane paved road. He didn't remember this.

"What the hell?" Kortel glanced at his netpad.

The truck's compass seemed to be working; it indicated the two-laner ran due east and west.

"Go west, young man." Kortel swung the Super Duty onto the road and headed toward the sunset, which was beginning to explode under a line of dark clouds on the horizon. He slipped on the Soris and set them for max. Their optics set up a faux eclipse spot that tracked with both the movement of the truck and his head. Occasionally it would lag, and the sun would form a corona to the side of it, but the Soris's filters adjusted and kept the glare to a minimum. After about 20 miles of nothing but sage and scrub oak, Kortel saw the lights of a building off to the right.

The last rays of the sunset were dying as he parked the Super Duty in front of *Deuces Wild, New Mexico's Hottest VidSlots*. Kortel seriously doubted that Deuces had been wild anytime in the last 20 years, but what the hell: he was lost, tired, and maybe due for a change of luck.

Deuces was the kind of relic that had vanished along with the landline and postal service. Gambling had become the exclusive domain of the big multinationals, and to find a casino with pre-holo vidslots was, well, quaint. Making his way past the watchful gaze of the gift shop girl, Kortel entered a carpeted room packed with vidslot machines. They were all playing a different theme, and the room's low ceiling and wood paneling made them blend into a hideous white noise that was probably 10 decibels above code. The carpet crunched under his boots with a texture brewed from thousands of parties, and it had an effluvium that Kortel swore he could feel on his skin. He found the bar and pulled up a stool. The bartender actually asked, "What'll it be?"

"Oban, over ice, please," Kortel answered.

"One J&B coming up."

Kortel was too beat to argue. Besides, this Native American was as big as the Super Duty, and Kortel didn't want to get sideways with him. The last time he had pissed off an Indian, his whole life changed, and people got killed. He took a sip of the J&B and winced.

"How's the drink?" the guy asked.

Swallowing, Kortel gave a reluctant thumbs-up.

The guy forced a grin, then lumbered to the other end of the bar. It was a classic: long, wooden, a huge mirror, and ancient neon liquor signs that either barely flickered hints of their products' former glory or else hung forlornly in darkness. The guy walked up to the other bartender, who had his back turned to talk to a semi-cute girl with rooster-spiked hair. Kortel felt a presence at his side.

"Reading?"

He turned to find a slightly heavier, older version of his high school girlfriend. He knew this girl couldn't be her, but the resemblance was still enough to make him choke a little on his drink. The girl wore bright pink lipstick with a hue that shifted as she moved, and her dress was a cheap off-the-rack type that filled the Trump Marts. His girlfriend had died in his senior year, but if she had lived, Kortel thought she might have looked like this girl.

"Excuse me?" he asked.

"I asked if you were *needing*...service?"

"Well, I, uh..." Kortel had never been propositioned so overtly before. "Look, all I need is this drink right now."

The pink lips smiled. "Not *that* kind of service. Net service!" She produced a tiny version of his netpad. It looked like it could have come out of a box of Japanese candy, all chrome and glittery in her palm. "It's cheap, easy and never gets affected by the dust." Her voice came across squeaky, like an old door.

Kortel eyed the pad.

"Aw, come on," she said, now with an edge of British Cockney. "I'll throw in global service! You'll even be able to connect to any of the Freedoms."

The resemblance to his high school girlfriend was eerie, and Kortel felt a little something pass over his heart.

"Okay," he said, facing her. "But what's the catch?"

"No catch," she said. "I swipe your credit chip, you get a week's worth of service. How long you gonna be in the area?"

"Good question. I'm trying to find an old friend, but I'm not having any luck."

"Well then, why not call him?" The pink lips broke into a big toothy grin that, unlike his high school girlfriend's, exposed too much gum.

As dumb as it sounded, what she was offering was probably the best thing he could do. With his netpad down, he was, as far as communications went, stranded. He didn't need to connect to any of the space stations, but the global service might come in handy.

Kortel fished for his chip-card and handed it to her. She placed the phone on the bar and swiped his card down a slot in its side. The little device lay dormant for a second, then blinked and buzzed to life. Miss Pink Lips clapped.

"Killer!" she said, and stuck her hand out. "Welcome to the Arroyo Network."

Kortel hesitated, then shook her hand. No discharge effect. "So what's your commission?" he asked, gingerly picking up the chrome rectangle with his thumb and forefinger. He placed it in his palm and it unfolded like a deconstructing origami.

Miss Pink Lips smiled again, this time showing off the little cracks that heavy smokers have around the edges of their mouths. Kortel thought she looked too young for that. But then again, maybe not in a place like Deuces.

"Fifty percent of gross, anything I sell," she said proudly.

"And how's business?"

"Better than you'd think." And with that, she turned and sauntered toward the vidslots.

Kortel studied the phone's interface panel: pretty standard, and about five years out of date. He hesitated punching in his friend's number, because his buddy spooked easily, and in that case Kortel would never be able to find him. But he was out of luck, no matter what Deuces' drink coasters promised, so he entered the numbers and put the phone to his ear. Its whole body pulsated a green glow for several seconds before it chimed.

"Hello?" a voice answered, coming across with surprising clarity. He should go find Miss Pink Lips and thank her.

"Tarris?" Kortel asked.

"Jonny?!"

"Who else would have this number?"

"That's true, no shit. Where are you?"

"I'm in your neck of the mesa."

"You are?"

"Yeah. I'm north of the park, somewhere off of 57. It's a little shit-hole called Deuces Wild–"

"Damn!" Tarris said, and Kortel thought he heard it from his other ear, too. Weird. Like old stereo.

"Hey," Kortel said, "you don't have to scream in my ear."

"Hell I don't!" Again the stereo, but even more pronounced.

"Look, Tarris, I was wondering if–"

"Turn to the fucking right, Jonny Boy!"

Kortel turned and saw that other bartender waving from the end of the bar. He had a similar phone to his ear.

"Tarris?!"

Tarris came walking up the bar. His smile was the best thing Kortel had seen all year. The biomedtronic implants that allowed him to walk were barely visible under his apron. Their micro-servos hummed slightly as he stopped in front of Kortel. He picked up the J&B and smelled. "Billy, shit!" he exclaimed. "Get the Oban for Christ's sake!"

The big Indian shrugged.

Tarris looked Kortel over. "You look like hell, but goddamnit, it's good to see you."

Billy set a bottle of Oban and two fresh glasses in front of Tarris.

"Good to see you, too," Kortel said.

Tarris smiled. "This is the good shit. We hold it back for special occasions." He poured generous shots for himself and Kortel, then raised his glass. "To old friends," he said.

They clinked glasses, and Kortel knocked back his shot.

"I see you've met Jen," Tarris said, pointing to the chrome rectangle.

"She's quite the little entrepreneur," Kortel said.

Tarris winked. "She's more than that, if you know what I mean."

Kortel didn't want to. The friend standing before him looked all right, but his youthful spirit was gone. And there was something raw about Tarris, as if his years of living on the edge had finally caught up with him. From the first time they met in grade school, Tarris had taken Kortel under his wing. When terrorists detonated an untested biothermonuclear bomb on the islands of Hawaii, over a million souls, including Kortel's parents, debiolized in less than 10 minutes. Kortel had been visiting his grandparents in the Midwest when "the Event," as the news analysis dubbed it, made him an instant orphan. Tarris had made growing up parentless more bearable, and Kortel had always been grateful.

"How the hell did you end up out here?" Tarris asked.

"I took the old road, but now it empties out onto a highway. I headed west until I got this urge to try my hand at the slots."

"Shit, not these." Tarris thumbed toward the vidslots. "The Indians have 'em so rigged, it's a surprise when anyone wins. But, really..." The wild ecstatic look was gone, and his voice now had a serious edge. "How did you find me?"

Kortel smiled. "I had Max do a probability run on where you might be hiding."

"Max is your loft's AI...back in Chicago?"

"Yes, and–"

"God, that thing is close to 10 years old by now. You need to upgrade it."

"Max has been. He's perfect for my needs. You want me to answer your question?"

Tarris motioned for him to continue.

"After all the shit that went down between you and Georgia, Max calculated there was a greater chance of you hiding out at your old Chaco lab than at any of the other holes you might crawl into."

"I'd like to see that program. You were always good at writing them."

"Still am," Kortel said. He sensed his friend's mood had changed.

Tarris took a long look down the bar. "Come on," he said in a low voice. "Let's go to my place and get our drink on."

Dragonfly. 4

BIXX wiped the steam from the bathroom mirror and sighed. Rocket told her once that she had the body of a dragonfly. Even though he had professed his love on many occasions, this single comment had wedged itself deep into her psyche. Steam began building again on the mirror, reducing her naked image to a patchwork of mottled cream. She wiped again, this time using the meat of her forearm, and stared at her 22-year-old body. Luckily she had been graced with her mother's Russian skin. Its porcelain sheen was a family trademark, but it also set off her delicate chest, which hadn't changed much, she felt, since her 12th birthday. Occasionally Bixx thought it would be nice to be able to wear certain clothes or flaunt her sexiness. And even though Rocket had declared that large breasts were overrated, she suspected he wouldn't complain if one day she came home with a pair of 34 C's. The Biolution had made changing your appearance as easy as changing your mind, but Bixx was a purist who didn't believe in augmentation. She was among a select few who chose to shun the perfection promised in the infomercials that littered the media landscape.

"Hey, Bixx?" Rocket yelled over a piercing guitar lick from the song *Crying Train*. He was somewhere in their cavernous loft, but she couldn't tell where.

Bixx leaned into the mirror. "Dragonfly?" she whispered. The steam began to blur her image again.

"Bixx? Shit!"

"What?" Bixx had half a mind to lock the door and never come out. She met his glare as he entered the bathroom.

"Girl, what is taking so long?" Rocket's expression suddenly shifted, and his eyes wandered across her body.

Bixx could tell that his frustration was sliding away. Although Rocket had been driving her nuts lately with his rants about how their kind should free themselves from their secret lives, she still loved that slide. "What are you looking at?" she asked playfully.

His eyes came to rest with hers. "Candy," he said. A mischievous smile began forming at the edges of his mouth.

Bixx pushed away from the counter and began to speak, but Rocket put a finger to her lips. He wrapped his hands around her waist and deftly lifted her onto the counter. Its surface was slick with heat and moisture. He knelt between her legs and the buckle of his belt passed down the curve of her inner thigh. She flinched from its metallic chill.

"Rocky," she said softly, "we can't–"

"Shhh," he replied. He was now cradling her buttocks with his palms, and his shoulders were gently persuading her inner thighs to part.

Bixx looked down at the top of his perpetual mop of red curls and felt Rocket raise her hips to his mouth like a chalice. "Rocket, come on–" She started surrendering, but quickly tightened and grabbed a tuft of red curls. She pried his head back, and he gazed up at her like he had been pulled from the frontier of a perfect dream.

"Hi there," she said, and smiled her little girl smile.

Rocket's brow furrowed.

"We can't," she said with all the sweetness she could muster.

The lines of his brow deepened.

"You know why..."

"Screw him," Rocket said. His warm breath tickled her.

She pulled him away, this time squeezing her thighs against the sides of his neck. "We'll have a date later. I promise."

Rocket nodded in resigned agreement and stood.

Bixx slid off the counter and turned to the mirror, where her image was clearing like a slow-focus camera shot. She felt the tip of Rocket's finger pass down the middle of her back.

"I miss you," he said. He was staring at her reflection, but past it at the same time.

"I miss you, too." Bixx caught his anguish in the mirror and sensed that empty feeling opening again, like a sinkhole for her soul.

"When are you going to be done with that project?" he asked.

Bixx hesitated. It was hard for her to leave her work behind.

Rocket came up behind her ear and whispered, "Even a computer genius needs a little release now and then."

"Hey, where is everybody?"

"Shit," Rocket said. "Kreet, we're in here. What do you want?" He leaned into Bixx's ear. "Did you have to invite him for the *whole* weekend?"

Bixx caught herself clenching her jaw. "He didn't have a place to stay," she said.

Rocket kissed her neck and whispered, "Then it's up to you to think of a way to get him out of here...for at least part of the night." He kissed her again and quietly slipped out of the bathroom.

Bixx studied her reflection. "Dragonfly," she whispered.

The sinkhole widened.

5 Another little bonus.

KORTEL fought back a yawn as the Oban washed over the ice of his fifth drink. He watched the amber liquor fill the glass with another round of liquid courage. *Liquid Courage.* A smile came to his face as he thought of better times.

Tarris wedged the cork back into the bottle and reverently nestled the 50-year-old Scotch between his thighs. With his leg implants turned off, he relaxed in his MotoTrak, which made him seem to Kortel more paraplegic than ever. His vigor, which usually dominated a room, had been replaced with a presence Kortel could only describe as aged.

"So," Tarris said, "Zvara's thinking it's time your kind came out from hiding?"

"Remember that club I told you about, back in Chicago?" Kortel mused, his attention firmly on swirling the cubes in his glass.

"Ah, yeah...the Liquid something–"

"Liquid Courage."

"Right. I remember it. Why?"

Kortel hesitated. "I went looking for Tam.... That's why I came back to the States."

"Jeez, man. Don't torture yourself like that. What's done is done."

Kortel took a long sip of his Scotch. It burned delicately, and he could feel its effects pushing his rational self aside. "I know," he muttered. "It's just–"

"Man, talk...you're not going anywhere, so spill it."

"I just wanted to know if she might remember me...remember us. So I met with Anari–"

"She was her best friend?"

"Yeah. Anari still works at Liquid Courage, and she filled me in on what had happened after the Agency performed a limited erase on Tam. She's done well. I was surprised when I saw her–"

"You didn't go see her, did you?"

Kortel nodded.

Tarris shook his head. "Man, you are out of control. You can't go doing that kind of shit. You could seriously mess her life up. Why'd you go do that?"

"Because when a person's memory is erased, especially if it's a partial erasure, sometimes it doesn't take all the way. There can be what's called leakage.... That's when fragments of memories surface, usually in dreams. And Anari told me about these dreams Tam was having. They're about a guy, and how she's so attracted to him, but she can never see his face."

Tarris's expression suggested he wasn't getting it. Or maybe it was just the Scotches.

"I think the guy in her dreams is me," Kortel said. "Anari mentioned these dreams had really affected Tam's life, especially when it came to men."

Tarris moved his chair closer. "Jonathan, listen to me. Take it from a guy who's lost more women than he can count. Don't do this to yourself. I know you love Tamara a lot, but you can't keep doing this to yourself...or her."

"Don't worry. When I finally saw her, I realized that I couldn't force my way back into her life, no matter how big of an opportunity there was. And believe me, there was. Walking away from her was the hardest thing I ever did."

"Well, it's like what my Japanese friend, Endo, says: When you fall in love with a comfort girl, you fall into hell." Tarris grinned. "It's only natural; these girls are wired to do that. I'll bet they're genetically altered to release some kind of megapheromone...one that puts you under their spell." Tarris emphasized this last point by waving his hands like some kind of magician. Then he activated his implants, stood, and walked zombielike around the room. "Yes, Mistress Tamara," he said, in a low monotone. "I am your slave." He staggered up to Kortel, eyes bulged and arms stretched. "Let me bang you, and I'll give you my condo, my car and my inheritance!"

Whether it was Tarris being a complete ass or the five Scotches, Kortel burst into such a hard laugh that his drink spilled over the side of his hand.

Tarris zombie-walked to the end of the couch and began humping it. "One million. Two million," he said, each emphasized with a clownlike thrust.

This brought Kortel almost to the edge of nausea. He couldn't remember the last time that laughing had brought tears to his eyes. He let his drink fall and desperately grabbed at his side.

"Three *million*!" Tarris yelled with another thrust.

Suddenly, an intense pain carved through the middle of Kortel's brain. The shock of it made him disoriented, and for a second he could see himself in the chair, as if he were floating up by one of the room's *vigas*. Then an inhuman sound erupted from his throat, and he was back in the chair. It felt like a scream, but it came out at a higher pitch and echoed off the tile floor. He looked at his left hand as it curled in on itself. The pain shot again to the base of his skull, and his hand tightened with such force that he thought it would snap from his wrist.

Tarris spun around at Kortel's scream. "Jonny!" he yelled, but the lamp on the table next to the couch exploded, knocking him into the MotoTrak.

"Tarris, in my coat!" Kortel could barely get the words out before another bolt of agony hit. His back arched, and the large bookcase by the picture window flew across the room. It barely missed Tarris before it slammed into the opposite wall, sending pieces of wood, paper and glass in all directions.

Tarris pulled himself into a standing position.

"My coat...pocket," Kortel managed. "The infuser."

Tarris looked madly about, then spotted the coat piled on a chair next to the fireplace.

Kortel pointed. "Get it now, before I–" Another wave crashed inside his head, and he fell out of the chair onto his hands and knees. He retched, and the sculpture awarded to Tarris for BioGame Programmer of the Year shattered in a violent spray of purple and green glass.

Tarris made it to the coat in four lunging steps. He dug out the infuser and charged over to Kortel.

"Switch it," Kortel said, forcing back another surge of nausea, "to the maximum dose. The yellow button...twice. Now, please!"

Tarris looked the infuser over and pressed the tiny yellow button. "Where?" he said, panicking.

Kortel held back the urge to vomit. "My neck," he said, between gasps. "Near the main artery." He pointed to the side of his neck.

Tarris pressed the infuser against Kortel's skin and pulled the trigger.

Kortel felt his heart instantly palpitate, and a chill gripped his body like he had been fast-dipped in a tank of ice water. The room's spatial integrity distorted, and his vision blurred. Clenching his jaw, he forced back another surge of nausea and waited for the next wave.

"Jonny," Tarris said, cautiously. "Is it working?"

Kortel couldn't answer. He held his position on his hands and knees, waiting. Slowly his heart returned to a normal rhythm, and he relaxed his jaw.

"Man, are you with me?" Tarris asked.

"Yeah," Kortel said hoarsely. "I think so."

Tarris straightened. "Damn," he said. "No more Oban for you."

"I doubt it was the Scotch."

Tarris helped Kortel into the chair. "Let me get you a cold towel," he said.

Kortel collapsed against the pillows. His mind was thick with disorientation, and the room was still a soft blur. There was a twinkling band of light moving across his vision. It appeared to be fading as the room came into focus.

"You want some water?" Tarris yelled from the bathroom.

Kortel cleared his throat. "Yeah...thanks."

Tarris returned and pressed a cool towel to Kortel's forehead. He handed him a glass of water.

Kortel took it with shaking hands and raised it to his mouth. As he drank, each gulp washed away the metallic taste and soothed his burning throat.

"What the hell was that all about?" Tarris asked, easing back into his MotoTrak. He warily eyed his drink on the table and shoved it aside.

"That," Kortel said, "is what the good doctor Shoalburg calls a little side effect."

"Damn, I'd hate to see a large one." Tarris twisted around and took account of the damage. "Aw shit," he said, spotting the empty shelf.

Kortel studied the fragments of the sculpture strewn across

the floor. "I'm sorry. I know that meant a lot to you."

Tarris leaned back. "Screw it," he said. "It was only an award...I'll just have to win another one."

Kortel wiped his mouth with the towel and then placed it over the puddle of vomit. "Give me second," he said, "and I'll wipe this mess up."

"Don't worry about it," Tarris replied. "We got a lot to clean up." He gestured at what was left of the bookcase against the far side of the room. "Besides, I'm too drunk and tired to deal with this right now."

Kortel eased his head against one of the chair's cushions and closed his eyes. The ribbon of light was almost gone, but his head was throbbing so hard he could feel it in his teeth.

"Shit, Jonny," Tarris said, "how long have you been having these seizures?"

Kortel cracked open his eyelids. "I guess about a year. They started just after I settled in Russia."

Tarris whistled. "Man, you need to get that checked out. Whatever the Agency put in your head is probably growing. And by the look of it, you can't control it.... Can you?"

Kortel shrugged. "That's the other reason I came back," he said, eyes closed. "There was nobody in the Russian Tel organization who could help me. This shit–" (he tapped the side of his head) "is too advanced. I'm just a walking experiment."

"So who knows anything about this stuff? That Dr. Shoalburg guy you told me about? He's with the Agency, right?"

"Mr. Nanogenetics himself." Kortel opened his eyes to find

the room in focus, but the color was off somehow. "He's a Tel, but a reluctant one. He's very hard core about going public. I'm supposed to meet with him in L.A."

"Maybe he can get you under control," Tarris said. "In the meantime, you should get some rest. You're welcome to stay here for as long as you want." Tarris eyed the infuser sitting on the table next to his drink. "So what's in this?" he asked with a nod to the device.

"A neurogenic cocktail the lab guys mixed up special for me after I complained about headaches. I didn't know at the time I had the tech in my head. I just thought I was getting headaches from all the tests they were having me do. Shoalburg says it's just a masker drug. It blocks the pain instead of fixing it. Whatever it does, I only have three infusers left. Each holds about 10 doses, so I'm hoping Shoalburg can make me some more...and maybe figure out what's happening so I can learn to control it."

Tarris's expression hardened. "Are you addicted to that shit?"

Kortel hesitated.

"Man, listen. I know about addiction." Tarris patted his legs. "Riding with Jack stung me good."

"So what if I am?" Kortel asked. "It's not like I've got a choice." He leaned forward. "I never asked to be telekinetic, or to be this powerful, and I sure as hell never asked for all this shit to be put in my head." Kortel rubbed his temples. "Tarris, I've done things...things I thought I'd never do."

"It can't be as bad as you think."

"It is, Tarris. I've killed people, and not just Trumble and Takeda."

Tarris reached over and rubbed Kortel's shoulder. "I know you better than anyone. If you did, I'm sure you had a damn good reason."

"There were these tests," Kortel mused. "They were public tests...of my telekinetic strength. I didn't know at the time they were tests; I just thought I was reacting to a random situation. One involved a bus, with kids..."

"Hey, Jonathan." Tarris had rolled closer, and Kortel noticed their knees were touching. "It's like I said before, what's done is done. You're right.... You never asked for that tech. But it's there now, and you're going to have to deal with it. You're never going back to your old life, so you might as well accept that you're in the major leagues now. Either you let shit happen to you, or you act first, and that means people might get killed. You have an extraordinarily powerful gift. It's also very dangerous...especially if it's getting out of control." Tarris leaned back into the MotoTrak. "You know, sometimes I wish I'd never told you about the Tels."

Kortel waved the comment off. "Their Recruiters would have found me eventually, especially with my level strength. It was only a matter of time."

Tarris stretched. "You're probably right," he said through a yawn. He looked around at Kortel's telekinetic damage. "Fuck this shit," he said, more to himself. "We'll deal with this later." He stood. "Well, I don't know about you, but I'm ready for some Z's. Your little fit wore me out."

"How are those new implants working?" Kortel asked, gesturing at Tarris's legs.

Tarris looked down. "The new interface program I worked out is a hell of a lot better than that crap I had before. I fatigue less, and the delay time is imperceptible, at least to my brain, which isn't saying much." He laughed. "I've killed so many brain cells, the delay could be two minutes, and I wouldn't know the difference."

"You're walking great – better than I've ever seen you."

"Yeah, it took me almost a year to write the program, and another couple of months to trial the technology."

"Whatever you did, it works great – a lot better than your old implants. You can hardly tell you were ever in an accident."

"Thanks, man," Tarris said. "Coming from you, that's a big compliment."

Kortel lightly touched the towel with the tip of his boot, and a large brown spot grew under his foot. He shouldn't have had the chili. It was much worse the second time around.

"What are you thinking?" Tarris asked.

"I was thinking that if I don't get this tech either out of my head or under control, my life is going to be pretty screwed."

"Don't count yourself out. See what Shoalburg says and go from there. It's a 'one day at a time thing,' you know?"

Kortel nodded, but time was what he didn't have. When Shoalburg had examined him two years ago, he guessed the tech would continue its integration process for up to a year or more, and he couldn't say for sure what it might do after that. Shoalburg was the father of the technology, but much of what had been put in Kortel's head was beyond even him. Kortel was on borrowed time, and the episode tonight was minor compared to some he had experienced in Russia. If it hadn't been for Reza, he probably would have killed himself. She had comforted him during many of his worst episodes.

Kortel looked down at his left hand. There was a slight tremor. "Well," Tarris said through a yawn, "I'm out of here. I put all your stuff in the laundry room. The couch is probably your best bet to get a good night's sleep. That is, if you can handle the smell of puke."

"Thanks," Kortel said. "I don't have much of an issue with smell anymore. It's another little bonus from the tech."

Tarris regarded Kortel with the big brother look he always used. "It's weird," he said.

"What's weird?" Kortel replied.

"You and I...we're kind of alike now, you know?"

"How's that?"

"We're both damaged goods." Tarris smiled. "Hang in there, man. I'll see you in the morning." He turned and disappeared down the dark hallway.

Kortel looked at his left hand and clenched it into a tight fist. He knew it was only a matter of time before he would lose control altogether. The question was when. He began to extract himself out of the large chair, but collapsed onto his right arm. There was a sharp, rhythmic tingling that ran from his shoulder to his palm, and the disorientation had returned. Kortel remained on the side of his face for a moment and took long, slow breaths. When he finally sat up, he tried to shake off the sensation, but it wouldn't let go. He examined his hands, turning them over in the soft light, and found his right shaking in sync with his left.

"Great," he said into the quiet of the room."Just great."

What a pity. 6

BIXX anxiously trained her attention to the rear of the club. The place wasn't too busy considering the time of night, and as gaps opened between groups of people she could see all the way to the bathrooms. They were easy to spot because of their door handles in the shape of question marks. They appeared to be carved out of a block of wood the size of a refrigerator, and since there was nothing else on the doors, it was a crapshoot which was which. Bixx had to keep reminding herself that this was the point – to get messed up, as if you weren't already at a club like *Up Yours*.

What the hell is taking him so long? Bixx was hoping to buy several hours alone with Rocket by dumping Kreet with some friends. Her plan was to introduce Kreet, have a drink, and sneak out to meet Rocket for a late dinner at Thai One On. But Kreet had gone to the bathroom 15 minutes ago, and there were no signs of him or her friends anywhere in the club.

She glanced at her watch. *9:36 p.m.* "Damn it–" There was a tap at her shoulder.

"Hi there."

"Kreet! Where have you been?"

"Just hanging in the bathroom. I met these girls from Georgetown. They say they want to go grab sushi later. I got their numbers, but I don't recognize the prefix."

Bixx looked at his netpad. "New zone on the other side of the Potomac. They're too money for you."

Kreet shrugged. "So where're these friends of yours?"

Good question, Bixx thought. "To be honest, I have no idea." She did a 360 of the club. "I told them nine o'clock, but maybe they blew us off." Bitches. She pulled out her netpad and placed a call to one of them.

Kreet took her hands and gently closed the pad. The music had kicked up a notch. "Bixxy, you don't need to entertain me." His voice had a sweet edge to it. "If you want to go meet Rocket, it's okay. I understand." He smiled and relaxed his grip. "I really do appreciate you letting me stay at the loft."

For all his faults, Kreet could be a decent guy – sometimes. He wasn't really that bad looking, either. (Sometimes.) He was a little short, and he dressed a bit street for Bixx. Maybe it was the silly scarves he always wore. To her, they made him look like he was trying too hard, and the animatics he programmed into them were always over the top. The scarf tonight had some kind of Japanese Kabuki image with big yellow eyes that kept following

Bixx whenever she moved. But what really unnerved her was what the Kabuki kept saying. With the club's music so loud, Bixx could hardly make it out: something about why Bixx should get wrapped up with it, and the next line was always too soft to hear, even when Bixx put her ear to the fabric. Knowing Kreet, it was probably something off color.

"Go on," Kreet said. "Have a good time with your boyfriend." He smiled. The Kabuki did the same.

Creepy, Bixx thought. "You sure you'll be okay?"

He grinned. "I think I'll go have some sushi."

Bixx gave Kreet a little hug (half expecting the Kabuki to bite her breast) and left him at the bar. On her way to the bathroom, she glanced over her shoulder and watched him walk over to two vapid blondes who towered at least a foot over him. She laughed.

The bathrooms at Up Yours were more like living rooms with stalls. Bixx never knew which question mark to pull, so she always went with the right one. Most women's bathrooms in Russia were on the right, so she figured it was the safe choice. The bathroom was surprisingly empty: just a couple of druggy club kids huddled on one of the couches. They were too engrossed in their netpads to notice Bixx – probably trying to hook up some Ride. Bixx knew. Six years ago she had been no different, but that was before an Agency Recruiter sat next to her late one night and explained that drugs weren't going to help her; her problem was unique, and she needed to be with her own kind. He even recounted the time she had moved her family's car without touching it. She had been across the yard when the car accidentally engaged the Interway and almost ran over her parents. They had been arguing and never saw it coming. That was back in Russia, and she had been barely 8. The fact that this guy knew intimate details from her early life hadn't surprised Bixx much, since anybody with enough digirubles could obtain information. The guy had been insistent, though, so like any good clubber she ran a bunch of attitude and told him to fuck off. But when the couch they were on rose off the floor, Bixx figured the guy was onto something. Besides, he was pretty cute and offered a way out of the stupid life she had sunk into.

One of the club kids shot a harsh glance at Bixx and said something into another kid's ear. Then they sneered and collectively rose and left. Maybe Bixx had spooked them. Or maybe she just reminded them that you could get off the Ride if you wanted to badly enough. Addicts of Ride could always spot one another, even after they were clean. Bixx could never figure out what it was, except that there was something. Base. As if the drug could genetically alter an addict so that others could pick up on the need.

Bixx stretched out on one of the bigger couches and activated her netpad. Maybe Rocket would still be at the restaurant and would understand why she was running late. They all had lived with Kreet for the better part of two years, so he would know. She hoped.

Rocket's image pixeled up. "Hey there," he said. His smile told Bixx things were cool. "Kreet being a pain in the ass?"

"As a matter of fact, no. He's actually being quite the gentleman." She laughed. "I think he knew that we wanted a date. Besides, he's already connected with some credit girls from the new zone across the river."

"What happened to Marley and Cid?"

"No-shows. It's okay. They would have blown Kreet off anyway, and I would have never heard the end of it."

"Well, get that pretty little butt of yours over here. I've already gone through an order of corn patties."

"Okay. Just let me get my face on, and I'll be there in 15 minutes. Love you. Bye."

Rocket licked his netpad's screen and his image cut out.

Bixx went to the mirror and dug in her bag for the new makeup enhancer she had bought. She was determined to make this a special night, so she had picked up a Jamma stick. They were very in, very expensive, and available only at the Jamma boutique on Pennsylvania. The girl at the counter told her that once it was applied, the base would keep changing color for a week, if she chose to leave it on that long. Bixx never kept any makeup on for longer than a few hours, but tonight was different. She owed Rocket, because he had been so patient with her long hours in the lab. Tonight was going to be her treat – and not just the dinner.

The lighting in the bathroom was dismal at best, but the makeup would know where to flow. The girl at the Jamma counter had scanned Bixx's contour and programmed the stick. All Bixx had to do was apply it in the right general area, and the makeup would do the rest. She didn't know how most people could stand having their makeup crawl over their faces each morning. She could barely keep from squirming every time she applied the stuff – and that was only for special occasions like tonight.

She anxiously raised the Jamma stick to her left cheek, and its tip quivered as it anticipated making contact with her skin. Suddenly, the bathroom door flew open and Bixx quickly set the stick next to her bag. She wasn't experienced applying the stuff and didn't need a bunch of club kids gawking and making fun of her. She thought she heard the stick make a sound, like a sigh. *Maybe it was just switching off.*

Into the bathroom strolled a pasty, taut woman in a pair of heels so tall that Bixx thought she needed a step stool to climb into them. She wore her shiny black hair in a high, tight cone that jutted out at an unnatural angle. It made her head resemble an alien creature in an old scary sci-fi vid Bixx had watched late one night on the Classics channel. The woman walked around the bathroom, sizing Bixx up like a lioness. Bixx tracked her in the mirror. This woman had the Bitch Chic act cold, and Bixx knew all about their kind. They were always at clubs like Up Yours, and they loved to pick a fight. It was the drug they took that made them so aggressive. The woman stopped directly behind Bixx.

"Got a hot date tonight?" she asked. Her accent was familiar, but Bixx couldn't place it.

Still facing the mirror, Bixx shifted to one side so she could see all of the woman's reflection. "Yeah, I do. Is that okay with you?"

The woman smiled, and the open-weaved pattern of her

fishnet outfit instantly shifted into a shiny black bodysuit. Bixx noted a slight glimmer during the change.

"Does your boyfriend like you wearing Jamma?" she asked.

Bixx turned and faced her. "For the record, he usually likes me wearing Jamma...and *nothing* else."

The woman reacted as if this declaration amused her. "I bet he would...Olga."

A spike of raw cold shot through Bixx. "How do you know my name?"

"I know all about you...Bixx. Isn't that what you call yourself these days?" The woman's smile disappeared.

This was getting very weird. Nobody knew her real name, not even Rocket. Bixx had always hated the name Olga. It didn't have any family tie and was so utterly…Soviet. Bixx looked at the door, wondering if she could grab her bag and make it out before things got any weirder. She'd probably have to leave the Jamma. Too bad; it had cost her a week's credits.

"How's your work at the lab going?" the woman asked.

The situation had moved into the serious range. Only an Agency Tel would know about her work at the lab.

"What part of the Agency are you with?" Bixx asked.

The smile returned. "I'm not with *your* Agency."

Bixx took a cautious step back and bumped into the counter.

"In fact," the woman said, "I'm not even one of your kind."

Shit. The woman was a normal, but how could that be? Tels were a secret society; even Bixx's parents hadn't known. They thought she had been killed in a car accident. The Russian Tel Agency had made sure of that. It was the best way, or so she had been told.

"I heard you had a meeting the other day with a certain telekinetic we all know," the woman said. "How is Mr. Kortel?"

Bixx wasn't sure how to play this. Whoever this woman was, she might know about Kortel and Kreet's plan. Straight up seemed to be the best course. "He's okay," she answered.

The woman widened her stance and put her hands on her hips. "You wouldn't happen to know where he's staying in D.C., would you? He's probably wearing a signature displacer, since we can't locate him anywhere."

"No I don't," Bixx lied. "But it doesn't matter because he said he was leaving the city. And before you ask, I have no idea where he went." At least that part was true.

The woman reached into a pocket on her leg, and the bodysuit rippled slightly. There was no pocket a moment ago, but suddenly it was there on the woman's quad. She removed an international credit chip-card. It was carbon black and appeared like an extension of her hand. The woman leveled it at Bixx, its edge disappearing at the perfect angle. "Are you sure you don't know where he was headed?"

Now Bixx was getting pissed. Bribery had become a fine art in Russia, and Bixx hated it. She decided it was time to show this normal who was in charge. "I told you the truth," she said, and produced a high-level grav field.

The woman's arms instantly slapped against her sides, and her body went rigid from the gravitational pressure. The chip-card flew out of her hand and was caught in the field. It hung motionless about a foot in front of the woman.

"Who do you work for," Bixx asked. "And how do you know my real name?" She had secured most of the woman's body, but had allowed her head to be free.

The woman didn't answer.

Bixx mentally lifted her off the floor and tightened her telekinetic grip. The woman gasped slightly.

"Are you going to answer me?–"

"Marcus," the woman called out. "I could use a little help here."

"What's the matter, love?" a disembodied male voice answered from one of the stalls. "Did a Level 4 get the best of you?" It was a distinctly British accent.

"Obviously she's not a Level 4," the woman replied, "or I wouldn't be floating off the floor!"

"You know they have little metal containers mounted to the walls in here. I don't think pubs have those back home. What do you suppose they're for?"

"Shut up and get the hell out here," the women said, trying to squirm in Bixx's field.

The toilet flushed in the middle stall. A man emerged wearing the same black bodysuit as the woman, but its cut was more masculine. His hair was slicked back against his head like plastic, which seemed to work with his thick features. He wore 'trodes over his eyes. *Jacked*, Bixx thought. He stepped over to the woman and looked up.

"Either our research is wrong," the Brit said, "or Olga here has advanced quite a bit since leaving Russia." He directed his attention to Bixx and smiled a set of perfectly crafted white teeth.

Bixx was on the edge of panic. She was totally clueless who these two were and why they wanted her. Sure, she had been in the meeting with Kortel, but she didn't really care if their kind came out or not. She tried to maintain her grav field, but was already pushing her telekinetic strength.

"How long are you planning to hold her?" he asked.

She didn't know what to say. "Well, I, ah–"

Suddenly Bixx was flying over the counter. She slammed into the mirror, and her head smacked against the base of a light sconce. She crumpled into the sink. The force of the impact almost caused her to throw up. Stunned, Bixx felt the back of her head and came away with blood on her fingers. She looked into the large mirror on the other side of the room and saw her reflection. A thin streak of blood ran from the base of the sconce to the top of her head. Her heart felt like it was coming out of her throat.

The woman had fallen onto her hands and knees, and she was picking the chip-card off of the floor. "Marcus," she said, straightening, "I distinctly said not to be rough." The wrinkles in her suit slithered away. "I'm already dealing with one lawsuit."

The Brit, ignoring her, strolled over to Bixx like he was about to ask her to dance. He smiled. More perfect teeth. "My colleague here is a normal," he said, gesturing. "I'm different. You're supposed to be a Level 4, but you held that grav field for…" he referenced his watch, "…two minutes. Not bad. You're probably a Level 5 now."

"Please," Bixx said. Her throat was tight and raw. "I don't know anything about–"

"Just hold her while I go talk to the scarf kid," the woman said, slipping the chip-card back into the invisible pocket. She shook her head at the mess. "Jesus."

"Yes, ma'am," the Brit said. He watched the woman leave and then got in Bixx's face. "You never answered her question," he said, pointing to the bathroom door.

Bixx felt herself yanked forward, as if invisible hands had grabbed the front of her sweater. She was inches from the Brit's face.

"Time to learn," he said.

He hurled Bixx against the mirror again, this time with such force that she bit her tongue. The room went out of focus, then came back. She looked past the Brit and into the other mirror. There was a new streak next to the first one. Bixx wanted to cry, but the shock of the moment wouldn't let her. All she could do was lie there and shake uncontrollably. Her crotch felt wet, and there was a faint smell of urine. The Brit leaned in.

"What a pity," he said, casually. "You've gone and smashed your Jamma stick."

Bixx looked down and saw the stick in three pieces next to her bag. Its brightly colored makeup had escaped and was halfway up the side of the wall.

"Bet that set you back a couple of quid," he said, now practically touching her nose.

Bixx could smell his breath. Gin.

The woman was at the door. "I can't find the kid with the scarf fetish."

The Brit turned and eyed her. "He's probably getting drunk at the main bar with Tolly and Brie. He's a bloody dolt, that one is."

Bixx's vision began to blur. There was a tingling at her temples. She tried to focus on the makeup as it inched its way up the tile. It disappeared into the HVAC vent just as everything went black.

Say hello. 7

KORTEL poured himself a coffee and stepped onto the porch. The morning sun had crested over the mountains and was flooding the small valley below with the quality of light for which New Mexico was famous. A dog barked in the distance.

A week had passed since Kortel had taken Tarris up on his offer to stay. He hadn't had another seizure since the first night, and the days had settled into a simple routine. He had breakfast with the sunrise, always sitting in the filtered shade of the blue cedars at the end of the porch. He spent the mornings walking the land around the compound, which was what Tarris called the architecturally arranged sections of an old 747 fuselage. The front quarter of the plane was partially embedded in a small mesa that ran along the edge of the property. Tarris made his bedroom in what had been the upper deck lounge, with the flight deck remodeled as a bathroom. On the ground level – which had been first class – was the kitchen and living room. Two sections from the middle of the plane sat at right angles to the nose, their bottom thirds sunk into the ground. They had been walled in on their ends; one served as Tarris's lab, the other his garage, which housed an antique, retrofitted Hummer along with various ATVs of his own design. Kortel always wondered how Tarris had gotten the sections to such a remote place – something about a favor being owed – but he had never asked for details.

Kortel spent most of his afternoons in the lab. Tarris had an on-again, off-again retainer with one of his former employers. EchoGame was a Pacific Rim conglomerate with its hands in everything from virt booths to holoporn. The gaming division was its brain trust, and Tarris had been its golden boy. But a decade ago all that ended on the night he mixed his love for drugs and motorcycles. Tarris was on retainer this month, and deep into developing a direct-link game that had promotional ties with a new action vid Kortel had only read about. It starred a new kind of virtual character whose name he couldn't pronounce. All Tarris could tell him was that it involved string-theory dynamics and was huge with kids 8 to 14.

In the evenings Kortel would prepare something: fish, steak, it didn't matter. It had been a long time since he had been in a kitchen that actually had modern conveniences. He enjoyed programming a meal again. Even grilling seemed refreshing. The nights were always capped off with a round of Scotch.

Tarris joined Kortel on the porch and took in a deep breath.

"Helluva morning," he declared. His robe's sash whipped in the wind, and the servos in his hips complained as he shifted weight from one leg to the other.

"The best one yet," Kortel agreed. He took a long drink from his mug, turned from the sun and faced Tarris. His hair blew across his eyes. "So, what will it be for today? More modeling of the heroine?"

Tarris stood staring at the valley. "No," he said, finally. "I think we're going to dive into the background architecture. I'm not sure it's structured right, you know?"

Kortel nodded and returned to the view. The barking echoed off the land again. "Whose dog is that?"

Tarris shrugged. "Not sure. I just feed him when he comes around."

The barking intensified into sharp, repetitive yipes.

"Something's got him pissed off," Tarris said.

Then Kortel heard it. Or rather, he sensed it: the faint audible drone of aircraft engines. Distant. Coming over the high desert wind like a messenger. "Hear that?" he asked.

Tarris put an ear to the wind. "Yeah. Sounds like two."

Kortel listened. "One," he corrected, "with two engines."

Both men put their hands up to block the sun's glare. Kortel pointed first.

"There it is," he said, "over that tall peak."

Where the sky met the mountains, a plane skimmed through the morning clouds. Reduced by distance to a sliver of gold, it was thick in the middle and had two tampering appendages.

The craft angled toward the compound, its engines barely discernable from the wind in Kortel's ears.

"You know anyone with their own personal jump jet?" he asked.

"CEO of EchoGame, but he'd never come out here." Tarris cupped both hands around his face and watched it approach. "There's no markings on it."

The jet banked and slowly circled the compound. Its mono-wing shape was more apparent as it came around.

"That's a shitload of money up there," Tarris said.

The jet slowed, leveled, and came to a stop near the north end of the property. It pivoted to face them and hovered about 100 feet off the tree line. Shadows from the clouds moved across the craft, dappling its skin with contrasts of gray and bright gold. A thin line of black bisected the fuselage horizontally from edge to edge. Probably the cockpit window.

"I've got something that could bring her down in a heartbeat," Tarris remarked.

"If we move," Kortel said, "my guess is we'd never make it to the back door."

Tarris cautiously lowered his hands. "They're here for you, aren't they?"

Kortel put his hands into the pockets of his jeans and felt the leftover dirt from a stump they dug up on Tuesday. "Not unless EchoGame's changed its policy on corporate travel." He kicked at an exposed nail in one of the deck's floorboards. "I knew it was only a matter of time."

"But you're wearing a sig displacer."

"No shit. But they've probably got a way around it."

"Can't you just throw up a grav wave or something and knock them out of the sky?"

"To move something like that fast enough to catch 'em off guard, I'd have to go into phase. I'm sure they're monitoring me right now, and I don't want to test their reaction time."

"But I thought you were faster than light."

Kortel sighed. "It doesn't work like that. I need motivation...to kick in the surge."

"This isn't enough motivation?"

"It has to be something radical," Kortel explained. "You can't alter that big a gravity field with just an idle threat. It's got to be severe. *Life*-threatening."

The jet began to move toward them, its engines now just slightly louder than before. It passed over their heads and disappeared behind the top of the lab. A large cloud of dust climbed into the sky, and the whine of the engines dropped an octave.

"Well," Tarris said, "what the hell do we do now?"

Kortel shrugged. "Go say hello?"

The dust kicked up from the jump jet's vertical thrusters was still settling as Kortel and Tarris rounded the east corner of the lab. Kortel could make out three figures standing about 10 feet in front of the nose. There wasn't a visible door, and the black line turned out to be the intake grill for the engines. At least that's what Kortel thought, because the only other apparent blemish on the craft was the windshield. It was gold, but a shade darker than the body. Kortel and Tarris stood their ground about 50 feet from the craft.

"I'll bet these are your people," Tarris said out of the corner of his mouth. "You go greet them."

Kortel laughed. "Pussy." He began walking toward the jet.

"All right, wait up."

The center figure was a large man with a shock of white through his dark gray hair. His face seemed fitted to his head, the skin unusually tight at the cheeks and jaw. He wore a black, formally tailored suit. It reflected the curved image of the fuselage, giving its dark fabric a golden hue. On his left was a small Asian woman in a deep blue jumpsuit. There were enough electronics across her outfit to be jacked into NORAD. Her hair was cut severely around her head, exposing her neck just above her ears. The cut apparently made it easier to wear the virtgear strapped to her head. She appeared to be the pilot. The guy to Mr. Shiny Suit's right was dressed like a garbage collector for a large European city. His coveralls were bright yellow and tucked neatly into a pair of black combat boots. He also had technology, but most of it was centered on his chest. His headgear spilled across his face, so Kortel couldn't make out the man's nationality. Or if "he" even was a he.

Kortel stopped about 20 feet from them. He put his hands in his pockets and felt for the dirt. Tarris stepped up to his side. His prosthetics were issuing an odd whining sound.

The suit and his associates slowly bowed.

The wind blew between them, and Kortel thought he saw the jump jet's skin quiver.

"Organic?" he said, finally.

The guy in the yellow coveralls turned to Mr. Shiny Suit. The pilot followed.

"Your jump jet," Kortel said. "It's mostly organic, right?"

"Yes," the pilot said crisply. "Micro-organics with a programmable titanium fuselage." There was a trace of an Asian accent...Korean, maybe?

"Bitchin'," Tarris said under his breath.

"Jonathan," the suit said, "how are you enjoying your vacation?" There was an air of sophistication in his voice, but it wasn't forced.

"Here, or the one in Russia?"

The suit smiled for the first time. "Here."

Kortel thought for a second. "The room service sucks, but the food's not bad."

The suit's smile faded. "It's time to become useful, Jonathan."

"I'll get useful on my own time," Kortel replied, and the jet began to rise slowly off the ground.

The pilot spun and watched it ascend.

"Is this the right way to say hello?" Tarris asked.

"It's a start," Kortel said.

The jet stopped and hung about 100 feet in the air. The pilot looked pissed.

"You're wasting your talent," the suit said.

Suddenly, Kortel felt numbness behind his left eye. It needled across his face and traveled down his neck. His throat began to constrict. The suit gestured to Mr. Coveralls, and the numbness stopped spreading. Kortel gasped slightly and fell to one knee.

"Jonny boy," Tarris said, "are you sure you want to play it like this?"

"Maybe...not," Kortel managed between gasps.

The jet quickly lowered and slammed to the ground, its hydraulics straining with the impact. Dirt flew, and the pilot scowled at Kortel.

The suit waved the dust from his face and cleared his throat. "I wouldn't test my patience, Jonathan. Or my client's." He walked over to Kortel and gestured again to Mr. Coveralls.

The numbness vanished, and Kortel gulped down a couple of breaths.

The suit helped him to his feet and dusted off his pant leg. "Now that we're past the one-upmanship," he grabbed Kortel's hand and shook it, "what a pleasure it is to finally meet you."

"Thanks, I guess," Kortel said, rubbing his throat. "Mr...?"

"St. John...Errol St. John." He turned to Tarris. "And you must be Tarris. My children have enjoyed your games for years. It's a pleasure." He offered his hand.

Tarris eyed it warily.

"Come now, Tarris, we're here just to talk with Jonathan. If we had wanted to cause harm, you would have never seen us coming." His hand was still extended.

Tarris cautiously took it. "Maybe," he said, and shot a sideways glance at Kortel, "but I got shit that can see right through stealth."

St. John pulled Tarris close and his expression went blank.

"Not ours," he said seriously, and then his smile returned, bigger than before. "There, now we're friends."

"Who are you?" Kortel asked.

"All in good time." St. John eagerly surveyed the compound. "Well?" he said, wringing his hands. "Isn't it time for breakfast in this part of the world?"

Tarris turned to Kortel. "You're the chef here."

Kortel sighed. Obviously, St. John was a man of means, and whatever he was peddling, he wasn't going away until he made his case. Regardless, Kortel wasn't sure if he would have a choice in the matter. "Okay," he said, "I think I saw a dozen eggs in the refrigerator."

St. John's smile grew, and he motioned to his associates.

* * *

"Extraordinary, Tarris," St. John said from the living room. "How *did* you get all this out here?"

Kortel was in the kitchen inputting a Southwest *huevos* dish he used to prepare at his restaurant. It had been his partner's recipe, so it took him a moment to remember all the code combinations. He glanced at Tarris, who was washing a knife in the sink.

"It was flown here in parts. I scavenged what I wanted and sold the rest for scrap," Tarris said. "You'd be amazed at what you can sell on the black net these days."

Kortel finished inputting the recipe and began setting

the table. St. John moved diligently through the room, as if taking account of every item, processing and storing whatever data he thought useful. The pilot and Mr. Coveralls remained by the door. St. John stopped at a wall that held many of Tarris's awards.

"Very impressive, Tarris," he said, examining the biogame interface patent. "I didn't know you invented the Opus Controller."

"How do you think I can afford all this?" Tarris said.

"I assumed it was the royalties from your games."

"No, what little I get of those goes to keep me walking."

St. John took a seat at the end of the table, and Kortel could feel his gaze. "You've been so quiet," St. John said. "Maybe we should have announced ourselves when we entered your country's airspace."

Kortel placed the last fork in St. John's setting. "This is your show. Maybe you should just get on with it."

St. John nodded and settled into his chair. "Jonathan, how many times has your life changed?"

Kortel leaned heavily on the back of a chair. "I don't get your question."

"Well, there was the death of your parents in Hawaii, the discovery of your gift, the loss of Tamara, the deception of Georgia, and the deaths of Trumble and Takeda...and that's not to speak of the technology now growing inside your head."

"Okay. Maybe a dozen times. I don't know. What's your point?"

St. John had done his homework, and it was beginning to creep Kortel out, especially his knowledge of Kortel's relationship with Tamara.

"What if you were to learn that the Tels were not the

deep secret you thought they were...that they've been in collusion with certain non-Tel factions?"

Kortel shrugged. He always suspected that the Tels had contacts in select industries, so the revelation didn't surprise him much.

Tarris walked in with a basket of biscuits and a platter full of Kortel's egg dish. He set them down and took the seat at the other end of the table. Kortel sat in the middle chair, his attention locked on their new guest.

"Jonathan," St. John said, "the world your Agency has been defining for you is not what it seems. Yes, the Tels have been in control of things behind the scenes, but not without help."

"Are you a normal?" Tarris blurted.

St. John didn't acknowledge the question. Instead, he scooped a rather large portion of eggs onto his plate along with two biscuits.

"He is," Kortel said.

St. John smiled as he buttered a biscuit. "That ol' Tel instinct kicking in?" he asked, and took a large bite.

"Something like that."

St. John swallowed deliberately. "He's correct, Tarris. I'm a normal, and so are my associates."

The hair on the back of Kortel's neck stood up. He glanced over his shoulder at the pilot and Mr. Coveralls. They hadn't moved.

St. John wiped his mouth in a manner cultivated by years of fine dining. "You see, Jonathan, the Tels have been in association with my clients–"

"Who are your *clients*?" Tarris asked.

"They're a consortium."

"What kind of consortium?" Kortel asked.

St. John played with the patch of hair below his bottom lip. "Let's just say that, like the Tels, they have their hands in almost every aspect of life. Don't believe everything they teach you at that Agency of yours. Be assured, there are only a few outside of the Tel culture who know of your kind's existence. And even fewer who know about you, Jonathan...and your power."

This statement punched hard at what was left of Kortel's feelings of security. He had been told that the Tel culture was a secret, hidden by layers of front companies and years of disinformation. He also knew about their influence in various governments. But St. John was a normal and seemed to know all about the Tels and the New American Agency. He even knew about Kortel's history. And about Tamara. What other revelations were there? And if St. John's coveralled minion had the ability to tap into the implants in his brain, what else could he do? Suddenly, Kortel felt very exposed.

"The people I represent," St. John continued, "have been in association with your kind for over 50 years. They have what I would call a mutually beneficial arrangement. My clients exert influence that helps the Tels, and certain people within the Tel culture respond in kind. What's the phrase...you scratch my back, I scratch yours? It's really that simple. Good Lord," St. John said with a chuckle, "how do you think anything gets done in this world?"

"Get to the point," Kortel said.

"I'm here to present you with an offer."

Kortel bit into some eggshell. "What kind?"

St. John grinned sinuously around a forkful of *chorizo* and scrambled eggs, then chewed slowly as if the act were a calculated effort designed to bring the conversation to an excruciating pace. "My clients," he said finally, "want to wipe your slate clean, so to speak."

"I don't follow you."

"They want to help correct one of those changes we were talking about. You see, they have considerable influence within the circles that would like to...oh, how can I put this?... seek revenge for your handiwork against Trumble and Takeda?"

"And the catch?" Kortel asked.

St. John smiled again, and Kortel noticed an undignified amount of chorizo lodged between his teeth.

"There's always a catch, isn't there?" He wiped his mouth and tongued his teeth. "Life has a way of creating points and counterpoints. Action. Reaction. What's being offered is merely a reaction to your action."

The chorizo was gone.

"Poof, just like that?" Kortel asked, gesturing.

"Poof," St. John said, and he took a drink of his orange juice. His eyes never left Kortel's.

"I'd be damn sure about the ground rules," Tarris said.

"Let me make sure I understand this," Kortel said. "What you're offering, I mean, what your clients are offering, is a kind of immunity?" His attention went to St. John's shock of white hair.

The guy was definitely a professional and obviously connected with a powerful group. But what kind? A corporation? A government?

St. John nodded. He had settled comfortably into his chair, his hands neatly folded across his lap. "That's correct," he said. "Total immunity."

"How can your clients guarantee that?" Tarris asked.

"At the moment, it's not important to know how, just that they can."

"You haven't answered my question," Kortel said.

"The catch," St. John said in a firm voice, "is simply this: for your immunity, you will be put on a retainer with my clients."

"To do what?"

St. John hesitated. "This and that...I really can't say at this time. It would be better if you met with them in person."

"This is bullshit," Kortel said, pushing away from the table.

"Before you go and erase us, Jonathan ..."

A pain shot through Kortel's head; he winced from its intensity.

"Consider the alternatives." St. John leaned onto the table, and Kortel noticed a large scar that started at the knuckles of his right hand and disappeared under the cuff of his suit. "Right now, your life is an abstraction. You're the greatest Tel ever, yet you're living as a fugitive hand to mouth. Jonathan, be reasonable." His voice was filled with earnest. "What do you have to lose? My clients aren't monsters – they're businessmen, just as you were once. This little demonstration is to remind you that you're vulnerable. They just wish to meet with you." St. John relaxed and leaned back in his chair. "Do you have a better option?" He motioned to Mr. Coveralls, and the pain disappeared.

"Okay," Kortel said, rubbing his temples, "new ground rule. No more making your point with pain. You don't need to keep reminding me that you've developed tech that can interface with my implants. I'm slightly more intelligent than a dog and can comprehend your intent without reinforcement."

Mr. Coveralls launched over the table and flew across the room, arms and legs flailing. He thwacked face-first against the bulkhead and fell to the floor in a tangle of yellow fabric and electronics. He groaned and tried to struggle to his feet, only to collapse onto his face. A small pool of blood spread from his cheek before he rose and floated toward the kitchen table, headgear hanging in pieces from his face.

Kortel maintained his focus on St. John. "Because," he continued, "if he uses that shit on me one more time–" Mr. Coveralls stopped above St. John, and a large drop of blood splattered across his plate.

St. John nodded tentatively. "You've made your point. There's no need for such drama. Please, put Mr. Kirasawa down and let's finish our talk."

Kortel moved Kirasawa toward the pilot and dropped him at her feet. She didn't react.

"What if I don't want to take you up on your offer?" Kortel asked.

St. John shrugged and took note of his right hand's fingernails. They were, like the rest of him, perfectly manicured.

"Then your life will plod along as it has," he said, still regarding one of his cuticles. "One pathetic day after another. The greatest living Tel ever, wasting his life away. A wanted man, who will eventually meet his fate. If we can interface with your biotechnology," his eyes went to Kortel's, "just think who else can. No one really knows what it will do for your gift. If you don't meet with my clients, there will be others who will want to *persuade* you. And they won't be as forgiving as I am." St. John stood and adjusted his tie. "Take your time. When you come back from seeing Shoalburg," he eyed Kortel again, "call me with your decision." He produced an old-fashioned business card and stuck it into the remains of his scrambled eggs. It had his name and a coordinate number in a delicate serif typeface.

St. John turned and walked toward the pilot, who now had Kirasawa propped against her shoulder. "Delicious breakfast, Jonathan," he said. "So wonderfully regional. And good-bye, Tarris. Please don't try anything that shows your ignorance when we leave." He went up to the pilot and spoke into her ear. She nodded, and they all started to walk out the original first-class exit of the plane.

"Hey, wait a minute," Kortel said.

The pilot and Kirasawa shuffled through the exit. St. John stopped, but didn't turn back.

"How did you know where to find me?"

"A word of advice?" St. John looked over his shoulder. "Don't buy discount Net phones from strange girls in casinos. You never know what kind of service you'll get."

Heritage. 8

"HEY," said a voice somewhere at the boundary of Bixx's consciousness, "I think she's coming out of it."

It sounded like Rocket, but she couldn't tell. She felt as if she were inside a dream – her mind soft, pliable, ready to liquefy and slide down the back of her throat.

"She's trying to open her eyes," the voice said, its tone rich with concern. It was Rocket.

Bixx felt someone approach and brush her arm. A smell wafted into her nose that made her flash back to summers at her family's farm and her grandfather fresh from the fields. It had been a thick odor that clung to his overalls.

"Should we keep her under?" she heard Rocket ask.

"No, it's time for her to wake up," another voice answered. This person sounded like Sanjiv.

Bixx felt someone gently squeeze her upper arm. "Hey you," Rocket whispered sweetly, "it's time to wake up." He was close to her face, and she could feel his breath on her cheek. Her mind went to the bathroom at Up Yours. The woman in the bodysuit. The Brit and his breath.

Gin.

"Nyet!" Bixx yelled, and opened her eyes to a stinging glare.

"Hey, hey. Easy there," Rocket said.

Bixx fought against the grip at her arm. Part of her knew it was Rocket, but another part could only see the Brit.

"Bixx, come on. It's me."

Another hand pressed at her shoulder. Rocket's face came out of the glare. Bixx focused on his eyes and stopped struggling. He looked scared.

"It's all right," Rocket said. "You're safe."

Bixx wrapped her arms around his neck and hugged him. She wanted to cry, but something instinctual was stopping her. Maybe it was her heritage. All Russian children were taught the history of their country: the struggles, the sacrifices, how the will of the Russian people was like a weapon, forcing back centuries of invaders. And now it was rising up like armor for her emotions. Rocket held Bixx and gingerly stroked her hair.

"It's okay," he whispered into her ear. "You're home, with me."

Bixx pulled away and felt the back of her head. A patch of hair had been shaved away, and a thick bandage covered the spot where she had hit the mirror. It was warm to the touch, and Bixx could feel a faint undulating under the film. She looked at Sanjiv.

"It's the nanomeds under the micropore's first layer," he explained. "They're, ah, eating the infection." He hesitated and smiled nervously. "They're in the wound glue."

Sanjiv wasn't a certified physician, but he knew a lot about medicine. Late one night during her first year in the warehouse when they were all living together, Bixx had overheard Kreet and Rocket talking in hushed tones. Something about Sanjiv and a lawsuit. She never heard the whole story but got the sense that something had happened that redirected Sanjiv's career path. Now he was a genetic researcher. And since it had never surfaced in any conversations, she never brought it up. Bixx fought the urge to scratch at the bandage.

"How did I get here?" she asked Rocket. The question sounded dumb even to her, but she really couldn't remember how she ended up in her bed.

"I waited at Thai One On for an hour," he said. "Then this girl called from your netpad. She said she found you passed out in a sink, and that a Bitch Chic had beaten you up. I blew every intersection to get to you, and when I got to the club, you were in one of the bathrooms, sitting on a couch with a towel full of ice to your head. Don't you remember any of this?"

Bixx didn't, which made her feel very weird. She pulled her legs close and hugged her knees. "No, I don't–"

"It's probably the drug I gave her," Sanjiv said. "It induces a deep sleep and sometimes causes a temporary loss of trauma-related memories. She might remember, but she might not."

"Can you tell us anything about your attacker?" Rocket asked.

"There were two," Bixx replied, and she proceeded to tell them everything she could remember about the bodysuit woman and the plastic-haired Brit. She explained how the woman wanted to know about their meeting with Kortel and where she could find him. Bixx even told Rocket that it all happened while she was putting on some Jamma, just for him, and that she was sorry for blowing their date.

"Shit," Rocket said, "that's the last thing I'm worried about. I'm just glad you didn't get killed. These two sound like they mean business. You're lucky you came away with only a scratch."

It didn't feel like a scratch to Bixx. She reached behind her head for the bandage.

"Don't disturb the wound," Sanjiv reiterated. "It won't heal if you start poking at it."

Bixx returned to hugging her knees. The nanomeds were beginning to itch like crazy.

"Let them do their job," Sanjiv said. "You're very lucky there was no concussion. It should take a day or two for the wound to heal completely."

"We should have expected this," Rocket said. He was pacing their small bedroom, arms folded tightly across his chest. "Leave it to the Agency to send in some goons to shut Kreet's plan down."

"Rocket," Bixx said, "they told me they weren't from the Agency. They never said who they worked for, but I know the British guy was at least a Level 6." She began to reach for the wound, but stopped. "And there was something else.... The woman was a normal."

Rocket stopped, and Bixx could tell this hit him hard.

He threw his hands up. "Shit, this isn't good. Fucking Kreet has gotten us into something stupid, I know it." His look went grave. "When's the last time you saw him?"

"I left him at the bar. When I was walking toward the bathrooms, I looked over my shoulder and saw him hitting on these two blondes–" Then Bixx remembered. The Brit's perfect smile. *What had he called Kreet...a bloody dolt?* "Rocket," she said, "you haven't heard from Kreet?"

"No."

"The woman asked the British guy about Kreet....She said she wanted to talk with him. The weird guy told her that he was with two girls. He called them by name, like he knew them."

"Shit," Rocket said to himself.

"Rocket," Bixx said, "how long have I been out?"

Rocket and Sanjiv exchanged tentative glances. "About a day and a half," Rocket said.

"Oh, my God," she said softly. "They might have erased Kreet by now." Then something began to rise inside Bixx. Hard. Guttural. She could feel her heritage pushing aside her anxiety and making a place for another emotion. "What was that guy's name?" she asked both Rocket and Sanjiv. "The one who got Kortel's incepts?"

Sanjiv thought for a moment. "McCarris!" he said. "James McCarris."

Bixx folded her arms, and her anger clicked into place. "Find him," she said, "and we'll find Kreet."

9

Serious as a heart attack.

KORTEL'S netpad chimed, yanking him from a dream he'd had before. He was sitting at an outdoor bar, somewhere in Northern California – the wine country, though he never understood how he knew this. His friend Carlton climbed onto the stool next to him and announced everything was fine, that Kortel shouldn't worry about him. The first time he had the dream was the week after Carlton had died of Netox, and although it had been more than seven years since his death, the dream still got to him.

Kortel wiped some sleep from his eye and read the salutation on his netpad's screen: *Get up. It's time for you to be great!*

"Hello?" he said blearily.

"Time to rise and shine."

Kortel read the time meter. *5:30 a.m.* "Shit, Sasha." He was having trouble focusing on her image. "It's 5:30 in the morning."

"Don't blame me. I didn't set the time for the meeting."

Kortel rolled back against the pillow and let the pad drop to his side.

"Hey, where did you go?"

"I'm still here," Kortel said to the ceiling.

"How's New Mexico?–"

"What meeting?"

"Didn't you get my message?"

"No, my pad's been off.... Hey, wait–" He grabbed the pad and brought it to his face. Its bandwidth meter was at full strength. "That's weird."

"I'm sorry, what did you say?" Sasha's hair was pulled up in a small ponytail. It set off her sharp cheekbones and bounced slightly when she spoke. "Stop moving your pad around; I can't see you."

"My pad...it was off-line, until...never mind. Now, what were you saying?"

"You have a meeting today."

"No I don't. I'm flying to L.A. this afternoon."

"We've canceled it."

"What? I need to see Shoalburg."

"First off, he won't be there. He's actually headed your way. Second, I did what you asked."

Kortel sat up. "He's headed where, and you did what?" He rubbed his neck, feeling for the injection bruise. Maybe two doses hadn't been a good idea last night.

"Will you wake up?! Shoalburg is landing in Albuquerque at 7:30 this morning."

"Why?"

"For the meeting. Will you focus?!"

"Hey, it's early. I'm still half asleep."

Sasha smiled.

"What?" Kortel asked.

"Your hair...It looks cute, that's all."

Kortel passed a hand through his hair. "Right, sure it does. And what did I ask you to do, again?"

"Find my dad."

"You did?"

Sasha nodded.

"What did he say?"

"Why don't you ask him yourself? You're meeting with him this morning."

* * *

Kortel had been driving for over an hour and now found himself traversing a narrow, rocky path. It had been years since he had driven a manually controlled vehicle, and never anything as archaic as Tarris's Hummer. It was hard to keep the huge vehicle away from the scrub sage. The path suddenly ended at an old metal gate that looked like it belonged on a ranch. There was a cattle guard in front of it, and the gate wasn't attached to any kind of fence, at least not within the last century. He put the Hummer in park and checked his position with his netpad. According to it, this was the point for the meeting. He confirmed the coordinates with the Hummer's SatNav and noted the time. *10:30 a.m.*

Sasha's instructions had brought Kortel to a remote area about an hour northwest of Tarris's compound. Tarris thought the coordinates would take him into the Navajo Indian Reservation, so he had given Kortel a handheld Light-Force. He said the Navajo were uptight about people on their land, now that 150 years of casino profit had transformed their lifestyle. The Light-Force was a low-power one, typical of early models, and Tarris had warned him to allow at least twice as much time for the loading sequence. Kortel glanced at it sitting in the drink holder of the center console, and hoped he wouldn't need it.

The land around him was pretty desolate, and the Hummer's SatNav indicated there was a drop-off about 200 yards past the gate. From all appearances, he was parked on top of a large mesa, but the Hummer's computer didn't have any information on the valley below. Kortel lowered the driver's side window and leaned back in his seat. A shaft of morning sun hit his face, so he pulled the visor down. A small holophoto fell into his lap, landing backside up. He turned it over, and a woman with long raven hair winked back. It was Georgia, Tarris's former lover.

It was a cheap print anyone with a holocamera could have made at home, and Kortel watched it cycle through her smile and wink. She had been captured from the waist up standing on a porch, but it wasn't at the Chaco compound; it was at Tarris's other home in Tres Piedras, probably at the height of their relationship. Her dark, almost black eyes followed Kortel.

"She was very beautiful," a raspy voice said over his left shoulder.

Kortel recoiled against the center console.

Armando Zvara's long, bearded face peered in from the window. It had been more than two years, but Kortel immediately recognized those sad green eyes.

"I'm sorry to have startled you."

Zvara took a step back, and Kortel noticed a slight awkwardness in his movement. The gray in his beard made him look old.

"It's okay; I was lost in a thought." Kortel wedged the holophoto under the butt of the Light-Force and concealed it with his coat before he stepped from the Hummer.

The last time Kortel had seen Zvara, Jacob Whitehorse had him telekinetically suspended over a fire like a rotisserie chicken. Whitehorse had wanted Kortel to join a group of loosely organized, disenfranchised Tels, but Zvara had wanted him for the Agency. At the time, Kortel wanted nothing to do with either, because things had gotten ugly between Zvara and Whitehorse – some old history about one screwing the other's wife. Both men had been top Recruiters, but Zvara had been made head of the Agency first. That, along with his wife's dalliance with Zvara, had sent Whitehorse over the edge.

"Do you ever think about her?" Zvara asked. He was leaner than Kortel remembered, and dressed in a blue work shirt, faded khakis and a pair of military boots. He looked rather ordinary, considering he was arguably one of the most powerful of their kind.

"Rarely," Kortel answered.

Zvara's expression challenged his assertion.

"Okay, sometimes I think about her. But it's weird."

"What do you mean?"

"To have known her as one person, then to find out she's somebody else, then having to kill her."

"But it was self-defense."

"Easy for you to say. You didn't see her die in front of you." The image of Georgia screaming as her molecular structure collapsed surfaced in Kortel's mind. That was the night that Georgia had revealed she was Whitehorse's daughter, that she had been fooling Kortel all along. She had played the part of Tarris's lover just to get close enough to kill Kortel. He had always rationalized that she had forced him to defend himself. A shiver cut through him.

"A hit from a Matter-Force can be an ugly way to die," Zvara remarked.

Kortel shot him a *no shit* look.

"She was just like her father."

"Crazy?"

Zvara's expression hardened. "Disturbed."

A hawk screeched above them, and both men watched it lazily ride the warm midday thermals.

"So," Kortel said, "are you really part of this plan to bring us out?"

"See that hawk?" Zvara said, still watching.

"Yeah."

"I think it is time our kind was free."

Zvara's contractionless speech pattern was a by-product of the tech the Agency had crammed into his head. Hearing it brought back a flood of memories for Kortel, and he found himself relating to the great Tel even more. He looked up again and watched the hawk glide over the top of a mesa and disappear behind its rim. "Do you think our culture could come out without repercussions?" Kortel asked.

"I think it depends on how it is handled."

"And you think Kreet is the man to do that?"

"No," Zvara said. "You are."

Kortel didn't know what to say.

Zvara gestured. "Walk with me?" he asked, and then started around the gate.

Kortel followed. "Is this the part where you bestow all your sagely wisdom on me?"

Zvara turned back. He had that look again. "No," he said, "this is the part where you grow some balls."

* * *

Kortel followed Zvara in silence along a tree-lined path that weaved down the side of the mesa. They approached what looked like an old military base, complete with long metal buildings and a tall barbed wire fence.

"What's this?" Kortel finally asked.

"Home," Zvara said.

The base was nestled near the north side of the valley. Much of it was overgrown with sagebrush, and when they drew closer, Kortel could see that many of the buildings were in various states of disrepair. Only a few looked like they had been restored.

They approached a gate, and two large men stepped into view, each brandishing a military-style Light-Force rifle. Their demeanor was all business. Zvara waved them off.

"How long have you been here?" Kortel asked.

"Since the night I last saw you, when Jacob had me compromised." The gate began to slowly open.

"I always wondered what happened to you. I thought you were dead that night. But Whitehorse put you on that call...when we were on that plane, just before–" The words caught in Kortel's throat as he remembered the flight that he, James McCarris and Tamara took trying to escape Whitehorse's wrath. He flashed on the missile's impact and the resulting horror.

"Are you all right?" Zvara asked.

"Yeah, I'm okay." Kortel tried to shake off the memory of the plane breaking apart.

Zvara studied him. "You should be proud. You saved hundreds of lives and demonstrated the true power of your telekinetic strength."

"People died because of me–"

"More lived."

Kortel threw his attention to the slowly opening gate.

"Jacob thought I would be more useful alive," Zvara said after a moment. The gate finished opening, and Kortel followed

Zvara into a maze of large shipping containers.

"After you killed Jacob," he continued, "what was left of the Rogues disbanded." They turned sideways and shuffled between some large self-sealing transport crates. Their third-world iconic hololabels kept saying hello to Kortel and telling him at which loading dock they should be staged. There was one icon whose character looked like an ancient *Samurai* warrior. It thrust its sword every time Kortel glanced at it, and after the third thrust, Kortel stopped ducking. Although he knew it was just projected light, it still creeped him out when the sword went past his temple.

"Only a few stayed behind," Zvara said. "They had no quarrel with me, so I was free to go." They emerged in front of a building that looked like it could have been a barrack. Its signage dated the installation from the time before America had merged with Mexico. This building was labeled number eight.

"So, what did you do?" Kortel asked.

"I stayed on. I was done with the Agency, and since most people believed me dead, it seemed fitting."

Kortel took account of the immediate area. There wasn't a person in sight – just sagebrush, packing crates and a row of three buildings, all standing on what had probably been the main street for the small base.

"These people needed a new leader," Zvara said. "Someone who could help them achieve what they wanted."

"What do they want?"

Zvara grabbed the handle to number eight's front door. "To be free."

Kortel followed Zvara into a small reception area.

"Good morning, sir!" a young boy said, quickly rising from behind an old military metal desk. He was Native American, and his bandanna had *Kick White Ass* in bold letters across its front.

Zvara gestured for the boy to sit, but the boy remained standing. He eyed Kortel with awe.

"Close your mouth, Billy," Zvara said.

The boy kept staring, and Zvara laughed.

"What?" Kortel asked.

"You are a legend around here," Zvara said. "Get used to it."

Kortel reluctantly acknowledged Billy with a slight grin.

Zvara led Kortel through the reception area and down a dark, narrow hallway lined with frosted glass doors. Dimpled shadows moved across the panes, and Kortel could hear muffled conversations as he passed.

Zvara stopped at the last door and knocked.

"Armando?" a distant voice asked from within.

"Yes," Zvara replied.

A shadow grew in the glass, then the lock clicked. The door opened, and a Hispanic man, probably in his 30s, greeted them. He gave a nod to Zvara; his eyes went to Kortel…and widened.

Zvara stepped into the room. "Alberto, this is–"

"Jonathan Kortel. Yes, I know...from the vids. I'm honored." The man thrust out his hand.

Kortel began to accept it, but an arc of static shot between them. The man jumped back.

"Sorry," Kortel said.

"I should have expected it," the man said, rubbing his palm.

The room was dark and crammed with electronics. Much of the equipment was post-Biolution organic, but some looked late 20th century. A large lab table dominated what little space remained in the center. Carter Shoalburg sat in the middle chair with two academic types flanking him.

"I think you know Dr. Shoalburg," Zvara said.

"Hey, doc," Kortel said. "It's good to see you again."

"It's always good to see," Shoalburg replied, edging his face into a shaft of light that illuminated the table. The two academics laughed, but the joke didn't register well with Kortel. It wasn't that he didn't understand Shoalburg's dry humor; it was simply that he felt more of a kinship with the famous scientist. After all, they both had tech running through their bodies. Shoalburg had invented the bionanogenetic technology that allowed people like Tarris to walk, or, as in the case of Shoalburg himself, to be able to hear, speak and see. Shoalburg's own need had been the mother of his invention, and its propagation into the mainstream had changed the lives of disabled people around the world.

"This is Dr. Robert Hammler." Zvara gestured to an unnaturally thin man on Shoalburg's left. "He is a normal, and one of the world's leading astrophysicists. He has taken a great risk to be here."

"Doctor Hammler," Kortel said.

"And this is Dr. Erin Richter," Zvara said of the other academic at the table. "You may be familiar with her work. Her pioneering theories on gravity are required study at the Agency. She, too, is a normal, and we are very pleased that she could join us. And you have already met my assistant, Alberto." Zvara shot a look at Kortel. "What is the matter? Shocked to be in a meeting with people other than our kind?"

Kortel didn't realize his expression was so telling. St. John's revelations the day before were almost too much to process, yet here he was in a meeting with two prominent normals.

"Jonathan, are you all right?"

For a second, Kortel felt disoriented. "No...no, I'm not." He rubbed his temples and faced Zvara. "What the hell is going on here? I thought we were going to discuss how to reveal the Tels to the rest of the world. Carter I understand; he's wanted to do this for years. But what's with these two? The world's leading scientists on gravity and astrophysics? And where's Kreet?"

"I told you he wouldn't take this very well," Shoalburg remarked.

"Jonathan, we are here to talk about revealing our culture, but there is something else."

"Save it," Kortel said. "Whatever it is, I don't want to know about it." He shook his head. "What is it with you people? Can't anyone be straight with me? I came back because I thought there was a viable plan to bring our kind out–"

"I thought you said he was on board," Richter said to Shoalburg.

"Jonathan," Zvara said, "there is a plan."

"Shut the hell up. First, it's McCarris hunting me down

for a bogus meeting with Kreet. Then, I'm approached by some shadow consortium that wants me to work for it to do God-knows-what. And guess what, they're all normals too."

Zvara exchanged tentative glances with Shoalburg and the academics.

"What, you're all surprised? Seems to me everybody knows about us."

"All right, Jonathan," Zvara said. "Yes. There are other normals who, ah...know of our existence."

"They do more than just know. I was told they've been doing business with Tels for years.... Right?"

This time Zvara and Shoalburg looked at each other. Shoalburg smirked and shook his head.

Kortel picked up on this. "Okay," he said, "you all can keep living in your little world, but I'm heading back to Russia. At least the Tels there are real."

"Jonathan–" Zvara said.

Kortel got in Zvara's face. "You don't get it, do you? I don't want to be famous, or powerful, or any other shit. I just want to be...I don't know...*free* of all of this!"

Zvara took his arm. "Please, Jonathan, just take a seat and I will explain everything."

"No!" Kortel jerked out of Zvara's grip. "Fuck all this! I'm out of here." The room suddenly felt much smaller, and Kortel began to back up.

Zvara's assistant stepped up and took ahold of Kortel's other arm.

"Get the hell off me!" Kortel yelled. The man instantly flew back and slammed against a stack of electronics. Kortel could feel a residual grav wave bow out in front of him, probably from his anger. It shoved the table into Shoalburg's chest, as its leading edge contorted to the shape of the invisible wave. It deformed to about the center of the table and stopped.

The two academics quickly stood and backed away.

"Jonathan, control yourself!" Zvara said. "No one is here to harm you."

Kortel wasn't buying Zvara's concern. He quickly turned and reached for the door.

"For God's sake, don't leave!" Hammler exclaimed. "You could be our only hope!"

Kortel turned the knob.

"Please! I beg you. Hear us out." Hammler's voice was on the verge of panic.

Kortel leaned his forehead against the doorframe. There was a sharp pain rising in his brain, but he couldn't tell if it was the tech or just his world closing in on him.

"I sorry, Jonathan," Zvara said. "I should have explained to you the whole reason I asked you here."

"Shut up," Kortel said. "Just answer me this question: who's the 'our' in 'you could be our only hope'?"

A cold silence filled the room. "The world," Shoalburg replied matter-of-factly.

Kortel reluctantly turned. Hammler had a pleading look on his face, while Richter was absorbed with examining the deformed edge of the table. She gave a quizzical look, but behind her eyes there was something else; to Kortel, it looked like fear. Shoalburg was still sitting, his prosthetic eyes void of any emotion. Zvara had his hands thrust deep into the pockets of his khakis, and his assistant was out cold at the base of a 6-foot equipment stack.

"Carter," Kortel said, "you're the only guy I trust here." He pointed at Hammler. "Is he serious?"

Shoalburg blinked calmly. "Like a goddamn heart attack, Jonny."

Kortel was numb. Maybe St. John was right about his world being full of shit. And what *was* there for him in Russia, except bleak safe houses and a lifestyle that probably wasn't any better than what he'd have here?

"I told you," Zvara said with a fatherly edge to his voice.

"What?" Kortel said, resigned to the situation. "What did you tell me?"

Zvara smiled. "That this was the part where you would grow some balls."

10 Was.

"THAT'S him?" Rocket asked.

Sanjiv referenced his netpad. "His displacement signature matches what's on file."

"How did you get his sig data?" Bixx asked. She shifted her position, trying to get comfortable in Sanjiv's new Familiagon. The front seats seemed too close to the dash, but Sanjiv had assured her this was the "roomier" model. Big enough for everyone who was important to him, he had said. That was key, because Sanjiv had a huge family.

"A friend of mine got it for me," he said. "He works in records."

Bixx felt her butt going to sleep. She slipped out of her All-Terrains and propped her feet on the dash. Sanjiv shot her a harsh look, so she sat up in the seat and crossed her legs.

"He doesn't look all that special," Rocket said. He was in the back seat leaning over Bixx's shoulder. His breath tickled her earlobe. He reached across the console and snatched the last fry from her lunch.

Bixx peered out the tinted Familiagon's windshield at James McCarris, who sat comfortably at an outdoor cafe. His table had attenuated legs that seemed to merge with the tile of the porch. The whole four-top looked solid – dense, as if it had grown right out of the floor. But it hadn't, because she had seen McCarris slide the table out of a shaft of light. The cafe was part of Colonial Market and situated in one of its commons. The area was canyoned by other buildings, which by midafternoon would create a tapestry of light shafts that would creep through the area. Finding a calm spot to read or talk was usually a challenge, but it looked like McCarris had accomplished the task, because he had been quietly reading his netpad, uninterrupted, for the last hour.

"He was once the head of Recruiting," Sanjiv remarked. "Before Kortel erased him."

"Yeah," Rocket said, "I never understood why Kortel did that."

"The story I heard," Bixx said, "was that when they first discovered Kortel, he was running this upscale restaurant in Chicago."

"It was real good," Sanjiv agreed. "I ate there once, before he was discovered. All biofood and very chic. His genetic matching was award-winning."

"Anyway," Bixx said, "he was dating this prostitute–"

"What?!" Rocket interrupted.

"Yeah, a high-end one. What's your issue? I have a good friend back in Russia who put herself through grad school that way."

"Okay," Rocket said, "I'm sorry. No disrespect to that noble profession. So go on, Kortel's dating a skank, and?..."

Sanjiv snickered.

Bixx, still watching McCarris, flipped them both off. "Rumor was," she continued, "that he was completely into this girl. I've seen classified photos. She'd make a straight girl gay. She had a friend, an Asian, who was equally hot. McCarris had been assigned to bring Kortel in, but when he ordered the back-end erasing, he didn't do everyone."

"You're shitting me," Rocket said. "Who he'd leave clean, the prostitute?"

"No, the Asian. Seems they had a little thing going on the side. Kortel found out a couple of years later and went crazy. He scratched McCarris's brain all the way to his childhood. I heard that when they went in to do the restoration, he had the intelligence of a 5-year-old."

Rocket whistled. "Man, that's severe."

"Why? If I learned a Recruiter erased you, but had left one of your buddies clean so she could fuck him, I'd go scratch her too. I guarantee you, when she woke up, she'd be looking for a diaper." Bixx put her feet back on the dash.

"I wonder how they built him back up?" Sanjiv mused. "I've never heard of anyone surviving that deep of an erasing."

Bixx shrugged. "One neuron at a time, I guess. I'm sure

that guys like McCarris have their brains backed up. I would if I were at his level."

"Well, maybe," Rocket said. "But 5 years old? Come on, that's–"

"Hey," Sanjiv said, pointing. "He's leaving."

McCarris paid the waiter and began edging his way through the maze of patrons and tables.

"Come on," Bixx said, slipping back into her All-Terrains.

"Do you have a plan or something?" Sanjiv asked.

"Something," she answered.

Sanjiv shot Rocket a questioning look.

"I just do what I'm told," Rocket said. "She's in control here."

Sanjiv shook his head. "That's what I was afraid of."

"Shut up, you two!" Bixx said, tightening the straps of her All-Terrains. She jumped from the Familiagon and crossed the street, falling into step about 20 feet behind McCarris. She matched his casual pace and tried to blend in with the crowd. Sanjiv and Rocket fell in behind her.

McCarris strolled away from the mall's perimeter shops and headed toward one of its large parking garages.

"I don't like the feel of this," Bixx heard Sanjiv whisper to Rocket.

"There's three of us and one of him," she said over her shoulder.

"Yeah," Rocket said, "but his Tel strength is stronger than the three of us combined."

"Not anymore," Bixx said.

McCarris crossed Pennsylvania Avenue and began walking up the steep ramp of the parking garage. Bixx started to cross, but Rocket grabbed her arm and pulled her back onto the curb.

"Hold up," he said. His fingers were digging into her bicep, and Bixx knew she was about to get a lecture. "Do you know who you're dealing with here?"

Bixx pulled away and rubbed her arm. "I think I've got a lock on what this guy is about. Why?" She glanced over to the garage in time to see McCarris take one of the side ramps to the upper levels.

"Why? Because he's a fucking Level 7!"

"I have it on good authority that James McCarris is, at best, a Level 3."

"And what 'authority' is that?" Sanjiv asked.

Bixx was losing what little patience she had. She got in Sanjiv's face. "Do you want to find Kreet?"

"Well, ah, yes...I do."

Bixx angrily pointed toward the garage. "Unless you've got a better plan, McCarris is our best hope of finding him!" She looked at Rocket.

"Baby," he said, "we don't know–"

"*Poshol nahuj!* I'll do it myself!" Bixx jumped from the curb and ran toward the garage, barely dodging two CitiCabs in the process. She could hear Rocket yelling at her, but she didn't stop. Something was pushing her, but it wasn't that she was particularly fond of Kreet – the little fart had gotten all of them into more trouble than she cared to remember. It was more about getting back at the latex bitch and the plastic-haired Brit. They had crossed the line with Bixx, and she was determined to get some revenge.

The ramp was deceiving, and about halfway up, the biomatrix of her All-Terrains shifted their soles' tread pattern to accommodate the grade. It was like having claws under her, and she opened her stride to catch up with McCarris. Bixx ran about 15 off-road miles a week, so she was used to her shoes thinking for themselves. The last she saw of McCarris, he was headed up the west ramp to the second level. It had only been about five minutes, so how far could he have gotten?

Bixx rounded the top of the circular ramp at full clip only to discover that it didn't lead to a parking level; it just kept going. Her thighs were beginning to complain.

Couldn't McCarris have taken the elevator?

She kept following the ramp as it curved upward until it finally emptied onto a parking level. All the vehicles were crammed two-high and looked like they were poured from the same vat as Sanjiv's Familiagon. Periwinkle blue seemed to be the color for this season. McCarris was nowhere in sight, and Bixx slowed to a trot. She craned her head to see over the vehicles, but there were too many, and with them stacked to the beams, she couldn't see the adjacent lanes.

"*Hooy na ny!*" Bixx's voice echoed off the old metal and cement surfaces. She stopped and gulped in some air. The soles of her All-Terrains shifted back to a walking tread, and the sensation made Bixx a little queasy, similar to what happened when she was stopped on a downtown lev and another tram slowly passed; it was a weird sense that she was moving, but she wasn't.

The parking area was strangely quiet, void of the typical tire screeches and impact warning signals. Bixx instinctually felt someone behind her. She turned. Nothing.

"Swearing isn't very ladylike."

The tread of the All-Terrains shifted to a climbing sole, and Bixx almost jumped onto the hood of an ugly green Familiagon. The imposing form of James McCarris loomed barely 15 feet behind her. He was backlit from a low-hanging mercury vapor lamp.

"But I have to admit," he continued, "when 'no fucking way' is said in Russian, it has kind of a sexy quality to it." He stepped forward, and his red hair caught the light from another lamp. He lit a cigarette and slowly exhaled the smoke upwards. "Where are your friends?"

Bixx hesitated and glanced over to the top of the ramp. She had run so fast, there was no way Sanjiv and Rocket could have kept up.

McCarris stepped closer and took a long drag. "Tell your Indian friend he needs to change the settings for the blackout filter on his van's windshield." The smoke lingered around his face. "It's not dark enough." He stepped closer. "You speak English?"

"Of course I do," Bixx said.

"Russian born?"

"Yes."

McCarris nodded, studying Bixx, then took another long drag. He wasn't at all what she had pictured. Not that she had a specific image in mind, it was just that he wasn't what she thought a guy who had been erased so badly should look like. He was taller than his photos suggested, and his red hair resembled Rocket's, though a deeper shade and not as curly. He seemed fit, his broad shoulders filling out the trim sport jacket he wore. For some reason, Bixx figured he'd be...well, scrawnier, like he had been bedridden or something.

"Am I what you thought?" he asked finally.

This caught Bixx off guard. "Pardon me?"

"Go ahead, get it over with. Take your vid, or whatever your friends put you up to." There was a frivolity to his voice, as if he sort of appreciated the attention. He blew three tiny smoke rings.

"Look," Bixx said. "I'm not here to–"

"Then why the hell are you following me?" McCarris's demeanor shifted, and his voice took on a hateful tone.

Suddenly Bixx felt all of her muscles lock down, and a crushing weight descended on her, as if gravity in her immediate space had tripled. She fought for a second, then dropped to her hands and knees.

McCarris stepped up and crushed out his cigarette inches from her right hand. He knelt. "When I was a Recruiter, bringing in Potentials, I used to feel like the weight of the world was on my shoulders. You ever have that feeling?"

Bixx struggled to raise her head and met his cold stare. There was emptiness in his eyes. She said, "I don't know what you're talking about."

"Oh, come on. You're not the first to try this. Because of

my accident, I've become somewhat of an enigma in our culture. Kind of a phoenix." McCarris looked away for a second, then back. "No," he said, "more like Lazarus...back from the dead!"

The elevator at the other end of the level chimed. Bixx slowly moved her head in time to see the doors open. Rocket and Sanjiv stepped out. Rocket saw her first.

"Hey," he yelled, "what are you doing to her?!" There was a surprising amount of authority in his voice. He started charging toward them.

"The boyfriend?" McCarris asked. He stood and pulled another cigarette from his pocket.

At about 20 feet, Rocket froze in midstride. He rose into the air until his head almost hit one of the crossbeams. Sanjiv, who had been running behind, skidded to a stop.

McCarris lit the cigarette. His demeanor had calmed, and he lazily exhaled the smoke. Bixx felt the pressure lighten slightly. She could now move her head more easily; breathing, though, was still a bit of a challenge.

Rocket floated toward them, his face caught in a strange mix of shock and fear.

"Please don't hurt him," Bixx managed.

McCarris now seemed intensely focused on moving Rocket, which struck Bixx as odd, because even for a Level 3, moving something as small as Rocket's body should've been child's play.

Child's play.

Rocket's bright red hair was a spray of curls, and they bounced slightly as he settled onto the pavement. When his feet touched, he gasped and began coughing.

"Man," he said between gasps. "Your field strength...it's too tight. You were choking me." He continued coughing.

Bixx felt the pressure lighten again, but not enough to allow her to stand. Her lower back was beginning to ache, and her calves started to cramp.

"You put her up to this?" McCarris asked.

"Hell no," Rocket said. "Now release your grav field or I'll–"

"Or you'll what? Kick my ass?"

Bixx watched Sanjiv cautiously approach. He kept a safe distance and avoided eye contact. *Wimp*.

McCarris looked at Sanjiv. "Join the party, friend."

Sanjiv suddenly went stiff, then slid over to Rocket and slammed into him, almost knocking them both down.

"Okay, take it easy," Sanjiv said to McCarris.

"Come on," Rocket said, straightening. "Would you please release my girlfriend?"

The pressure on Bixx disappeared, and she collapsed onto her stomach. Rocket rushed to her side.

"Oh, my back," she exclaimed. Her left calf began to cramp. "Shit, my leg!" She rolled over and began desperately massaging her calf.

Rocket jumped to his feet and lunged at McCarris. "You asshole!" he screamed. He got within an arm's length of McCarris and froze.

McCarris didn't flinch. "Good ol' fashioned chivalry," he said. His attention went to Rocket's hair. "Nice color."

Suddenly the air around Rocket's body began to distort like a wall of water was washing over him. Bixx's ears popped. Then McCarris was thrown violently about 30 feet and crashed into the side of a small cargo van. At the same instant, Rocket yelled something unintelligible and stumbled forward, almost falling to his hands and knees.

"Damn, that was incredible," he said, looking himself over.

Bixx had never seen Rocket so angry, and definitely not that powerful. To break a grav field like that meant he must have jumped a level. In an odd way, the whole thing was kind of flattering.

Rocket turned to her and grinned. "You thought I'd never do something like that, did you?" he said.

Bixx smiled.

"Nice move," McCarris said. He was leaning against the cargo van and dusting off the arms of his coat. "Tight threshold, clean focus, and a hell of a punch."

Rocket faced McCarris. "You fucking deserved that."

"Yeah, you're probably right." McCarris began to walk toward them, but doubled over and clutched his left knee. "Man, that smarts." He straightened and forced himself to walk.

"All she wanted was some information."

This stopped McCarris. "I thought you were out to get my image or something." He rubbed the side of his knee and continued hobbling.

Bixx stepped up to Rocket's side. "We came here to see if you knew anything about our friend Kreet."

"What's a Kreet?" McCarris asked. He limped over to a late-model silver Street Hugger.

"BACK OFF NOW!" it commanded. "You have violated my security perimeter!"

"It's me, you fucking piece of bioshit. ID: McCarris, James."

"My apologies, sir. Voice recognition confirmed."

Bixx thought she saw the color of its body redden slightly.

"Retard rental," McCarris explained while he sat on its hood. He began gingerly rubbing the side of his knee. "Now, who's this Kreet guy?"

"You gave Jonathan Kortel's incepts to him," Sanjiv said, finally doing something besides standing.

McCarris was now leaning heavily against the Hugger. He folded his arms tightly across his chest. "Oh, that guy. Always wore a scarf. Yeah, I remember him. He paid well. Had a big stupid plan to spring our kind out. So what's the problem? He get caught?"

"We don't know exactly," Bixx said, and she proceeded to tell McCarris about her encounter with the Brit and the woman.

At one point, McCarris's face went blank, like he either didn't buy that part of the story or he didn't understand its relevance to him. When Bixx finished, he just sat on the hood of the Hugger and stared forward.

"So," Bixx finished, "if you have any–"

McCarris raised his hand. "Hold on, I'm thinking...which is a little hard for me to do these days."

"Sorry."

McCarris sat there for what felt to Bixx like forever before sliding off the hood of the Hugger. He walked over with a slight limp, but less labored.

"I think I know one of these characters," he said. "I don't know who the woman is, but if your description of the guy is accurate, I think he's..." McCarris looked away, like he would find his answer among the Familiagons.

"What about him?" Bixx asked.

McCarris looked back, but acted like he was listening to something only he could hear. "He sure sounds like a guy I used to know," he said, finally. "But he can't be." His eyes lost focus again.

"Are you okay?" Sanjiv asked.

"Hmm, what? Oh, yeah... I'm okay, I guess. I mean, as okay as a guy can be given my condition."

"What is your condition, exactly?" Rocket asked.

McCarris's expression hardened, and Bixx thought he and Rocket would start in on each other again. But he relaxed and lit up another cigarette.

"I was told I was in a diagnostic accident." He made quote marks with his fingers, and the smoke from his cigarette formed little puffs that rose delicately into the air. "Hell, I don't know. When you lose most of your memory, you don't know what to believe. It's not like I had a choice in the matter. My brain got wiped pretty good...back to my childhood. At least I had that left." He took a long, thoughtful drag and exhaled. "I had my memory backed up, but they couldn't download all of it.... Something about a graying of the neural compatibility, so they did the next best thing."

"What was that?" Sanjiv asked.

"Connected me to my backup." He took another drag. "Via the Net. Bioimplants. They say I have enough tech in my head now to run a small city."

"That's why you looked like you were listening to something," Bixx said. "Just a minute ago, right?"

McCarris smiled and tapped the side of his head.

"You mean that some of your brain functions are being fed to you...right now?" Rocket asked.

"Kind of. It's not like my breathing or digestion is done for me – just some of the higher functions. You don't really use all of your brain anyway. When I need to access info or a skill I used to have, I just go online...in my head, sort of. It's complicated, but you get the idea." He laughed. "It's great for golf, and don't play chess with me. I'll kick your butt every time." He took another drag. "The only issue is storage. I gotta keep going back to the well."

"But what about this British guy?" Bixx asked. Her lower back twinged, and she rubbed at it with her knuckles.

McCarris's demeanor went serious, like a switch in him had been thrown. Maybe it had, Bixx realized.

"Right, the guy with the plastic hair. Well, that's got me puzzled. See, when I met him – about nine years ago – he was a corporate mercenary...a suit soldier. He did work for the Big Five, mostly around the Pacific Rim."

"So what has you puzzled?" Bixx asked.

"You said his grav wave, the one he hit you with, was a Level 6, right?"

"I think so. At least that's what it felt like." Bixx fought the urge to scratch at the bandage on the back of her head.

McCarris shook his head. "That's weird."

"What is?" Rocket asked.

"If this *is* the same guy, he didn't have that power when I met him..." McCarris's voice trailed off, and Bixx couldn't tell if he was thinking for himself or if he was being helped.

"Maybe he grew in level since you knew him," Sanjiv offered.

McCarris shook his head again. "No, you don't get it."

"What?" Rocket said. "Tels grow in strength all the time. You got a taste of that tonight, I'd say." He took Bixx's hand and gave a slight squeeze.

"I'm not talking about level strength."

"Then what are you talking about?" McCarris wasn't making any sense, and Bixx was beginning to think that his link with the Net was screwed up.

"This guy who attacked you, and probably took Kreet, shouldn't be able to do what he did." McCarris's voice was now filled with earnest. He threw his cigarette to the ground and got into Bixx's face. "The Suit Soldier came out of the SAS...*British* Special Air Service."

"Oh my God," Sanjiv said to himself.

Bixx was confused. She looked at Sanjiv then back to McCarris. "Okay, wait a minute. Does somebody want to explain this to me?"

Sanjiv cleared his throat. "If he was in the British military, he has to be a normal."

"Correction," McCarris said. "Was a normal."

Great. 11

KORTEL couldn't find any comfort in the faces across the table. Richter, Hammler, Zvara, even Shoalburg with those androidian eyes of his, were all looking at him as if he should say something profound. *Something profound?* he thought. *Hell, I'm still trying to get my head around what I just heard.*

Halfway through Richter's explanation, Kortel got lost when her holopresentation segued into the mathematics underpinning her theory. He started watching her lips. They reminded him of an old receptionist's of his, but fuller, and not so peaked. They puckered slightly when Richter said the word radiation, which she did about a hundred times. And the edges of her mouth curled into little dimples...just like Tamara's. He had loved that about Tamara and was beginning to enjoy it with Richter, who looked pretty damn good for nearly 50.

He leaned forward, and the bulb from the lamp above the table, which had been hidden by its shade, flared like a little sun. Even though he knew he shouldn't look at it, he did, and its glare burned into his vision. He rubbed his eyes and tried to will away the negative image of the bulb, along with the nightmare he had just heard.

"Are you all right?" Zvara asked.

Kortel leaned back and looked vacantly at him. The afterburn had died somewhat, replaced by a little crescent that floated in the center of his vision. He felt a headache coming on. "What kind of a question is that?" He couldn't think of anything better to say.

"Jonny, I know this is a lot to take in," Shoalburg said. "Hell, I work with this stuff, and it still takes me a while to absorb it all."

"I was with you until the part about extinguishing all life on the planet."

Richter gave a slight shrug. "It's just a theory," she said. "But, then again...the numbers don't lie."

The numbers. There was that math shit again. Kortel had a rudimentary knowledge of astrophysics, but this stuff, with its helioseismology data and CME stats, had his brain swimming. Richter had used more acronyms in her presentation than his Agency quantum grav teacher had in a whole year. It was the CME acronym – coronal mass ejection – that gave Kortel a particularly bad case of the willies. For the last decade, Richter had been tracking the eruptions of plasma on the sun's surface, which on a normal day kept the earth bathed in a steady, all-sustaining glow. But for the last eight months, there had been a disturbing amount of violent ejections that had bombarded the earth with ever-increasing amounts of radiation.

"I still don't get it," Kortel said. "Our sun has been cooking along for the last four billion years, and now its nuclear furnace is going to melt down? Why now?"

Richter exchanged an uneasy glance with Hammler.

"You see, it's quite simple," Hammler said. "Data from the NCAR's Coriolis 4 satellite confirms that the turbulence in the fraculae between the granules accounts for the disgorging of the mega CMEs."

Kortel felt his head beginning to throb. He rubbed the side of his temple.

"Umm...I think Mr. Kortel needs it explained in a more understandable way," Richter said. She grabbed her chair and walked around the table, careful not to touch its deformed edge. She sat, and her dark bangs fell across her forehead, revealing a look Kortel had sometimes glimpsed in women her age – that how-she-looked-when-she-was-20 look. The bangs also gave her a retro appearance that worked well with her biofabric cargo shorts and runner's warm-up top. When she approached, her shorts changed to the color of the aluminum chair, even matching the shadows that spilled across her legs. Kortel noticed that they were lean and muscular. Her quadriceps flexed as she settled in. He scooted his chair around and faced her. Up close, Richter had fine lines around her eyes – which Kortel had heard Tarris's mom call "crow's feet" – and a narrow white streak cut a path through her dark hair. Obviously, Richter had shunned the cultural pressure to bioaugment, which most people had done by the time they left high school.

"The sun isn't melting down," she explained, brushing back her hair. "It's actually doing the opposite. CMEs have been happening for millennia, and for the most part usually cause only minor disturbances such as power outages and communication disruptions.... It's the radiation that does it."

There was that word again. Kortel's attention was drawn to her lips. "I wouldn't call any of those minor," he said.

She grinned and her dimples reappeared. "Compared to what's going to happen, they are."

"*Might* happen," Hammler said. "It's still a theory."

Richter smiled curtly. Her eyes didn't leave Kortel. "Well, yes...it might happen. But as I said before, the numbers don't lie."

"What do you call this killer CME?" Kortel asked.

"A Tsunami Ejection," Shoalburg interjected, "but this one would be the mother of all ejections." He gave a nervous laugh, which no one else joined.

"Could it really do that much damage?" Kortel asked.

Richter gathered Kortel's hands into hers. The gesture caught him off guard, but for some reason he didn't resist. His attention went to her pale green eyes.

Richter leaned in. "Jonathan, what I'm telling you *will* happen. It's just a matter of time."

Her use of his first name came across with an intense

intimacy, and her inflection on the word *will* hit Kortel somewhere near his survival instinct.

"If my calculations are accurate," she continued, "then within one, maybe two years, the earth will experience a coronal ejection on a level it's never seen before. When it arrives, it'll cause massive destruction in a matter of hours. It might even reduce the planet to a lifeless rock."

Kortel shuddered at this last statement. Although he tried to subtly slip from her hold, Richter pulled him back. There was strength to her grip, but it didn't feel like the result of the weight training she obviously did. It felt more like someone who was scared and didn't want to let go.

"I–" she began, but couldn't manage the rest. She nervously averted Kortel's gaze, and her grip fell away. The tough woman-in-charge who had just lectured Kortel about the possible end of the world had vanished. She folded her arms tightly across her chest; the reality of her numbers seemed to weigh heavily upon even her.

"Hey, come on," Kortel said, "it can't be as bad as–"

Richter's gaze cut him short. "I've been studying the sun for most of my adult life. You never think it could happen." She looked away again, struggling to find the words. "You're correct, you know.... The sun *has* been steadily burning for billions of years, but now I think something is changing." Richter composed herself and swallowed deeply. "Gravity," she said to herself.

"What's that?" Kortel asked.

The woman-in-charge had returned. "The earth is protected from CMEs by its gravitational field," she said. "But this kind of ejection will be too powerful. It will hit us with a southward magnetic orientation, the opposite of the earth's, and compress our protective magnetosphere. Its force will peel back the field lines like an onion and expose the planet to a radiation hit. It'll make Chernobyl look like a pinprick."

Kortel was stunned by this revelation. Chernobyl had been the worst nuclear accident in history. The plant had been partially shut down in the late 20th century by a similar, much smaller incident, but the energy crisis of 2032 had forced the Russians to reopen it, supposedly safeguarded by new technology. Kortel was well aware that the term "new" was subject to debate in Russia. Today, a 100-mile radius around Chernobyl was still kept closed to human traffic.

Richter's intensity was beginning to make Kortel uncomfortable, and he shifted in his seat. The data from her research seemed plausible, but despite Hammler's insistence that her global destruction theory was weak, Richter's passion was carrying the day with Kortel. He could sense something about Richter's conviction that suggested she wasn't basing her theory on just the data. He also sensed the direction of her line of thought on gravity. "I'm not that powerful," he said.

"We don't know that yet, Jonny," Shoalburg countered. "You've demonstrated incredibly powerful grav fields. Hell, you're altering matter, for God's sake." He gestured at the deformed part of the table. "Hammler's right – you could be our only hope."

Kortel spun around. "Carter, you're talking about the earth! I could never produce a field that large!"

"You wouldn't do it alone," Shoalburg said. "You'd be the, ah, I don't know...what's the word?" He glanced at Hammler for help. "Lens?"

"Don't you see?" Zvara said. "It's your destiny.... It's why God gave you your gift."

Kortel felt nauseated, but at least he couldn't feel his headache anymore. He turned and faced Richter. She smiled thoughtfully with an expression that said, "Go ahead, ask the question."

Kortel hesitated. "What do you think, doctor?"

Richter took in a breath. "I don't know a lot about the technology in your head. That's Dr. Shoalburg's field of expertise. But from the technical data that I've seen on you, in theory, you have the potential. It's your... " She hesitated, and Kortel thought the woman-in-charge was vanishing again.

"The what?" he asked.

Richter nodded to herself, like she was doing some kind of mental bolstering. "I've read your, ah, psychological evaluations."

This hit Kortel squarely in his ego, as if he hadn't been hit with enough already. "And?"

"Let's just say that for this to work, we're going to have to work on your mental stability."

Kortel looked down and shook his head. It was almost impossible to wrap his brain around everything that had been handed to him over the last few days. And to make matters worse, now he was a neurotic fuck in need of therapy. He felt Richter stroke the side of his face: the touch comforting, familiar, like something borne on the wings of a memory. He raised his eyes to find Richter smiling.

"How do you feel?" Her voice suddenly put him at ease.

"Like a reluctant superhero in need of some self-actualization."

"Jonny, you've had enough life-altering presentations for one day," Shoalburg said, standing. "Come on. Let's get out of here and grab some dinner." He patted Kortel's shoulder and walked over to Zvara.

Kortel caught Richter staring at him. "Would you like to join us for dinner?" he asked her.

"Only if I'm not intruding."

He waved her comment off and stood. "Tag along. I'll have Carter show you one of his eyes. You'd appreciate its technology."

Kortel and Richter followed Zvara and Shoalburg out the door into the dark hallway. Her boots squeaked on the old linoleum as they walked along in silence. Closer now to her, Kortel could smell her bath wash – or whatever she was wearing. It was citrusy and had an expensive edge to it, like something from an exclusive African spa.

"Mikado," she said suddenly.

"I'm sorry?" Kortel asked.

"My body spray – it's called Mikado."

"How did you–"

"You were practically sniffing my hair."

Jesus. "I'm sorry," Kortel offered. "I-I don't know why–"

Richter laughed. "Don't worry. I'm not offended. I

grew up with three brothers. There's not much that fazes me."

Down the long hallway, Kortel mentally chastised himself for being such an ass. He felt for the infuser in his pocket and fingered its reassuring shape. He caressed its trigger, fighting the urge to help himself to a dose. "Can I ask you another question?" He placed his hands behind his back.

"You can ask me anything, anytime," Richter said.

"How long will it take this CME to reach us?"

"A typical one takes two to three days to reach our magnetosphere."

"But I thought light from the sun took minutes."

"It does, but a Tsunami Ejection is different.... It's made of matter, not photons. Plus, we don't know how fast it will travel. It might take a day or less."

"At least you'll be able to detect this thing before it happens, and give me time to do whatever it is I'm going to do, right?"

Richter stopped and faced Kortel. Her expression suggested he wasn't going to like her answer.

"It doesn't work like that," she said gravely. "We can't accurately predict when an ejection will occur…yet. We could be hours, even days off. When it happens, you'll have to react instantly."

Richter quickly turned and continued walking. Kortel noticed her shorts had returned to their preset color of fatigue green. He watched her reach the end of the hallway and disappear into the harsh light of the lobby.

"Great," he said to himself. His headache had returned.

Media circus. 12

BIXX stared into her fresh beer and watched its head slowly dissipate. She never understood what the big deal was about getting the foam just right – to her, beer tasted the same, head or no head. Rocket and Sanjiv had indoctrinated her with the virtues of finding the perfect beer. For them, it was practically a religion.

"You need to start drinking...before it all dies," Rocket said, gesturing toward the foam.

"I know," Bixx said. "Before the head dips below the 1-inch mark." Beer, she had been informed, needs to be tapped with at least a 2-inch head in order to be considered a good draft. And to qualify as a perfect beer? Well, that was for the gods to decide.

"See," Sanjiv said, "she's learning."

Bixx raised her glass and proceeded to down the 16 ounces in one continuous gulp. It was a technique she had perfected in

Russia, when she made 100 digirubles a night off of stupid freshmen by betting they couldn't beat her in a chugging contest. She'd just open her throat and let the beer flow. Most guys' gag reflex would end the competition before she had to finish her glass. Bixx had learned to relax her muscles and control the urge to puke. It had been a useful trick that had helped pay for her apartment during school.

"That's right, baby," Rocket said, sarcastically. "Go ahead and savor *every* drop."

Bixx shrugged. "Beer's beer. It all tastes the same to me. I drink for the effects." She turned to Sanjiv. "Wanna race?"

He shook his head. "No way."

Bixx let out a belch that caused the pool players to stop and turn.

"Excuse me," she called out.

"My, aren't we the lady," Rocket said. He scooted closer. "Why don't you order some food? That's your third one."

"*Yaytsa kuritsu ne uchat!*"

"What did she say?" Sanjiv asked.

"It's an old Russian saying," Rocket said. "I think it means: eggs cannot teach a hen, or something like that."

Bixx laughed. Rocket was always screwing up her language. "Do not give advice to someone who is more experienced than you." She raised her empty glass in salute. The beers were beginning to affect her, but she didn't care. Their encounter with McCarris had left her melancholy, but she couldn't put her finger on the reason. Sure, she was concerned for Kreet's well-being, but something else was unsettling her. Maybe it was the fact that for the last couple of weeks, Rocket and Sanjiv had been talking so much about the possibility of their culture revealing itself. Bixx never really cared if their kind came out or not, but all the talk had gotten her thinking. She wondered if this was how gays and lesbians had felt ages ago, before the Gender War and all the resulting legislation.

Rocket asked, "Bixxy, what's bothering you?"

"I don't know," she said, staring.

Sanjiv smiled. "I wouldn't worry about Kreet; he's a survivor."

"Besides," Rocket said, "McCarris promised he would do some digging on that British guy. Maybe he'll find something. He sure seems to be nicer than we figured, don't you think?"

"McCarris is just like all other senior Tels," Bixx said. "Memory or no memory, his loyalty will be to the Agency." She faced Rocket. "You think we'll ever come out?"

Rocket pondered the question for a second. "Honestly? I doubt it. Kreet's plan is cool and all, but I don't know. I can't imagine it coming together. I was surprised that he got Kortel to meet with us.... I guess everybody gets lucky now and then."

He thought for another second.

"No," he said, "it would be too difficult. Besides, there're too many higher-ups worldwide who would shut down any grassroot attempt. Kreet was right; Kortel was his ace." Rocket dropped his attention into his beer.

Suddenly, their holowaiter appeared. "Another round of

Darrion's Ale?" it asked. "Genetically mapped for authentic taste." It was a tall, 20-something male, probably modeled from extensive focus groups where upwardly mobile women detailed to marketing experts their perfect man. He wasn't quite white or black, and as Bixx studied him, she concluded he wasn't quite anything. He appeared to be an amalgamation of every popular male star of the last five years. His eyes were a complete rip from Jordan Cash, the Australian action hero currently number one on the Net, and his cleft chin was from the sim star of a couple of years ago – Tora something – the one who had dominated all the war games. He was one virtual character Bixx could get pixeled with.

"I'll take another," she said.

Rocket rolled his eyes. "Hell, why not? Make it two."

"Make it three," Sanjiv chimed in.

The holowaiter batted his Jordan Cashes and disappeared.

"I think he likes you," Sanjiv said to Bixx.

"It's not a he, it's an it," Rocket corrected.

Bixx sighed. "It, he, who cares? I'd jack with him in a heart pound."

Rocket chuckled. "It's beat, baby. Heart *beat*."

"Vhatever." Bixx's accent was showing, which happened after a few beers. One more round, and Bixx was seriously considering taking on the big guy at the pool table in a game of Eight Ball.

Soon enough a waitress approached, carrying their drinks. "Here you go," she said. "Three cold ones from the best that Ireland has to offer." Bixx's head was turned toward the pool table, but she recognized the voice. Kara was a Tel who worked with Kreet, monitoring the virt booths at the Agency. She didn't hang with their gang, and the only time Bixx ever saw her was when she was working at the bar. Bixx had always wanted to know her better, but the timing never seemed right. Kara set the fresh beers down, then their empty glasses floated onto her tray.

"Watch it there," Rocket said to her.

Kara smiled. "In this place? I doubt anyone would even notice." She placed her tray on the table and slipped new coasters under each drink. "Have you guys seen Kreet? He wasn't at his station this last week."

Bixx, Rocket and Sanjiv exchanged glances.

"No," Sanjiv said, "we were hoping you might know something."

Kara shrugged. "He's done this before. I'm surprised they let him get away with it so much."

"Get away with what?" said a voice behind her.

"Kreet!" Bixx exclaimed.

"I was just telling them how much shit you get away with," Kara said while she grabbed her tray. "I knew you'd show up sooner or later. Just like a cat." She turned and walked away.

It took Bixx a second, but then she registered who the figures were behind Kreet. The tall-heeled woman stepped forward, and the Brit gave a little wave. Bixx sunk into the booth, her heart racing.

"Is that the guy?" Rocket whispered.

Bixx nodded.

Both Rocket and Sanjiv slowly stood. They didn't even acknowledge Kreet.

"You!" Rocket yelled, pointing at the Brit. "I'm going to fuck you up!"

"Whoa, easy, cowboy!" the woman said.

Sanjiv looked at Rocket sideways. "Remember what McCarris said.... He's powerful."

Kreet stepped up to Rocket and put his hands on his chest. "Stand down, Roc. These are my business associates."

Rocket glowered at him. "That asshole almost killed Bixx."

Kreet turned to the Brit. "You told me you only pushed her once."

"Right," the Brit said, flashing his perfect smile. "It was a little more than a push. Kind of a throw, I'd say." His attention went to Bixx. "Sorry, love. I got into the Ride that night, and that stuff gets me going. Hope you're okay and all. I know a good doctor–"

"Shut up!" the woman said. She turned to Bixx. "I am sorry, honey. Marcus here can get a little enthusiastic about his job. Ex-military, gung-ho and all, you know the type. Did he hurt you much?" She turned to the Brit. "You hurt her, didn't you?" She shook her head. "Good God."

Bixx didn't know how to respond. The whole scene was surreal: the woman standing there in those heels, her jumpsuit styled out in a crisp, businesslike manner. She wore a pair of heavy framed glasses, which meant she was jacked, because no one needed glasses anymore. Then there was the Brit, dressed in that same suit from the night in the bathroom. He was leaning against a chair, casually considering the decor of the bar. Bixx kept thinking about what McCarris had said about him, how he had once been a normal.

The woman gingerly touched the side of her glasses, and the lenses went dark. "Cindy, in the morning, get me the name of that doctor who did Jordan Cash's face, after the accident.... No, he's in L.A. How should I know? Look him up. No, keep this away from the front office.... And get me the folks in legal." She looked in Bixx's direction. "I don't think we have a problem, but you never know. We'll be back on Monday. Oh, and can you get me a reservation with Billie? My back is killing me. Thanks, you're a peach." The lenses became clear. She walked up to the table and folded her arms. "So these are them?" she asked Kreet.

"That's right," he said. "What do you think?"

The woman looked them over, and her lenses went dark again. "Cindy, get me a meeting with Tony on Wednesday.... I don't care if he's still in tech, get me a meeting." She pulled the glasses from her face and chewed on the end of an earpiece.

"Is everything okay?" Kreet asked.

The woman was studying Rocket. "I love this hair," she finally announced. "It's going to resonate with our demos beautifully." She turned her attention to Bixx. "And you, we'll fix the nose in post, but this whole Russian thing is perfect right now. The country is so out they're in again. And the waif look, ha! We haven't seen that for a hundred years. They'll eat this up in New York."

"Kreet!" Rocket yelled. "What the hell is going on?"

"Relax, mate," the Brit said. "Your life's about to change."

"Wait a minute," Bixx said to the woman, who was slipping her glasses back on. "Who are you?"

The woman didn't respond. She pulled from her pocket a tiny wafer of green glass and handed it to Bixx. As soon as Bixx placed it her palm, a tiny holojection began running through a montage of some of the biggest vids produced over the last 10 years. Full music came up while a voiceover declared the achievements of SecondSight Studios. Then the woman appeared, standing in Bixx's palm. She introduced herself as Megan Toffler, senior executive producer.

Bixx looked from the holo Toffler to the real Toffler. Things were getting weirder by the minute.

"The studio likes these," Toffler said. "I think they're too over the top, but they get the point across, don't you think?" Her lenses went dark, and she stepped away, barking orders to Cindy. The Brit followed.

"Kreet," Rocket said, "what have you gotten us into?"

Kreet smiled, and Bixx noticed for the first time the scarf he was wearing. On it was the famous Hollywood sign, cycling through an entire day, complete with time-lapse weather and a faint, cheesy soundtrack. She could barely hear a woman singing, but couldn't make out the lyrics.

"What have you told her?" Bixx asked. "If you've exposed us, I swear I'll break every bone–"

"She already knows everything," Kreet said. "Our

culture, the levels. She even knows about the Agencies."

"How did she know all that?"

"She won't tell me. She wants to protect her sources. She originally wanted to do a vid on Kortel's life. I have no idea how she knows about him, but she does. *Everything*."

"This is very dangerous!" Sanjiv said.

"No," Kreet said. "She wants to help us come out. She wants to make it a worldwide media event. It's about sell-through and cross-platform synergy."

"More like a media circus," Rocket said.

"She thinks it could be the biggest marketing event since the opening of the Disneyverse space station." Kreet looked at Rocket with a pleading expression. "I thought you, of all people, would understand this. You said it yourself: We can't do this by ourselves. Well, then, here's the opportunity, dropped right in our laps."

"There are 10 different Agencies around the world," Bixx said. "How are you going to get them all on board with this...*producer*?"

"Zvara's the man for that–"

"And how are you going to convince all the Tels around the world that this will work?"

"That's going to be my job."

"You already have this all worked out, don't you?" Rocket asked.

"Not everything, just the big-picture stuff. We have people who will–"

"You have *people*?" Sanjiv asked.

"Okay, Megan has people."

"You got shit without Kortel and Zvara," Rocket said.

Bixx was furious. "Kreet, we're a culture, not a product–"

"Culture is product," Toffler said, strutting back to their table. She was chewing on her frames again. "How many of your kind exist in the world?"

"Oh, I don't know," Bixx said. "Two, maybe three thousand."

Toffler smiled, and Bixx felt her stomach tighten.

"Young lady, I've created worldwide netcasts that involved hundreds of thousands of people. Uplink, downlink, transglobal feeds bounced off of the moon...you name it, I've done it. I think I can handle a few thousand outcasts." She turned to the Brit. "Did you check on our rooms in New York yet?"

"Yes," he said. "We're booked at The Thin, downtown."

"Oh, thank God. They have a wonderful spa. My blood could use an updating." Toffler began to leave, but wheeled around. "We'll be in touch. Great to meet you all. Kreet, we'll be out front." She and the Brit walked through the bar like they owned it.

"I need you guys to do something for me," Kreet said.

"Let me guess," Sanjiv said. "Find Kortel for you, right?"

"Actually I was thinking Zvara, but find one and you'll find the other." Kreet looked at Bixx, and his expression softened. "I'm really sorry you got hurt. I had no idea. I was at the bar the night Megan approached me. She never said anything about what happened to you."

Bixx folded her arms. "I'm probably going to have a scar, you know."

"A small price to pay, considering what's at stake, don't you think?" Kreet read her look. "Come on, this will work. It's what we've wanted–"

"You've wanted," Bixx corrected.

"Okay, maybe, but think about it. No more hiding. No more false names or lying about our power." He faced the others. "Wouldn't it be nice to use what God gave you for a change, without having to keep it in check? You've always said you wanted to do good in the world. Maybe now you'll be able to. But we'll never know unless we try."

"Kreet..." Bixx bit off the rest of her thought and let her anger cool. There was no changing Kreet once he had his teeth sunk into an idea. "You be careful," she said resignedly. "I don't trust those two."

Kreet inched closer. "I will. Thanks for the thought."

As he turned to leave, Bixx caught a few lyrics from his scarf. It sounded like the lady was singing *That's Entertainment*, but she couldn't make out the rest.

Adios. 13

THERE was something about a New Mexico sunset that could lock up Kortel's attention for a good hour. He had seen his share of spectacular ones: Tortola, Hawaii, and a stretch of Trans-Russian Interway where during the summer the sun never quite set but rather skipped on the horizon before ascending again. But for Kortel, a New Mexico sunset set the standard by which all others were judged. And if he had his way, he'd package it and present it to every person from New York to Atlanta. God, he hated that sprawl. His netpad hummed inside his pocket, and he fought the urge to toss it into the creek bed that ran by the base.

Tarris's holographic figure appeared above the netpad's tiny screen. He had been captured from the waist up and was outside somewhere. "What are you doing?" he asked.

"Trying to enjoy one of your state's best assets," Kortel replied.

Tarris turned to his right. "Yeah, it looks like a beautiful one tonight."

"Where are you?" Kortel asked.

"I'm at my old compound near Tres Piedras. I'm doing a little cleaning before the real estate agent gets here tomorrow."

"So you're really going to sell it?"

Tarris looked to his right again and lingered on the sunset. Shades of orange and burnt yellow contoured his face. "Too many bad memories," he said, barely audible through the gusts of wind.

"You don't need two places anyway," Kortel said.

Tarris nodded in agreement. "So how's it going?"

Kortel placed the netpad on a large rock and rubbed his temples. "They're killing me, Tarris. Shoalburg and Richter have me doing all these extreme grav tests. And Shoalburg says he'll have to enhance my level past 10.... Says he's 'tweaking' the tech in my head to be more 'parallel,' whatever the hell that means."

"Isn't Richter the one who thinks you're unstable?"

"Yeah. She's got me in these therapy sessions twice a week with a guy from the Middle East. His last name sounds like you're hocking up a fur ball."

"Is he helping?"

Kortel shrugged. "I don't know. He says I have some kind of deep-rooted trauma from the deaths of my parents."

"Well...do you?"

"Sure, me and about a million other survivors of Hawaii. He says we're close to making a breakthrough, but it feels more like a breakdown." Kortel rubbed his temples harder.

"I have a therapist," Tarris offered. "He's a 12-year-old Tennessean who weighs about 750 milliliters."

Kortel burst out laughing, and he could hear his voice echo off the dry creek bed. "Shit, what I would give for an Oban right now."

"What? They have you off drinking?"

"It's all natural for Richter. Strictly juice and water."

"Screw that," Tarris said. "I can't cope without Mr. Daniel. He's my stabilizer, especially now that I'm not Riding."

Kortel turned his attention back to the sunset. Ashen clouds edged in purple and orange hung like heavenly flotsam on the lip of the horizon. He watched a hawk tack into the wind, then dive behind a row of ponderosa pines.

"How long have you been there?" Tarris asked.

It took Kortel a second to remember. "I don't know," he said. "Six, maybe seven weeks." He thought harder, trying to recall, but the days and nights had fallen into a tedious pattern of level testing, psychoanalysis and fitful sleep. He felt a burning behind his eyes. "Six, I think."

Tarris stepped closer, and his figure loomed within the constructs of the netpad's holoparameters. "How are you holding up?" His voice had the edge of a big brother, like when they were kids.

"Good, for the most part. But I'm having these dreams." Kortel was dying for a drink. "They're, ah...I don't know, just intense."

"And?"

Kortel watched a jackrabbit scamper through thick scrub sage, its form barely visible in the fading light. It cut four hard angles and disappeared over an embankment that led to the creek bed. "They're about Tamara," he said.

"And?"

"They're kind of sexual in nature, but kind of not."

"That figures. You're lonely."

"No, it's more than that. She's been on my mind lately."

"Quit torturing yourself. You've been down that road, and you made your decision. A good one, I might add."

Kortel glanced at the sunset again. Only a few fingers of light splayed on the horizon. Then he caught the glint of a metallic wing skimming the bottom of some dark, wispy clouds. It was gold and approached at a high rate of speed.

"Fucking *hell*," he said to himself.

"What's the matter?" Tarris asked.

Kortel scooped up the netpad, clicked its imager for maximum zoom and pointed it in the direction of the craft. "Check it out," he said. "We've got company."

* * *

The only visible evidence of the jump jet's downward thrust was the slight distortion of air 30 feet below its fuselage. It had been motionless about a hundred feet above the creek bed for more than 20 minutes now. Its golden profile had been reduced to a sliver of black shadow as the evening sky gave way to night. Kortel removed the high-imaging field glasses from his eyes and stepped from the lab's bank of third-story windows.

"Tell me more about this St. John person," Shoalburg said. He pushed away from the console, but the tether of fiber optics connected to his eye implants didn't allow him to go very far. He twisted toward Kortel, and the optics slapped against the counter.

"It's like I told you," Kortel said. "He reps a consortium of companies that want me to work for them.... You know, dirty ops and crap like that. He stinks of big business and has a team of ex-Agency types who've figured a way to tap into my tech."

Shoalburg looked about, riding a wave of information only he could see. "I can't find a thing on this guy in the grid. If that's his real name, he plays under the netdar. I wouldn't worry about him interfacing with your tech. I've got this base so packaged, even the spy satellites can't see us. To them, we look like that old river bed out there."

"Then how did St. John know where to find me, assuming that is St. John out there?"

Shoalburg raised his eyebrows and looked more buglike to Kortel. "Good question."

"So where're Zvara and Richter?"

"They're in town," Hammler said, "but should be back any minute." He was busy across the room at another console and didn't seem particularly bothered by the presence of an unmarked aircraft hovering a thousand feet from the front gate of the base. Hammler had his attention buried in the latest data of Kortel's grav testing.

The door to the lab opened, and Zvara and Richter rushed in.

"Why did you not contact me about this?" Zvara asked Kortel.

"Because we didn't want to take a chance and breach the security grid," Shoalburg replied.

"Looks like it already is," Richter said, pointing to the image of the jump jet on Shoalburg's console vid screen.

Zvara picked up the field glasses and aimed them out the window toward the plane.

Kortel cleared his throat. "I think I know who that is out there."

"Errol St. John," Zvara said, still looking through the field glasses.

"Yeah, that's right. How'd you know?"

"Errol and I go back a few years...to my time as head of the Agency."

Kortel leaned against the counter and folded his arms. "Of course, I should have known."

"Jonny says he reps some conglomerates that want him on their credit roll," Shoalburg said.

Zvara slowly lowered the field glasses. He kept staring at the jet. "Mr. St. John does not work in the corporate sector," he said gravely. "He works on the fringe."

"You mean he's a freelancer?" Richter asked.

"No," Zvara replied. "He is a *consigliere.*"

"A consi-who?" Kortel asked.

"A counselor," Shoalburg said. "But I'll bet this guy's more of a consultant. Nasty sons of bitches." He quickly turned in Richter's direction. "I'm sorry."

Richter waved it off, and then realized what she was doing. "No worries," she said to Shoalburg.

"You mean St. John works for the Mafia?" Kortel asked.

"Of a sort," Zvara said. "For decades the Tels have been in…oh, help me, Carter, what is the expression?"

"In bed?" Shoalburg offered.

"Yes, bed."

"I don't get it," Kortel said. "Why would we do that?"

"No other organization can keep a secret better than the Mafia. Even with our ability to erase minds, we always had leakage with our corporate clients. But with the Mafia, there was never this issue. And like us, they, too, live out of the mainstream. They help us, and we help them." Zvara faced Kortel. "I did not want this arrangement. I inherited it when I took control of the Agency, and believe me, I am not proud of it. I fought to end it, but you do not end something like this. When you get into bed with these people, you are in for life."

Kortel looked out the window. "Shit, it's gone!"

"Carter," Zvara said, "can you see where they went?"

Shoalburg sat motionless for a second. "They're masked. I can't find any trace of their presence."

Suddenly an explosion rocked the building. The lab's lights flickered, and Richter stumbled into Kortel's arms. They both went to the floor, along with Zvara, but Shoalburg clung to the counter. Hammler shrieked as he spilled from his chair. Then there were shouts, and the sound of boots running past the lab's door. The image of St. John pixeled up on Shoalburg's vid screen. Zvara frantically motioned for Kortel to crawl out of its imager's range. He did, quickly scooting around Richter and behind a lab station.

"Good evening, Armando!" St. John bellowed from the screen.

"Errol," Zvara said, struggling to his feet, "what did you just do?"

"Some of your men got a little excited by our presence."

"If you hurt anyone–"

"No one has been harmed, Armando. You know I don't work like that unless provoked. There is a vehicle, though, that won't be of much use to you now. And you can come out, Jonathan. I can see all of you, so there's no point in hiding."

There was a thunderous drone outside, and the glass in the old windows rattled in its panes. A dark, featureless form slowly lowered into view. Kortel could barely make out the jump jet's contour as it glided to a stop above the parking lot, slowly turned and faced the windows. Lights came on inside the cockpit, and Kortel could finally distinguish exactly where the windshield was on the jet. In the pilot's seat was the Asian, her interface gear strapped to her face like an articulated metal octopus. St. John was in the copilot's seat, bottom-lit in a red glow by the cockpit's instrumentation. He was grinning from ear to ear, but his skin remained smooth, as if defying nature to create any wrinkles.

"Jonathan," St. John said, "we need to talk...*now*."

Kortel shot a glance at Zvara, who motioned for him to come out from behind the station.

"He cannot be bought," Zvara said.

St. John chuckled. "What, are you his agent now?"

Richter and Shoalburg were standing in a dark corner to Zvara's right. Kortel looked at Richter. She smiled stoically, but he could see she was unnerved. Hammler was cowering behind his station. He looked terrified, and his eyes darted frantically between the jet, Kortel and Zvara.

"I am just a friend, Errol. That is all."

St. John's grin disappeared. "Doubtful."

"I'm not interested in working for organized crime," Kortel said. He and Zvara were now looking at St. John inside the cockpit, rather than his image on the vid screen.

St. John leveled his attention at them. "Armando, is that what you told them?" His smile came back, but it had a devilish look in the light of the cabin. "Jonathan, if you think I'm associated with the Mafia, you've been misinformed. The companies I represent are legitimate global enterprises."

"I don't care if they're part of the Pac 100," Kortel said, stepping to the window. "I'm not interested."

St. John leaned over to the pilot and said something into her ear. She nodded and the whine of the engines raised an octave. The jump jet began to pull back from the window.

"Armando," he said in a low tone, "I'm not leaving without Jonathan."

Zvara looked at Kortel knowingly, and then slowly closed his eyes.

Suddenly, the jump jet began to list to one side, its port wing coming dangerously close to the ground. Its engines roared, drowning out the audio feed to the lab, but Kortel could see St. John yelling at the pilot. The fiber optics attached to her interface gear swung madly about as she fought to get control.

"Zvara!" Kortel yelled. "Hang on, I'll join you!"

The jet violently recoiled, as if the force that had been causing it to tilt had instantly vanished. The craft rolled wildly and its starboard wing tip clipped the top of a light pole. The engines' thunderous whine cut the air as the pilot overcompensated.

"I have not gone into phase yet!" Zvara yelled.

Suddenly, the jet lurched at their building, its port wing rising toward the lab's large bank of windows.

"Look out!" Kortel screamed. "It's going to hit!–"

The jet's port wingtip tore through the wall of the building, hurling large chunks of cinder block into the lab. The leading edge of its gold biotitanium fuselage crashed into a scanning station, obliterating it in a spray of organics, metal and glass. The room's lights went out. Kortel instantly phased and launched himself at Zvara. He scooped the older Tel into his arms and landed, tumbling, behind a workstation.

"Jonathan!" Kortel barely heard Richter yell through the deafening sound of the jet's engines. He spun and saw Shoalburg on the floor. He was leaning against the wall, with Richter crouched next to him.

The wing began to exit, dragging parts of a desk and chair with it, but then it came jabbing back into the lab and slammed into the ceiling. The building shuddered as the body of the plane grazed the roof of the second story.

"It's Shoalburg!" Richter screamed through the chaos.

Kortel phased again and flew across the room. Richter's eyes were filled with awe as he landed in a skid next to her.

"My, God, it's true," she said.

"What's the matter with Carter? Shit!–"

The jet's wing was heading toward them. Kortel draped himself over Richter and Shoalburg and instantly created a grav field to protect them. The wing bounced off of it and plowed through the wall to their right. Shards of cinder block and wallboard rained over them, but the grav field acted like an unseen umbrella. Kortel watched the jet through the gouge in the wall as it moved away from their building, still pitching and rolling above the parking lot.

Richter stared at Kortel. "Thank you," she said.

Kortel just nodded. "What's the matter with Carter?"

"I think he was convulsing."

Shoalburg was still tethered to a remote interface pack that he held in his lap. Kortel watched his fingers dance across its control surface.

"Carter," he said, "are you okay?"

"It's really like one of those old vid arcades," he replied, scooting himself into a sitting position. "Once you get the hang of it, it's pretty fun. Watch this...." He pointed to the jet.

Kortel and Richter peered out though the gash in the wall. The plane was hovering about 50 feet above the parking lot when it suddenly started spinning like an old amusement ride: slowly at first, then gaining speed until it was hard to watch.

Kortel glanced from the interface pack to the 'trodes inside

Shoalburg's eye sockets. "Carter, are you controlling that jet?"

"I am now. It was hard to figure out its computer's protocols. But once I did, it was surprisingly basic." He moved his head as if glancing around the lab. "Sorry for all the damage. The jet's core was tough to wrangle, and it put up quite a fight before I managed to disable it." His fingers danced again, and the jet slowed to a stop.

The door to the lab burst open, and three men rushed in. The beams from their flashlights cut erratic patterns through the dusty air.

"Mr. Zvara, are you all right?" one of them called out.

"I am, Louis," Zvara replied. He was kneeling next to Hammler, who was crumpled on the floor and bleeding from his head. "Get a med kit up here immediately."

"I thought you were convulsing," Richter said to Shoalburg.

"Nah, just some body English fighting the jet's AI core." Shoalburg looked in Kortel's direction. "What do you want me to do with St. John?"

"I've got an idea." Kortel rushed over to one of the active vid screens. It cast the room in hot edges of blues and greens. St. John's image was still projecting, although now his hair was tousled and his suit was torn at both shoulders. He was angrily shouting something, but the sound had been cut.

"Carter," Kortel said, "can you get back the audio?"

Shoalburg's fingers danced again.

"–if you don't release my jet," St. John yelled, "I'll–"

"You'll what?" Kortel asked as Zvara came to his side.

St. John passed a hand through his hair. "I never had any intent of taking you by force–"

"Right, and that blast earlier was just a warning shot?"

St. John tugged a bit at his suit's shoulders, but quickly gave up and settled into his seat. "Sometimes I have to emphasize my position," he said arrogantly. "Besides, your men gave me no choice."

"Errol," Zvara said, "I would say that you have made your point. I think it is time for you to leave now."

St. John started to protest, but Zvara motioned for Shoalburg to cut the audio. "Carter," he said, "can you program that jet to return to its point of origin?"

"Sure. It's just a reverse-out of its inbound flight parameters. Looks like they came out of a private airport just south of London."

"Then send them on their way, before they regain control of their craft."

Shoalburg took the interface pack into both hands and began programming. As he sat on the floor with his legs folded, humming to himself, he reminded Kortel of a kid with one of Tarris's original biogame units.

"Let me know when you're ready, Carter," he said, walking over to him. "I want to personally give St. John a little nudge."

Shoalburg looked up and smiled before he returned to his programming.

Kortel helped Richter to her feet.

"Your grav display was amazing," she said. "I didn't know

you could reverse your polarity and move yourself like that. You were *flying*." She started to laugh.

"Done!" Shoalburg announced.

"Carter," Kortel said, "give me audio again."

"–my business associates won't tolerate this, Armando–"

"Mr. St. John," Kortel said, "if you ever come near me or any of my friends again, I won't be as nice as I'm about to be." Kortel motioned for the audio to be cut.

"What are you going to do, Jonny?" Shoalburg asked.

"Give him a kick in the ass. On my count, angle them for their flight home and engage their main engines. How's the air space around us?"

Shoalburg sat for a second. "We're all clear under 10,000 feet for 100 hundred miles in all directions...except south of us, of course, around Albuquerque."

"Good. Let's do it. Ready?"

Shoalburg nodded.

"Mark. Three, two, one."

The jump jet turned, and its nose angled toward the full moon rising just above the horizon. Its main engines engaged, but the jet remained in place. The jet began to shake as it fought the physics holding it captive.

"Jonny," Shoalburg said, "that fuselage can't take much of this stress. If you're going to let her rip, you better do it quick."

Kortel held the jet in a narrow grav field while its engines struggled to break free. A drop of blood slid down his upper lip.

Richter gasped. "Jonathan, don't." She started to approach

him, but Zvara stopped her. "He knows what he is doing," he said. "And believe me, this is only a fraction of his capability."

Kortel felt another drop of blood slide, and he glanced at the vid screen. St. John was frantically strapping himself into the copilot's seat.

Shoalburg quickly stood. "*Jonny* ..."

"Now, Carter," Kortel said. "Kick in their afterburners."

Shoalburg passed his index finger over the upper corner of the interface's control pad, and flames shot from previously unseen exhaust outlets.

Kortel glanced at the vid screen. *Adios, asshole.*

The jump jet shot away from the base in a flash of orange and white. In the time it took for Kortel to exhale, it disappeared into a thin layer of clouds backlit by the glow of the full moon.

Kortel wiped away the blood from his lip. He examined it for a second between his fingers, and then rubbed it off on the side of his pants. *That's weird*, he thought. *I haven't bled like that in a long time.*

Richter came to his side. "Are you okay?"

"Oh, yeah. That's not that big of a deal to pull off. It's all in how you structure the grav field."

Zvara started chuckling.

Kortel turned. "I don't think I've ever heard you laugh before. What's so funny?"

"Nothing," Zvara said. "I just had a mental image of St. John cleaning out that cockpit."

"I hope he hurled into every nook and cranny on that plane," Shoalburg said.

Zvara approached Kortel. "You know this will not be the last time we see him."

"I know, but we'll be ready for him, right?" Kortel looked questionly from Zvara to Shoalburg to Richter. "Can I get a 'hell yes' here?"

"Jonathan, you have to understand something," Zvara said. "With these people, losing is not an option."

MEGAN Toffler frowned behind the thick black frames of her Net glasses. "I thought you said she was good at this...a real natural."

"She is," Kreet said defensively. He leaned into Bixx's ear. "Bixxy, Megan has a six o'clock out of Dulles, and we need for you to start in *this* lifetime."

2:08 p.m. Bixx stared at the virtgear disc on the counter. Its inert presence could fool you into thinking it was just another of the inane tchotchkes collected from her travels that littered her workstation. Rocket had warned that one day she wouldn't be able to find her netgear amidst all the crap. *Maybe he was right. Maybe she should just dump it all into the waste can. And while she was at it, trash the virtdisc, too*. Bixx turned to eye Toffler. An eyebrow slowly rose over the top of the Net glasses.

Bixx let out a deep sigh. She loved being in the Net, but hated the way the new virtdiscs attacked your head. “Okay, let’s get this over with.” She spun and faced her workstation.

“That’s my girl,” said Kreet.

Bixx grabbed the disc and shoved her chair away from the station. The top edge of its lumbar support stabbed Kreet just above his crotch. He groaned and doubled over.

“Sorry,” Bixx said, “I need a little room for this.”

“Sure, right,” Kreet managed. “Anything for a genius.” He hobbled over to Toffler and parked himself on the counter of another workstation.

Bixx raised the disc to her forehead.

“Remember,” Toffler said, “just locate Kortel. Don’t try and collect any other data. I don’t need to know what he’s been eating or who he’s been sleeping with. The less you gather, the less likely you’ll expose yourself. The last thing we need is somebody getting to him first.” She turned to Kreet. “She knows how to mask her movement, doesn’t she?”

Bixx glared.

“She’s the best,” Kreet said.

This associate of Kreet’s was beginning to piss Bixx off. With her marketing studies and genetigraphic mood charts, she had been into everyone’s shit for the last two weeks. She had flown in three times from God knows where just on “dialogue” with Bixx, Rocket and Sanjiv about their “take” to approaching Kortel. Rocket finally lost it and suggested Toffler should let Bixx search for him, because she knew more about navigating the

Net than all of Toffler's console jocks combined. Rocket's opinion of Bixx's ability was always flattering, but this compliment was a bit of a stretch, considering she only had a fundamental knowledge of nodal dynamics. But the door had been opened, and surprisingly, Toffler agreed.

Bixx hesitated, the virtdisc inches from her forehead.

"Today?" Kreet asked.

Even before Bixx placed the disc to her skin, its biomatrix sensed the impending union and released its interface tentacles. Bixx gritted her teeth while its fiber optics slithered across her face and neck, seeking the optimal points of contact. The last tentacle found the port at the base of Bixx's neck and clicked into place. Toffler, Kreet and the warehouse space melted away as the Net's vastness pixeled up in her vision.

"*Bliad*," she heard herself say before the Net completely engulfed her reality.

Bixx was now floating in what the Guardians for God labeled "the Devil's Playground." But for her, the Net was a gateway to an endless supply of information…and hope. As a little girl in St. Petersburg, she had often sneaked onto her father's old computer and explored the realm of cyberspace, although she never understood why it was called that. It was neither space nor cybernetic. After her parents had died in one of Russia's many mass transit accidents, Bixx had been shuttled through a maze of state structures. She luckily ended up in a *dyetskii dom*, a children's home for "educable" children. There, she begged the staff to let her log hours past the allotment mandated by the Ministry of

Education. Around the age of 17, Agency Recruiters approached Bixx, and her life changed forever. She once tried to find out how they had discovered her, but she could never hack into the Agency's main grid. Nestled in the Tel culture, she continued studying the intricacies of the medium. When she learned of its history, she was amazed that the Net had been developed for something as archaic as email.

Suddenly, Toffler's image appeared, floating in front of her. She looked the same, except the lenses of her glasses were dark. The chaos of the Net swirled behind her to jarring effect.

"Hello, honey," Toffler said, her mouth and words out of sync. "I can't stay long. This netwear is a loaner from corporate, and it doesn't interface well with my chemistry. Gives me a hell of a headache." Her form jittered slightly, as if something had interrupted the feed. "I wanted to tell you that our boys lost Kortel a month ago outside of Albuquerque. I swear, ever since our country did this merger with Mexico, all those border states have gone Wild West on us. You might want to start there. Here are all the incepts we have from him." A menu box unfolded to the left of Toffler, and a series of inception codes cascaded down its screen.

"What's that one?" Bixx asked, pointing to the last code entry.

"Looks like startup protocol from a cheap credit phone. He must have bought one on the street, but I'm not sure why." Toffler shrugged. "Who knows? The more I learn about this guy, the more I question the whole concept. Anyway, you go do whatever you Net folks do, and we'll chat when you come out. *Ciao*." Her image vanished.

The Net always smelled to Bixx like long-chain monomers and lettuce. The plastic smell she could understand, but lettuce? That always creeped her out. It took Bixx a minute to get used to the rhythm of the Net. When Rocket asked her to describe it, she said it felt like an ocean of vegetable oil, the data like schools of neon fish on the Nature Channel, except there were trillions of them, and they were the size of your fingernail. Even this description paled in comparison to the real thing. Another aspect she could never get used to was the speed. The mass of data moved at an incredible rate, though it never looked blurred, at least not to Bixx. She could always capture individual bits if she focused hard enough; it was similar to looking at the spokes of a spinning wheel and catching a single spoke by blinking. One of her professors at the Agency said she had an "infinite perception," but Bixx just thought she was good at math. In the Net, the data seemed to speak to her. She couldn't explain it, and she never said anything in front of Sanjiv. He thought all her talk about nodal points and data textures was a bunch of crap. When Bixx suggested Sanjiv try the Net, he almost bit her head off, exclaiming he wouldn't be caught dead in there; besides, his body wasn't the right fit for a port connector. Bixx had to admit that only a small portion of the population had the correct "acceptance threshold" for porting. She had gotten her first one from an off-line vendor when she was at the orphanage. It was cheap and not very reliable. When she arrived at the Agency, its techies retrofitted her with a bioptic model custom-grown for her. They said it was more than she would ever need. One of the techs liked Bixx, and on her 18th birthday added a range booster to her port.

Bixx had learned practically everything she knew about the Net from her teachers at the Agency, especially her Construct professor, who taught her the finer points of nodal perception – or "listening," as he liked to call it. He told her that less than 1 percent of the people who worked in the Net had the gift, and that she should consider herself extremely blessed. Bixx had never considered herself extremely anything until Dr. Yanez had enlightened her to the subtle tones than ran underneath the data. "It's like rhythm," he had told her. "Either you hear it or you don't." Bixx had heard it all her life, but never knew what it was until Yanez taught her to open her mind and listen.

Bixx accessed a map port and jumped to the New Mexico grid. Toffler was right. It had become a little wild. Data around mega grids like New York had a certain essence about them. They were rich in texture and highly evolved technically. But the data streams in the New Mexico grid were a *mélange* of bio, digital and analog: everything from state-of-the-art bioptics to century-old T-lines. It was hard for Bixx to get a read on where to start. The incepts from Kortel's credit phone placed him in the north central part of the state. He had used the phone to make one call and buy a pack of cigarettes. But it was the call that caught Bixx's attention. It had an odd pattern, and the signal appeared to have looped in the grid, like Kortel had called someone within just a couple of feet of himself. The cigarette machine was leased to a corporation called Enchanted Entertainment, which had a gambling subsidiary named Deuces Wild. Bixx cross-referenced Deuce's address with the incepts from Kortel's credit phone. They matched.

Good, she thought. *At least I know where you were. Let's see if I can find where you are.*

Bixx started with the model number of the phone Kortel had called. It was difficult to trace, because it had been bought on the black net, which suggested that the person Kortel called lived off the grid. Since New Mexico was a haven for such people, trying to find this one might be impossible. But Bixx remembered a tip a friend at the orphanage had told her: most credit phones, like netpads, utilized the new living micro-engines, and almost all of these batteries where made in the new nation of Caribbeatan, specifically on the island of St. Lucia. Every battery had a genetic marker code. If Bixx could get the code, she could do some reverse indexing. She jumped to the Caribbeatan grid and easily located the battery company. After a little digging, she found the marker code. She then chased its history to an after-market refurbisher in Mexico City that resold to home-based companies throughout the Southwest. The one in the phone Kortel had called had been bought in Taos with a credit chip registered to a T. Finn.

Didn't Kortel have it out with Jacob Whitehorse in Taos? Bixx thought. She tried to recall the story. Wasn't there something about Whitehorse's daughter trying to kill Kortel? Hadn't she been married to a friend of his? A guy named Terry...Tarris? T...Tarris Finn.

Bixx quickly searched the Net for the name and found an extensive history on Tarris Finn. He was the inventor of the biosensory headgear that revolutionized the gaming industry and had developed many of the games Bixx had grown up on. He had battled a severe addiction to Ride and became a paraplegic after a bad accident. Then he dropped off the grid, settling onto property he had inherited outside of Tres Piedras, New Mexico. Bixx found its address, but it was up for sale and, according to the listing, not currently occupied.

What do I do now? Bixx glanced at the time code. *3:08 p.m.*

Most of Finn's data was untraceable. He definitely didn't want people finding him, and Bixx was out of ideas. She began to close the menu box when she heard a subtle droning beneath the data. It sounded like the old trains she had seen in museums in Russia – the type that ran on little black pellets. The drone sounded just like the trains when they were far away and heading toward you. Bixx closed her eyes and started to "listen." The image of Dr. Yanez came into her mind, along with his classroom and vast collection of music memorabilia. Maybe that's where she had gotten the bug to collect. Bixx listened while the drone increased, slowly at first, then building until she could feel it in her chest.

She opened her eyes on James McCarris, his form perfect in every detail.

Bixx let out a yelp. Her heart was racing. "Vhat are you doing here?"

McCarris contemplated her for a second. "Playing chess. I was retrieving an old Bobby Fischer closing move when you entered my stream. I'm taking a bathroom break, but give me a minute, and I should finish this guy off." He winked. "I know it's cheating, but this guy's a jerk. I'll be right back." His image vanished.

The droning had been replaced with the Net's usual white

noise, which always reminded Bixx of the murmuring in a theater just before a play started. For many Net people, this noise was too much of a distraction, but Bixx had learned to ignore it. That talent might have been her salvation, because if she couldn't tune it out, the idea of 5 billion people communicating all around her might be overwhelming. She floated and watched the textures resolve.

"Okay," McCarris said, his form suddenly appearing. "That went well."

"What did you end up doing?" Bixx asked.

"Do you play chess?"

Bixx shook her head.

"Then it wouldn't make any sense to you. Let's just say I checkmated his ass. And he deserved it."

Bixx shrugged. "If you say so."

"How did you get into my data stream? It has more security around it than most banks. It's my lifeline."

"I-I don't know. I just did."

McCarris studied her. "Are you one of those nodal readers? I've read about your kind. What do they call it?"

"Infinite perception."

"Yeah, that's it, I.P. So, what are you trying to perceive today?"

"Jonathan Kortel. Or where he is, to be precise."

McCarris's expression hardened. "Why?" he asked.

Bixx explained the whole story about Kreet, the Brit and Toffler. McCarris listened, nodding occasionally.

"Sounds ballsy," he said finally.

"I call it crazy," Bixx replied. "I could care less if we came out or not. I just have a bad feeling about it. Like once we do, our lives will be at risk."

"If there's one thing I've learned...or, ah, relearned, it's that people basically hate change."

"That's for sure," Bixx said.

"So this producer really thinks she can get Kortel and Zvara to go along?"

"That's what she says."

"Good luck with that. From what I know about Kortel, he's too wound up for something that big. Now, I know Zvara...well, sort of know him, at least what I've read. He's an idealist and would probably go along with the plan if he thought it could be pulled off." McCarris appeared to think for a moment, or possibly just retrieve more information. He nodded to himself. "Maybe this producer's onto something. Taking it prime time might be good. Anyway, did you find Kortel?"

"Not really–"

"You're in the right state. He always goes back to his friend Tarris Finn when things get bad."

"Yeah, so I've read. But Tarris's compound is up for sale...and he's not living in it."

"He's probably at his lab outside of Chaco Canyon."

"Do you know where it is?" Bixx asked.

"Well, kind of. When Zvara and I were assigned to bring Kortel in, we searched *everywhere*. Tarris's lab was one of the first places we went. It's in the case file, and I've got clearance. Hold on; this might take a minute." McCarris's image disappeared.

Bixx glanced at the time code. *3:46 p.m.* Something from behind tapped her shoulder.

"Shit!" Bixx said, spinning.

Toffler's staticky image smiled curtly. "How we doing?"

Bixx scowled. "Give me a few more minutes, and I'll have his location."

"Splendid." Toffler's image quivered and vanished.

"Here you go," McCarris said, appearing. A menu box unfolded next to him. It showed an address and some coordinates, then folded to the size of an old-fashioned envelope and glided into Bixx's hand before it dissolved. "That info's in your netgear's wetdrive now. Trash it as soon as you can. And we never had this conversation, *right?*"

Bixx nodded.

"Good girl. Now I've got to run." McCarris's image faded, but quickly returned. "Oh, I'm still working on the info on that Brit. I'll let you know what I find out." And he was gone.

The droning had returned, but it was fading. Bixx closed her eyes and listened. She had read once that a powerful stream like McCarris's was similar in concept to an old-style hologram. You could sample a tiny section anywhere along the flow and see everything carried by it at once. She wondered what kind of patterns and textures his stream would contain. She took a deep breath and focused her perception at the core of the droning. Then she let go, releasing herself into the mass of data that was James McCarris....

Instantly, the stream consumed her, digesting the almost

infinite algorithms of her program like a digital reptile. Bixx frantically looked down at her form, but couldn't see it. She tried to pull away, but found she was caught in the riptide that was McCarris's life. Suddenly it all was there, every memory and thought, saturated in a thick torrent of emotion and pain. Bixx panicked and tried to rip at the virtgear disc, but her arms and hands were now phantom limbs. McCarris's life swirled around her. She tried to focus on individual elements, but the sheer volume was too much. Even when Bixx pinched her eyes closed, the data was still there.

She opened them to find herself floating outside of a building, several stories in the air. It was night, and Kortel stood at an open window, laughing.

"I'm not going to kill you," he called to her.

She remembered the story of how McCarris had used Kortel, and how Kortel had punished him for it. He had telekinetically suspended McCarris outside of his office window on the Agency campus and toyed with him until he had gotten the truth....

"I'm going to do something a lot worse," Kortel continued.

Bixx gasped, but it felt like someone had done it for her. A terrible fear gripped her. "How far back are you going to erase?" she heard herself ask. Again, she felt like a puppet through whom someone else was speaking. There was a perceptible lag before she heard her own voice.

Suddenly, the scene shifted. McCarris was now in the window. Kortel's eyes narrowed. "All the way," he said.

Kreet was pulling at the virtdisc, its tentacles stubbornly releasing their grip. "Stop screaming," he said. "Come on, you're okay." Toffler was next to him, her arms folded tightly across her chest.

Bixx sensed more than felt her lower lip quivering, as it had on frigid winter mornings in St. Petersburg. Her breathing came in gasps. She leaned back in her chair and stared at the virtdisc in Kreet's hand. Everything had a slight halo, and the color was off somehow.

"Jesus, girl," Kreet said. He placed the disc on the counter. "What the hell happened?"

"We have to get to New Mexico," Bixx said.

"Okay, but–"

"He lied about his memory loss.... He knows everything."

"Who lied...about what?"

"McCarris," she said, still staring. "I think he plans to kill Kortel."

Breakthrough. 15

KORTEL watched the psychiatrist enter something into his netpad. "Can we continue?" Kortel asked, his impatience building.

The portly man casually raised a finger and continued inputting. Barely a minute passed, but it could have been an hour to Kortel, who had already suffered through a long session.

"All right," the psychiatrist said, snapping his netpad shut. His dark brown eyes met Kortel's, which were bloodshot and seemed to carry all the anguish he had ever seen in his practice. "Let's move on to where we left off last time.... We were so close to a breakthrough."

Kortel sighed. *There was that word again.*

"Would you like to talk about something else?" the psychiatrist asked.

"No, it's just...."

"It's all right, Jonathan. Please, go ahead."

"Look, doc. It's not like I don't appreciate what you've been doing in these sessions. It's just that I've been through all this before."

The psychiatrist nodded. He referenced his netpad. "I gather you're referring to the Albers Mandate?"

A dead feeling began to rise in Kortel. His attention moved to the windows and the mountains beyond. A cloud formation that vaguely resembled the shape of a car he had owned in his third year of culinary school hung above the farthest peak. Shortly after the destruction of Hawaii, then-President Albers had decreed that all survivors of "the Event" should receive counseling for their grief. She brought the power of the government to bear and convened a panel of medical experts who were given the task of implementing the mandate. She had proclaimed it was necessary for the collective mental health of the nation. Kortel thought he had locked that time away, but Dr. Furball's questioning dredged it all up again. Now, the memories came rushing back on a wave of guilt and shame. He studied his right hand. His fingers twitched slightly. He rubbed them and watched the clouds shift the late afternoon light, as if God had slipped a filter across the sun.

The psychiatrist's eyes went to Kortel's hands, then to his netpad. He entered something. "Would you like to talk about that period of your life?" His voice was clinical and emotionless.

Numbness coursed through Kortel's body as he fought

the urge to tell the doctor to piss off. But something was pushing him to spew out his angst. Gripped by the flood of memories, he stared out the windows. A bird flew past.

"Jonathan...are you all right?"

"I'm fine." Kortel leveled his attention at the psychiatrist. "One night, my grandfather came into my room. I was...I don't know, ten? Eleven? Does it really matter?"

The psychiatrist didn't respond.

"He said that my number had been drawn...that I was to begin my sessions. He said it would be good for me...set me straight."

"Did it?" the psychiatrist asked.

Kortel felt something shift in his brain, like his tech was advancing toward a new part of his nervous system. His heart began to race. He swallowed hard, and tightness wrapped around his throat. "I told those doctors everything they wanted to hear," he said. "They just sat there and listened."

The psychiatrist nodded and referenced his netpad again.

"They assured me I would be fine.... All I had to do was grieve. They said it was a natural function of the human spirit...that all victims went through it. They called it a disorder...post-trauma something."

"Yes," the psychiatrist said, "go on."

"I was only 10 years old!" Kortel tasted the salt of a tear at the corner of his mouth, and it startled him. His mind slipped back to the hot classroom. That summer, the Department of Intelligence had taken over an abandoned school and used it for processing survivors who lived in the Central Midwest zone. Like an assembly line, the doctors saw people around the clock. The team assigned to Kortel had informed him, rather casually and without remorse, that their primary job was to "cushion" him from the reality that his parents were dead. A boy his age wouldn't understand the consequences, a nurse assured him.

Something shifted again.

A bowl of fruit on a small table behind the psychiatrist exploded, sending bits of oranges and apples arching in all directions. A large chunk landed in the lap of the psychiatrist. He regarded it calmly and made another notation.

More memories quickly surfaced, one after another. Kortel could taste them at the back of his throat. They were bitter and acrid, like cognitive bile his body was trying to expel. "They said I would get over it," he continued. "That...that I was still young. That I would be able to recover with 'minimal damage.'"

"And?"

"They didn't know," Kortel said, feeling the salty echo of another tear.

The psychiatrist leaned forward, clearly puzzled at this statement. "What, Jonathan?... What didn't they know?"

The room blurred as the memories began to pile up at the door to Kortel's soul. A voracious edge of pain tore through his mind. "I saw their photos," he said, wincing.

The psychiatrist's face screwed into question.

The team that had treated Kortel sat before him now, their faces heavy with the burden they had been assigned. One of them gestured. Kortel felt himself stand.

"Jonathan?" the psychiatrist asked.

Kortel glanced around the office, and its spartan furnishings seemed to morph into that room.... He was 10 again. "I saw them, sir," he heard himself say.

"You saw them?... *Who?*"

Kortel felt himself step forward, but the movement was vague and dreamlike. "I saw photos of my parents...as they were."

The psychiatrist shifted uncomfortably in his chair. "Do you mean *after* the Event?"

Kortel felt his lips moving, repeating what he had just said, but no sound came.

"How?" the psychiatrist demanded. "Those were highly classified!"

Kortel's attention ricocheted around the room until it landed on the bloodshot eyes of the doctor. He poured all of his pain into them. "I hacked into the government's database, into my parents' case file," he admitted. "I saw what happened to them, after they had debio..." He couldn't finish the word.

"You should have never seen those images!" the psychiatrist said. "They were...oh my God."

Kortel felt a scream emerge from his throat. All of his pain erupted in a guttural torrent of grief. "Mother! Father!" he screamed. He called out to them over and over until his throat was raw, the words coming out in hacks and coughs. He began hyperventilating as mucus and tears streamed down his face. It felt as if his body had been torn open and his guts were spilling. A hot spike of pain cut between Kortel's eyes. He screamed and stumbled into a chair. Suddenly, an intense white flash split the room.

As Kortel's eyes adjusted, he could make out only edges of detail. A brilliant glow roughly the size of a human floated by the windows. The psychiatrist was cowering in his chair, pointing the netpad toward the apparition. Like a small sun, the glowing mass floated about a foot off the tiled floor.

The psychiatrist swung his netpad at Kortel, then back to the apparition.

Kortel instinctively stepped toward it.

"No!" the psychiatrist ordered.

The apparition's shape quickly gained form. A head and extremities emerged, then eyes appeared, defining a face. Its pure light transformed into hair that spilled down the sides of its head, along with skin and clothes. The brilliance began to ebb, and it coalesced into a more discernable form.

It was a woman.

"Mother?" Kortel whispered.

The form's light flared slightly.

"Fantastic," Kortel heard the psychiatrist say.

The apparition's glow calmed, and the room fell into a greenish hue. Kortel could now make out the form of his mother: her dark shoulder-length hair, the lab coat and the ankle-length khakis. Even the belt she always wore when she worked in her lab – the one with the old mud flap image of the reclining naked girl set in chrome relief on the buckle.

The psychiatrist came up to Kortel's side. "Have you had

these visions before?" The netpad had been put away.

Kortel felt dizzy and barely heard the question. "Yeah," he replied. "I've had three, maybe four of these."

"Amazing."

"Jonathan," the apparition said. Its voice was transparent, as though it had been reprocessed a dozen times over. It sounded to Kortel like it was coming to them at great risk. Maybe it was.

The psychiatrist gasped and took a step back. His attention vacillated between Kortel and the apparition. He quickly pulled his netpad from his coat and began scanning again.

Kortel approached it. "Yes, Mother?"

"You must release your father and me."

"But, Mother–"

The form extended its hand and put a finger to Kortel's lips. He felt an icy sensation at the point of contact, but didn't flinch. "You're very powerful, my son. Your destiny is before you. You can't live in the past anymore."

For a moment that felt like forever, Kortel teetered between shock and reverence. "Mother," he said, finally, "I…I miss you and Father so much."

The apparition's glow brightened. It took Kortel's face into its hands. "And we miss you." It passed a finger down his cheek, and he instinctually leaned into it.

"Jonathan, please," the form said, lifting Kortel's face by the chin. "You must let go of us and live your life."

Kortel's heart collapsed. He began to cry and sank to his knees. The apparition moved with him. It was close to his face now, and he could see its form was dissipating. It smiled.

"Remember, your father and I will always be here." It placed its hand against Kortel's chest.

"I love you," Kortel uttered.

"We love you," it mouthed before its form dispersed in a delicate mist of gray and pink and green.

Kortel remained motionless, staring at the floor. He felt something cold and delicate pass over the back of his neck. The psychiatrist knelt next to him.

"Are you all right?" he asked. He started to place his hand on Kortel's shoulder, but hesitated.

Kortel took a moment to find his voice. "Yes," he managed, still staring.

"Jonathan, I...I didn't realize the extent of your trauma. I would have never pushed you as I did. I'm truly sorry."

Kortel wiped the tears and mucus from his face with the sleeve of his shirt.

"Let me help you up," the psychiatrist said.

He took Kortel under the arm and helped him back into his chair. Kortel could feel the doctor's hands shaking. He leaned back and rubbed his temples.

The psychiatrist stepped to his desk and poured a glass of water from a metal decanter. "Here," he said, handing Kortel the glass, "this should help."

The cool water washed away the burning at the back of Kortel's throat. He emptied the glass in four vigorous gulps.

The psychiatrist sat in his chair. He clicked open his netpad and began entering data. His hands were still shaking.

An uneasy calm settled around them.

"Are you okay?" Kortel asked.

The doctor stopped inputting and raised his eyes. "I can't define what we just witnessed," he said. "Your ability to alter matter has developed to a point where your thoughts, even your memories can become manifest. I've never seen anything like this before. It's extraordinary."

"It might be extraordinary to you, doc, but it scares the hell out of me."

The psychiatrist contemplated Kortel's statement for a second. "It scares you because you don't understand what it means, and you haven't learned to control it. Once you have, the fear will be gone." He went back to his netpad.

"So, ah...was that the breakthrough you were looking for?" Kortel asked.

The psychiatrist looked up and snapped his netpad shut. He smiled, and his eyes seemed to have lost their sadness.

BIXX was jolted from her sleep by the rental's inability to compensate for the rough road they traveled. The pothole must have been particularly deep, because her head smacked against Rocket's bony shoulder harder than the last dozen times. She'd been able to drift back to sleep after those, but this one definitely woke her up. She leaned forward and peered out the windshield. The van's argon beams cut through the New Mexico night with a precision that could only be found in German-grown vehicles. The road was empty, and the sky was darker than Bixx had ever seen. Kreet was driving and must have been plugged into his netpad, because he didn't notice her, and his fingers were tapping out a rhythm on top of the steering toggle. Toffler was passed out in the passenger's seat, her head mashed against the side window.

"Hey there," Rocket whispered, shifting to face her. His

hair was pushed into a mass of red curls that spilled over the side of his headrest.

"What time is it?" Bixx asked.

"About 3."

Bixx peeked back over her seat into the van. Sanjiv was curled across the third row of seats, his jacket pulled up to his shoulders.

"Where's the Brit?" she asked. "You know, I don't even know his name."

"He's on the floor in the back, next to the equipment."

Bixx craned over her seat, but couldn't see him. She snuggled into the crook of Rocket's arm. "He gives me the creeps."

"I know what you mean.... He never says anything."

"Why does she keep him around?"

Rocket shrugged. "Insurance, I guess."

"What's insurance?"

"My dad told me it was a form of protection against anything bad, like an accident or something. You'd pay a company a lot of money just to protect you."

"Sounds like the Mob."

Rocket chuckled. "I think this was legal."

"So why does she need insurance?"

"I don't know. Some people just like to have others around.... They're paid to kiss ass, I guess."

"In Russia, we call people like that politicians." Bixx laughed. Rocket gave her a little hug.

"Can a guy get some sleep around here?" Sanjiv whispered between their headrests.

"Sorry," Bixx said.

"Where are we?"

Bixx tried to read the nav screen in the cabin's dim light. "I think we're about an hour from the casino."

The van hit a small bump, and the Brit coughed. Sanjiv's eyes widened. "I hope he doesn't wake up," he said. "I like him like this."

Bixx nodded. They all waited, but the cabin remained silent.

"I don't know why he came along," Sanjiv said. "He doesn't do crap except carry the equipment cases and fetch Toffler's iced Chai."

"You know how it is with Toffler," Rocket said. "It's not our place to question."

Sanjiv rolled his eyes. "I'm going back to sleep." He curled onto the seats and pulled his jacket over his head.

It had been more than a week since Bixx had sampled McCarris's data stream. She was certain that he was planning to erase Kortel, though it had taken a lot of convincing to get Sanjiv on board with her conclusion. He argued that the Net wasn't reliable, that studies had shown being jacked could alter your perception and change your reality. But it was Toffler who came to Bixx's defense. She said the Net was the new reality, and Sanjiv better get used to it. She cited the fact that there were hardly any human actors left anymore.... They had all been replaced with virtual ones. "Why waste your money with an untested actor," she declared, "when you could have classics like James Dean or Tirk Bradford." She said her company was in negotiations with the estate of a guy named Christopher Reeve for the rights to his likeness. Bixx didn't recognize the name, but Toffler assured her that he was pure money.

What really irked Bixx was that Toffler had taken five days just to get her act together. Something about her gear being so "on the edge" that Canadian customs didn't know what to do with it. Regardless, all Bixx knew was that more than a week had passed, and Kortel could be dead by now. Toffler said that for the sake of her career, he damn well better not be.

Another pothole pitched the rental, and Toffler snorted awake. She stretched and looked into the van, her Net glasses hanging around her neck.

"Morning," Rocket offered.

Toffler grinned and turned to Kreet. "Where are we?" she asked. He didn't acknowledge her, his fingers still drumming. She slapped his shoulder, Kreet jumped, and the van swerved slightly, throwing Bixx into Rocket's chest.

"What?" Kreet said loudly, obviously jamming to some kind of music.

Toffler reached over and clicked his netpad off. "I asked, 'Where are we?'"

Kreet referenced the nav screen. "Fifty-eight minutes from Deuces Wild." He pointed at it, as if to say, "Couldn't you have read that?"

Toffler stretched. "Right, I can get some more sleep." She propped her legs onto the dash, folded her arms and settled against the window.

The hum of the road filled the van.

"Oh, and by the way," Toffler said through a yawn, "his name is Marcus Nichols. And for the record, I pay him handsomely to kiss my ass."

* * *

"Are you sure this is where we can find him?" Kreet asked.

Bixx couldn't take her eyes off the woman's bright pink lips. They seemed plastic, almost stuck on like some terrible clown accessory. At least they matched the woman's hair, and there was something comforting about that.

The pink lips parted in a smile. "As far as I know, that's his address."

Bixx peered over Kreet's shoulder and read the coordinates on his netpad. She couldn't tell where the location was.

"Thank you," Toffler said.

"No problem. Since each of you bought service, it's the least I could do. Besides, I know Tarris, and he wouldn't mind the company. So, are you really going to do a documentary on him?" Bixx thought she caught a bit of Cockney in the woman's accent.

"That's correct. Look for it on the *Where Are They Now?* Channel."

The pink lips whistled. "Tarris is going to be so excited." She slipped her credit chip into her clutch. "Tootles," she said with a wave, and headed toward the vidslot room of Deuces.

"That was too easy," Kreet said. He tossed his credit phone into a trash can. Everyone else followed.

* * *

Kreet handed the field optics back to Toffler. "That's unbelievable," he said.

Toffler passed them to Nichols. "What's your assessment?"

Nichols scanned Tarris's compound. "It's an old Boeing, all right. A 747. I'll bet they disassembled it and 'coptered it out here." He swept the length of the compound again, stopping once to zoom in. "Probably bought it on the black net. There's a junkyard for planes like this, probably somewhere out here. And I'd lay down a quid that it's wired to the gills." He handed the glasses back.

Bixx had never been to the desert Southwest. The sun was rising, and the air was crisp with a freshness she hadn't smelled since she and Rocket went to upstate New York to "decompress," as he called it. All she did was scratch herself raw from mosquito bites. Rocket had assured her New Mexico didn't have mosquitoes, but Bixx could swear she felt something biting her. She slapped her neck and checked for a welt. Nichols gave her a sideways glance.

"What do we do now?" Sanjiv asked the group.

Nichols retrieved one of Toffler's silver cases. He carefully laid it down and tapped a code across the interface panel. The case hissed and slowly opened. Inside were several devices nestled in green foam that looked like the putty Bixx had played with as a child. Nichols removed one of them, and the space it left started to fill back in, as if the foam were healing itself. With a sucking sound, the wound closed. Bixx was a techie and knew a lot about certain hardware, but the instrument Nichols held in front of him didn't look like any conventional scanner she'd ever seen.

"This Tarris Finn is a tricky little bugger," he said. "He's got this place tighter than my mum's purse." He scanned to his right and stopped. "What's this?" He clicked a button. "Smile everyone, we're being watched."

"Can you tell by who?" Toffler asked.

Nichols clicked again. "Hard to say, love. I can't get a fix on the point of origin. But I can say there's nobody home, if that helps."

"The place is empty?"

"Roger that. By the looks of it, I'd say they've been gone a long time.... More than a month probably."

"Damn it," Toffler said under her breath.

"What's the plan, boss?" Kreet asked.

Toffler shot him a look. "Since they know we're here, we wait. They'll come to us."

"We're not going to have to wait long," Rocket said, his attention focused behind them.

Bixx turned and saw two large men walking toward them through the scrub sage. Each held a military style Light-Force rifle, the butts tucked tightly into their armpits and the muzzles pointed down. One wore a bandanna and the other a wide-brimmed hat that was pinned to one side of the crown.

Nichols stepped toward the case, and the bandanna wearer

dropped to one knee and raised his Light-Force. The other held his ground. Nichols stepped back, and the men resumed walking.

"I thought you said the place was empty," Toffler said to Nichols out of the side of her mouth.

"They must be wearing sig displacers or something. I can't be expected to read *everything*."

The men walked to within 20 feet and stopped. They stood silently. A hawk screeched in the distance, and a cold chill ran through Bixx. Finally, Wide Brim stepped forward. "This is private property," he said.

"Yes, we know," Toffler replied. She took a step, and Bandanna raised his weapon. "Easy there," she said. "We just want to talk with Mr. Finn."

"Why?"

"We're here to do a documentary on him. My name is Megan Toffler. I'm with SecondSight Studios. This is my crew."

"We weren't told about this," said Bandanna.

Toffler smiled. "Often, celebrities like Mr. Finn keep certain things from their staff. In this case, our pre-pro team tried on several occasions to confirm our arrival date with Mr. Finn. But, with all our busy schedules and flight arrangements, you know, things can fall through the cracks. I'm terribly sorry you weren't informed. Is Mr. Finn available? We'd be more than happy to wait."

The two men stood silently, and it occurred to Bixx that they were probably jacked and receiving instructions from whomever Nichols had spied watching them. A hawk screeched again, closer this time.

Wide Brim looked around, then nodded to himself. "Right," he said into the air. His attention came back to the group. "Mr. Finn knows all about the documentary and would be more than happy to grant you time. Please follow us back to your vehicle." Both men shouldered their Light-Forces and began walking in the direction of the rental.

Toffler and Kreet exchanged tentative glances before falling into line behind the two men. Nichols returned the scanner to the case, and the foam ate it like a sandwich. He gathered the case under his arm and trotted off to catch up with Toffler.

Sanjiv came up between Bixx and Rocket. "What documentary?" he asked.

"Toffler's just bullshitting to get us to Kortel," Rocket said.

"It doesn't make sense."

"What doesn't make sense?"

"Those guys...with the Light-Forces. Why does Finn need bodyguards?"

Bixx had been wondering the same thing. Something didn't feel right. If this was Finn's compound, why were these guys leading them back to the rental? "Yeah," she said, "something's wrong here. Why does he need them?"

"Insurance," Rocket replied, and gave her a little grin.

* * *

It had been over an hour since they had left Tarris's compound. The rental's nav put them somewhere northeast of Chaco

Canyon, but exactly where was up for grabs. The two men drove an old-fashioned gas-guzzler called a Bronco LX. The LX Bixx got, but what the hell was a Bronco? For the last 30 minutes, they had been traveling a dirt road, and the rental's filter system was having a tough time with their dust. Bixx was beginning to taste it herself.

"Is anybody else getting a little nervous?" Sanjiv asked.

Toffler was on her Net glasses, "dealing" with New York. Kreet was jamming and driving, and Nichols was sleeping again.

"Not yet," Rocket said.

"I don't know enough to be nervous," Bixx said.

"Well, I don't like this," Sanjiv declared and angrily folded his arms.

The Bronco suddenly veered into a field filled with cactus and small rocks. Bixx could hear the rental's leveling system try to compensate for the terrain.

"Kreet, can you fix this?" Toffler asked as she bounced in her seat. "I'm in the middle of a conference call."

Kreet just looked at her and gunned it. The rental violently jerked, throwing Sanjiv against the back of his seat and sending Nichols into the equipment cases.

Bixx looked out the windshield and saw the back of the Bronco coming up fast through the dust. She punched Kreet's shoulder. "Look out!"

Kreet engaged the brakes, and everyone flew forward. The rental stopped inches from the Bronco's bumper. "The faster you get through it, the quicker it's over," he said as he switched off the rental's organics.

Sanjiv said earlier that New Mexico was called the Land of Enchantment, which, right now, Bixx was finding hard to believe. She watched the two men climb out of the Bronco, their Light-Forces glistening in the midday sun.

"Okay," Kreet said, "this is getting a little weird."

Sanjiv came up to Bixx's ear. "Now do you know enough to be nervous?"

Bixx nodded.

"Where are we?" Toffler asked.

"In the middle of fucking nowhere with two rowdies with Light-Forces," Nichols replied.

Bixx flashed on a vintage movie about World War II, where German soldiers had marched Russians into a field and shot them. She tucked her knees against her chest and watched Bandanna approach Kreet's window. He tapped it with the muzzle of the Light-Force.

"We'll be walking the rest of the way," he said while the window slipped into the door. "Just take what you think is essential." He abruptly walked away.

"Marcus?" Toffler asked.

"Yes, love."

"If you had to, could you take these two out?"

"With my enhancements, I'm fast, but not faster than a Light-Force."

"Great," Sanjiv blurted.

"Come on," Kreet said. "We might as well gear up. What choice do we have?"

Bixx and Rocket stuffed what they would need into Rocket's backpack. Sanjiv, Toffler and Kreet had small duffle bags, but Nichols didn't have anything. He just carried the equipment. Maybe his stuff was buried somewhere inside the silver cases, Bixx figured, down in that living goo with all the tech gear.

They followed the men through a thicket of white-barked trees whose leaves fluttered delicately in the breeze. When they came to the edge of a drop-off, Bixx remarked that it was a tall hill. Sanjiv informed her that it was actually called an arroyo. Bixx asked if everything in the Southwest had more than one name. He looked at her like she was crazy.

They continued along a narrow path that angled down the side of a mesa to a dry riverbed. The sun was beginning to heat the landscape, and as they trudged across the dry clay, Bixx couldn't decide which was more obnoxious: the mosquitoes of upstate New York or the dust of New Mexico. They followed the riverbed for about a mile. As they rounded a bend, buildings began to appear, followed by a whole complex of old wooden-framed structures, complete with a high barbed wire fence.

"What the hell is this?" Toffler asked.

Nichols put his hand to his forehead to block the sun. "Looks like a military installation." He studied it more. "From the Old War, if I had to guess."

They approached a large gate guarded by more men brandishing Light-Forces. Wide Brim made a gesture, and the gate started to open.

"Stay together," he said to the group.

Bandanna exchanged nods with him and walked off.

They were led through a maze of tall shipping containers just like the ones Bixx's dad had off-loaded on the docks of St. Petersburg. No one said anything. Sanjiv kept glancing over his shoulder.

They followed Wide Brim across what looked like the main street of the installation and into one of the old buildings. Just inside was a lobby, of sorts, and a young boy seated behind a metal table. He also wore a bandanna. Bixx was beginning to suspect it was some kind of uniform. The kid snapped to attention. Wide Brim waved him off, as if it were embarrassing.

"Which room, Billy?" he asked.

"Twelve, Mr. Aarons."

"You can all drop your gear," Aarons announced. "It'll be secure here. Right, Billy?"

"Yes *sir*!"

Aarons laughed under his breath and motioned for them to follow.

Near the end of a long, dim hallway was a frosted glass door marked with a black 12 trimmed in gold. Aarons unlocked the door with an old-fashioned key and held it open for them.

As Bixx filed past, she brushed against Aarons. Something quivered under his shirt. Bioarmor.

The room had a metal table of the same style as the one the kid had sat behind, along with a several metal chairs with green vinyl seats. A light bulb attached to a wire hung above the table. Bixx stared. She hadn't seen a *glass* bulb on a wire since Russia.

"Wait here. Mr. Finn will be right with you." Aarons forced a grin and closed the door as he left.

"So far, so good," Toffler said, walking around the table.

"Are you kidding?" Sanjiv declared. "We're in the middle of who knows where, and you think everything is *good*. Where are we, and why do these guys have weapons?" He stormed around the table and got in Toffler's face. "What's this crap about a documentary on Finn? If you've gotten us into trouble–" Suddenly, Sanjiv's body went rigid. He hacked out the word "Shit," twisted around and slid into Nichols's outstretched hands.

Nichols pulled him close and smiled hideously. "Listen, mate. You're in the big show now. You gotta tighten up." On the word "up," he telekinetically raised Sanjiv into the air until his head disappeared into the rafters of the ceiling.

Toffler sighed. "Marcus, for the love of *God*, put him down."

"Yeah, Marcus, put him down," a voice said behind all of them.

Bixx turned to find Jonathan Kortel standing in the doorway. The light from the bulb cast him in sharp contrast. He looked bigger than Bixx remembered, though it might have been merely the shadows.

Nichols eyed him, still holding Sanjiv aloft.

Kortel's demeanor hardened. He stepped into the room and pointed at Sanjiv. "He's a friend of mine, Marcus. Put him down now." There was an inflection in Kortel's voice that cut through the room.

Nichols smiled coolly, and Sanjiv slowly lowered to the floor. "No harm done," he said, straightening out the wrinkles he'd made in Sanjiv's shirt. "Good as new."

Sanjiv adjusted his collar and threw back his shoulders. He glared at Nichols and walked over to Rocket's side.

A woman in a lab coat stepped into the room, followed by an older gentleman with a close-cropped beard. Then a rough character appeared. His hair was tousled, and he had a slight hunch. There was a whirring sound like tiny servos, and Bixx figured this was Tarris Finn. If she didn't know so much about him, she would have passed him off as just another of Aarons's men.

Toffler strutted around the table, and Bixx suddenly noticed the suit she had been wearing had changed style. She was still dressed in a professional manner, but it was sexier somehow. Her skirt was a little shorter, and her coat seemed to fit more tightly around her waist. Even her face looked slimmer, which is when Bixx noticed that her hair had changed style. It was now darker, shorter and curled delicately under one side of her jaw. She walked over to Kortel and stuck out her hand.

"Mr. Kortel, Megan Toffler, with SecondSight Studios."

Kortel regarded her hand. "Normally I'd accept your handshake, Ms. Toffler. But right now, given my conditioning, that could be a little dangerous."

Toffler looked at her hand like it was somehow offended. She cleared her throat. "On behalf of SecondSight Studios–"

"Pardon me, will you?" Kortel walked over to Sanjiv. "Are you okay?"

Sanjiv nodded, surprised. "I am, thank you."

Kortel scanned Rocket and Kreet before his attention landed on Bixx.

She smiled.

"It's good to see you all," Kortel said. "Come on, have a seat and tell me all about this vid you want to make. I assume it has something to do with your plan, Kreet, to bring us out?" Kortel glanced knowingly at the bearded guy.

"It does," Kreet said, taking a chair.

Bixx and the others sat. Nichols remained standing, though he had stepped back from the light that surrounded the table. This attracted Kortel's attention for a second. Tarris and the bearded man sat on either side of Kortel, but the lab woman stood behind him. This gave the appearance that she was protecting him, which seemed silly, considering his power.

"Our project has evolved since we last spoke," Kreet said. "I've had the fortune to become part of Ms. Toffler's business unit. Her group adds a certain dimension to the original concept."

"What is it that you add, exactly?" the bearded man asked. He had an accent that Bixx couldn't place.

"Sorry, everyone," Kortel said. "This is Armando Zvara."

"Whoa," Rocket said under his breath.

Bixx knew the legend, but never imagined she would actually meet the man in person.

"And this is Tarris Finn," Kortel said.

Tarris smiled and saluted with two fingers.

"And this lady behind me, you may have heard of.... This is Dr. Erin Richter."

"*The* Erin Richter?" Sanjiv asked.

Richter smiled. "In the flesh."

Bixx couldn't believe who she was looking at. Between Zvara and Kortel alone, there was more telekinetic power than most Agencies...at least according to the rumors. And Richter practically rewrote the book on gravitational theory.

Kortel gestured. "This is Bixx, Sanjiv, Rocket and Kreet. These folks helped me once." He glanced at Bixx. "Okay," he said, settling into his seat. "Armando had a question."

"What I add," Toffler said, standing, "is the global reach a concept like this requires in order to be successful. Here, let me show you what I mean." She produced another of those thin glass wafers, but this one was twice as big as her personal card, and it glowed bright orange in the harsh light. She placed it in the center of the table. "What I propose is a media event that would rival anything to date." At the word "date," a holographic presentation appeared. It took up most of the tabletop, and Bixx got a sense that from any angle, it would appear as if it were playing strictly for you. It quickly advanced through a montage of SecondSight history, then sequenced into a four-part plan for revealing the Tel culture, complete with projections about lifestyle issues and potential product-centric endorsement opportunities. It even contained a breakdown of which religions would be the most accepting of the Tels. Much of it went over Bixx's head, but Kortel studied it intently, only looking away occasionally to eye Nichols. When it ended, Toffler pocketed the card. The room grew quiet, and Bixx didn't know whether to clap or not.

Kortel chuckled to himself. "Ms. Toffler," he said, rubbing his forehead, "do you really make a living with this kind of stuff?"

"I have, Mr. Kortel, for over 20 years."

"I remember the Disneyverse opening."

"Most people do."

Kortel looked at Zvara and Tarris. They weren't smiling, which set Bixx on edge. She couldn't read Richter's reaction because her face was hidden in shadow. Toffler was still standing with her arms folded.

Kortel's expression became serious. "What you're proposing is very impressive." He leaned back in his chair and drummed the table with his fingers. "Unfortunately, something has come up that might, um, preempt this. I'll let Dr. Richter spell it out for you."

Richter stepped out from behind Kortel and took the only empty seat left. She motioned for Toffler to sit, which she did, reluctantly.

Richter's demeanor was grave, like she was about to tell them they had Netox or worse. "Do you all know what a solar flare is?" she asked.

Bixx looked at Rocket, then exchanged questioning glances with Kreet and Sanjiv. They all nodded.

"Good, then what I'm about to tell you shouldn't be that hard to understand." For the next 20 minutes, Bixx listened as

Richter explained the deadly mechanics of a Tsunami Coronal Ejection. At one point, when she was describing what would happen to the earth's magnetosphere, Rocket gathered Bixx's hand into his under the table. She got a little lost with all the acronyms, but by the time Richter had finished, Bixx grasped the gist of the situation: Earth, in the very near future, was basically fucked.

A collective numbness settled over the table. Bixx could feel Rocket's hand shaking and saw in his face a fear she had never before seen. Sanjiv looked like he was about to cry, and Kreet leaned on the table with his head in his hands, staring at Richter. Toffler, on the other hand, didn't seem fazed by the pronouncement. In fact, she had an odd little smile on her face, as if this were the best news she had gotten all year.

Curtains. 17

KORTEL watched Richter explain the inevitable to Kreet and the group. Toffler was definitely the only professional in the group, but it was Marcus who gripped his attention. Even before Kortel had entered the room, the man's presence passed through him like an acid – burning and corrosive. And the displacement Marcus emitted lacked the integrity Kortel usually felt from other Tels. It was almost like the guy was bluffing his telekinetics, which didn't make sense. Either you had it or you didn't.

Richter started in on the results of the Tsunami Ejection on the magnetosphere, and Kortel caught Bixx flinching, like something had touched her under the table. He liked Bixx. She was smart, intuitive and, like him, an orphan. She looked thinner than the last time he had seen her, which wasn't good. It wasn't that she looked sickly; wiry was the word that came to mind.

There was no doubting her toughness, either. Kortel had seen it displayed before and was amazed that so much power could come out of such a small body.

A spike of pain suddenly forged itself into Kortel's brain. With all the exercises he had been put through during the last month, headaches had become a regular feature. He shrugged it off.

Richter concluded her lecture on the end of the world, and Kortel waited for reactions. Both Rocket and Kreet appeared stunned, and Sanjiv was shaking his head. Bixx didn't show much of a reaction; she just kept looking from Richter to her boyfriend. It was the producer Kortel couldn't figure. She had a look on her face like she had just won a Peabody.

The pain struck again, this time deeper and more concentrated. Kortel fought the urge to wince. He grabbed his head. "Shit," he said, abandoning any manners.

Richter turned, alarmed. "Jonathan?"

"I told you," Tarris said to Zvara. "It's those damn APT tests."

The pain crashed through Kortel's nervous system. He shuddered from its intensity.

Richter scooted closer, her chair scraping across the old concrete. "Come on," she said in a low voice, "you're done here."

"I'm okay."

"The hell you are. I'm getting you into the med bay right now." Richter had the look she used when she wanted to ramp up the serious factor. She hung on every word now as if Kortel's life depended on it.

"Come on, doc."

More of the look.

Kortel studied Richter. She wasn't backing off. "Sure," he agreed, "let's go."

Toffler cleared her throat. "Mr. Kortel…"

"Ms. Toffler," Zvara said, standing, "Mr. Aarons will show you and your friends to your rooms."

Aarons had suddenly appeared in the doorway.

Kortel stood, his limbs feeling cold and disconnected. He leaned onto the table.

"Can you walk?" Richter asked, taking his arm.

Kortel nodded, but he knew the next few steps would be a bitch.

"Do you need any help?" Bixx asked.

The question, pure and genuine, hit home with Kortel. He turned, accepting Richter's support a little too much. Her fingers dug into his bicep.

"Not right now," he said, straightening. "But we will."

* * *

"You're pushing Jonathan too hard with the APT tests," Richter said.

Shoalburg was studying the med screen that hung above Kortel's head. It was angled such that Kortel couldn't read what was being displayed; he could only watch Shoalburg's eyes as they darted back and forth. The technology within them could process light a hundred times faster than organic eyes and feed it to the biochips inside his head. Only God knew what their processing power was. The movement of those eyes was beginning to make Kortel dizzy.

Shoalburg pointed at the screen. "This colored mass isn't the result of the APT tests…or anything else we're doing."

This clearly hit Richter hard. She folded her arms against her chest.

Kortel sat up and swung around to see what Shoalburg was referencing. An enhanced holoimage of his brain projected off the screen's surface. A tiny blue spot nestled among the textured pink layers of his neocortex. At the Agency, Kortel had taken several advanced classes on the brain and could read a medgram about as well as a doctor. Even though he didn't know what the spot was, he sensed that it wasn't good. "I see my tech's grown."

Shoalburg glanced at the screen, his eyes doing their dancing thing. "Yes, but not in the area of this mass."

"What do you mean?" Richter asked, walking up to Shoalburg's side. Her attention remained fixed on the screen.

The holoimage shifted to an extreme close-up of the mass while technical data ran down the left side. The streaming stopped, and a section of data enlarged. It moved through the close-up and became the center of focus.

"These numbers verify your tech is growing at a substantial rate everywhere except the area adjoining this mass," Shoalburg said.

"Is it slowing the tech's growth or stopping it?" Kortel asked.

"I think it's stopping it, but it looks like the tech just shifts around and continues developing."

"What's causing it?" Richter asked.

Shoalburg shrugged. "I don't know yet. It just showed up a day ago, and I've only had a couple of hours to analyze it. At first, I thought it was harmless – the result of the tech's growth.... You know, like the trail a snail leaves. But the data doesn't support that."

"What does it support?" Kortel asked.

The close-up shifted along with the highlighted data, and a new stream began to cascade down the screen. Then another data box detached and enlarged.

"The mass might be more like a by-product of the tech," Shoalburg said.

"What do you mean by a 'by-product'?" Richter asked.

"He means crap," Kortel said.

Richter looked from Kortel to Shoalburg. "You're kidding, right?"

"No," Shoalburg said, "Jonny's correct. The medical biotech used today is basically alive, though engineered not to create waste. But the tech in Jonny's head is radical, and I have no idea how it was engineered."

"Kind of makes you rethink the phrase 'shit-for-brains,'" Kortel said.

Either Richter and Shoalburg didn't get the humor, or the mass was more serious than Kortel thought. They continued studying the data and began talking to each other, their techno-speak far over Kortel's head.

"You want to let me in on the conversation?" he asked after another round of acronyms and nods.

Shoalburg started to speak, but Richter stopped him.

"I'm sorry," she said, "that was rude of us."

"That's okay," Kortel said. "Just tell me what you think it is."

"I need to study it more," Shoalburg said. "But the preliminary data shows that it could be doing a couple of different–"

"It could be harmless," Richter blurted.

"Possibly," Shoalburg said. "But not if this data is correct."

Kortel folded his arms, frustrated. "Get to the point."

Shoalburg motioned for him to look at the screen.

Kortel complied, and a chill shot down his spine. The blue spot was bigger. "Damn it," he said to himself.

"Now don't get all crazy about this," Shoalburg said. "It might be something that gets absorbed by your body."

"But that's not what the data suggests, *right*?"

The thing about Shoalburg's eyes was that they didn't reveal what he was thinking. Even though they were exceptionally realistic, they were not what Tarris's mother called windows to the soul. Kortel was looking into them now, trying to gauge how screwed his situation really was.

Shoalburg hesitated. "It's too early to say.... I need to run some tests to be certain."

"Carter, just get to the damn point!"

Suddenly the med screen exploded, spraying plastics and electric colored organics throughout the med bay. Shoalburg went to the floor covering his head, and Richter ducked behind the bay's scanner station.

A fine red mist dissipated around Kortel, as hot orange

biocables quivered from the end of the screen's ruptured armature.

"Easy, Jonny," Shoalburg said, picking tiny elements of the screen out of his hair. Some of the holojection fragments still carried the complete image of Kortel's brain, creating a disturbing effect that resembled an installation Kortel had once seen in a Chicago gallery.

Richter slowly stood, brushing a bright green dust from her shoulders. She shook out her hair, and Kortel watched a dozen tiny holojections of his neocortex flutter gently to the floor.

"Sorry," he said.

Richter regarded him as a mother would a mischievous child. "We're going to work on that," she said, arranging her hair into a makeshift ponytail. She turned to Shoalburg. "What were you about to say before Jonathan had his little hissy fit?"

Shoalburg hesitated again, and Kortel seriously considered letting go of his anger and seeing what else might blow up. "*Carter*..."

"I really need to study the mass further, so I can rule out something."

"What's that?"

Shoalburg leveled his attention on Kortel, his eyes somehow revealing the graveness of the situation. "I think this new substance isn't stopping the tech," he said. "It's replacing it."

* * *

"Man, I didn't sneak this Oban in just for you to stare at," Tarris said. He propped his feet on the coffee table and settled back against the couch. "Time to go off-line," he declared, and clicked something on his lower back. The organics in his leg's servos hissed into their dormant setting. "Hell, yeah. That's what I'm talkin' about." He took a sip of his drink.

Kortel looked into his glass of Scotch wondering about the mass and what it might do. Would it replace the biotech and slowly take over his central nervous system? Maybe it would alter his DNA, and one morning he would wake to find he was something different. Shoalburg thought that it was the next phase of his tech and that he had never seen anything like it, which was pretty unnerving. Just as Kortel was wrapping his brain around his new responsibility for saving the world, now he had to deal with something that had the father of nanogenetics scratching his head. He looked into his drink again and knocked it back in one continuous gulp.

"Easy there." Tarris said.

"What do you think?" Kortel asked, staring into his empty glass.

"About what?"

"All this, you know...shit."

"You mean the stuff in your head?"

"No, I'm talking about the Tsunami Ejection, Kreet's plan, St. John...all of it. What the hell's going on?"

Tarris took another sip. "If you ask me, I think most of it is a bunch of bullshit."

Kortel grabbed the flask of Scotch off the table and poured himself another. "I don't think a cataclysmic solar flare is bullshit," he said, easing back against the bed's headboard.

"Richter's own calculations are spotty at best," Tarris said. "Is it possible? Sure. But there're too many factors that have to line up exactly right to produce the planet-destroying flare she's predicting. Now, damaging the atmosphere? Yeah, maybe. I'll give her that. But total annihilation? Puh-leez."

"And what about Kreet's plan?"

Tarris laughed. "Do you really think the other Tel Agencies are going to go along with it? Come on–" He waved it off. "There's no way in hell."

"Zvara's pretty powerful. He can wield a lot of influence."

"Zvara is old news. Besides, why would they?"

Kortel had to admit, Tarris was probably right. There wasn't really anything to gain from their kind going public, except a lot of grief. He took a long drink of his Scotch, and his thoughts went back to the new growth in his head.

"You think Shoalburg's right about this shit in my head?" he asked.

Tarris shrugged. "Take a wait and see. Carter's a smart guy; he'll figure it out." He pulled his now-inanimate legs off the table and propped them where he could lean on them. "You know what I think you should be worried about?" he said, swirling the Scotch in his glass.

"Let me guess...the price of biochip futures?"

Tarris grinned for a second before his demeanor tightened. "I'd be worried about this St. John character. You don't piss off the Mob and live to brag about it. Especially those Pac Rim tech boys. I've dealt a little with those sons of bitches. You don't say no to them. Mark my words – St. John will be back, and he won't be polite."

"He wasn't polite the last time we saw him."

"I know. That's why next time, we'll open a little can of good ol' fashioned whoop-ass on him." Tarris patted a small chrome briefcase next to his feet.

Kortel eyed it with suspicion. "I don't even want to know what's in there," he said.

Tarris laughed. "Just a little new-tech I've been working on, in case St. John or any other bastard wants to fuck with you."

Kortel climbed off the bed and stretched. "I think I'm going to crash."

Tarris engaged the tech in his legs and grabbed the case. "Okay then," he said, standing.

Kortel hugged Tarris and could feel the tiny strips of processing packs that lined the sides of his spine. They were warm to the touch, and one of the packs moved under his fingers. He led Tarris to the door. "Thanks for the drink," he said. "And for listening."

"I'll always be there for you, Jonny.... You know that."

Tarris left, and Kortel locked the door.

Silly, he thought, securing a door that any Level 4 could rip apart with the simplest thought. He let the old-fashioned key slide from his fingers onto the nightstand. Its polished brass surface caught the light and reflected into his eye. Sitting on the bed, he wondered how the person who made the key had found the machine to make it. He pictured one of Aarons's men researching the Net and finding it in some forgotten corner of the country. He clicked his boots into their off setting and watched as they unwrapped from his feet like a flower in a time-lapse sequence. BioBoots were one of the few luxuries Kortel afforded himself. He settled back onto the bed and punched his pillow into the perfect shape. He didn't bother with the covers, because the base was vintage, right down to the lack of HVAC in any of the buildings. The screened window helped a little, but there was no wind to bring the cool New Mexico night air into the room.

Sleep was slow to come, and the distant howling of a coyote didn't help matters any. He tried to empty his mind, but Tarris's words kept cycling through his head.

What the hell, he thought through an especially big yawn. *Whatever happens,s happens.* He nestled his head into a soft groove in the pillow and let the world slip away.

Something cold at the side of his neck brought Kortel out of his dream. He had been watching Tamara as she worked in the gallery, wondering if she would notice him, but her face had been replaced by the room's darkness. The moon was up, back-lighting the sheer curtains that hung motionless on either side of the window. He tried to focus on them, but all he could see was milky forms.

"Don't even think about phasing," a voice whispered into his ear. It had an accent. Familiar.

British.

The coldness at the side of his neck was like ice now.

"Okay," Kortel replied.

The ice turned into a sharp pain, needlelike and deep.

"Time to go."

"Where?" Kortel managed, as whatever had been injected began its duties. He could feel it coursing through his system. His fingers were getting numb.

A small laugh. "Hell," the voice said, and the curtains blurred away.

Surprised. 18

SOMETHING brought Bixx out of her sleep. It usually didn't take much: a drop in temperature, a faint noise, even the slightest air movement. Ever since the orphanage, her sleep pattern had been altered. When she was a little girl, her parents had been proud that she could sleep through an entire night. Her mother used say "Our little Olga, such a young woman!" But at the orphanage, all that changed. Sleeping in a room filled with more than 100 children meant getting a full night's sleep was rare, at best. During her early years, she often woke in the middle of the night screaming for her mother and father. And when she grew older, she could hear the *moy angelochek* – little angels – crying out just as she had. Their high-pitched wails haunted her dreams. The orphanage never had enough "adult" beds or sheets, and Bixx's toes were always numb from pressing against the footboard's cold iron.

"I'm sorry; did I wake you?" It was Rocket's voice, cutting through the fog of her past.

"No," she said, sitting up, "not really." She began rubbing her toes.

"Dreaming?" he asked. His tall, blurred form stood by the window. Bixx's eyes adjusted to the dark, and she saw he was smiling.

"Yeah," she said, the word sticking in her throat.

"The orphanage?" The smile was gone.

Bixx couldn't answer.

Rocket left the window and came to the bed, a dark figure settling next to her. "It's okay," he whispered. "You're not there anymore." His fingers tenderly traced the line of her jaw.

"I know." A tear had formed at the edge of Bixx's eye. She could feel it building on the lip of her lashes. Usually she would wipe it and the pain away. But tonight, she fought the instinct and let it fall.

"Oh, baby." Rocket caught the tear against her cheek with his fingers. He leaned in and kissed her forehead. "You have nothing to be sorry about."

"Why are you up?" Bixx asked, changing the subject.

"I was hot. I went to open the window and ended up watching them take out the trash."

Bixx laughed a little. "Was it entertaining?"

Rocket clicked the light on his watch, casting his face and hair in a cerulean hue. "Best I could find at 3 in the morning."

There was a rustle of movement from outside. Bixx and Rocket went to the window and looked down into the street.

"See what I mean?" he said, gesturing.

"I wonder why they're doing it in the middle of the night?" Bixx watched a guard maneuver a hoverlift past the front gate to the back of a small transport truck. It was carrying a cargo container, the kind that filled the bellies of commuter jump jets. As the guard angled it onto the truck's lift, its metal surface caught the moonlight and sparked a reflection.

"Probably 'cause it's cooler at night," Rocket said.

The guard leaned on the container to rest as the lift rose to the level of the truck's bed.

"Kind of big for trash, don't you think?" Bixx asked.

"Not really," Rocket said. "The recycle containers we had at *Clone World* were about that size, and that place was 10 times bigger than this base."

"You worked at Clone World?"

"Yeah. When I was a kid, before they discovered me. I was a stocker, working hoverlifts." Rocket pointed out the window. "Bigger than that one. The kind you sit in."

Bixx giggled.

"What?" Rocket asked.

"I can't see you driving one of those. How old were you?"

"Sixteen."

"How'd you get around the labor laws?"

"My dad had a friend who got me the job."

"Ah-huh, sure...a *friend*."

"Shut up." Rocket playfully dragged Bixx from the window, and they fell onto the bed stifling their laughs. "You sure went to bed early," he said.

"I was really tired," Bixx replied. "Where'd the others end up?"

"Down the hall. They gave Toffler and her boy toy separate rooms, and put Sanjiv and Kreet in one room."

"Oh, God," Bixx said. "That's a big mistake."

"No shit. I bet Sanjiv doesn't survive the night. Kreet'll talk his ear off."

"They won't fight, will they?"

"Nah," Rocket said. "If Sanjiv gets pissed enough, he'll just knock his ass out."

"He's gotten that powerful?"

"I think so. He's moving up in level pretty quickly. It's getting harder to beat him in the grav tests."

"I'll make a note of that," Bixx said and rolled over onto her side. Rocket snuggled next to her, and they quickly assumed spooning positions. "Good night," she said.

Rocket didn't answer, but Bixx could feel him getting excited against her lower back.

"I'm not tired," Rocket whispered, then ran his tongue delicately down the side of her neck, ending with a soft kiss at the top of her shoulder.

"*Really*."

Rocket laughed and pressed himself against her. "What was your first clue?"

Bixx rolled over and nestled into his arms. Rocket was rarely subtle about wanting to make love, but compared to her last boyfriend, he was downright shy.

"Hey, you," Rocket said tenderly. His look had an edge of little boy, as if he were surprised at how aroused he was. But his expression shifted, and Bixx sensed a seriousness filling him. He gathered her tightly into his arms.

"Tell me," she whispered. "What are you thinking?"

Rocket hesitated, his eyes searching her face. "How much I love you," he replied, and pulled her close.

A strange warmth wrapped around Bixx's heart, and another tear formed at the corner of her eye.

"I...I love you too," she replied.

Useless. 19

"TIME to rise and shine," the British voice said harshly into Kortel's ear. The effect was jarring.

Kortel coughed up some phlegm and spat on the floor. "What was your name again?" he asked.

"Nichols."

Kortel opened his eyes, fearing a bright welcome, but was greeted by a twilight of monochromatic shadows. A silhouetted figure stepped in front of him and knelt, his hulking form backlit by what little light there was.

"How is he?" another voice asked from somewhere deep in the room. Like Nichols, it carried a British accent, but older and with a film of tiredness overlaying it.

"Considering he's been packed in a crate for the last 12 hours, he looks pretty shipshape," Nichols said over his shoulder.

Some light caught the rim of his ear, and a diamond stud winked at Kortel. Nichols stood and stepped into the folds of the blackness.

"Raise the lights to full level," the voice ordered.

The light in Kortel's immediate space brightened. The glare stung his eyes. He reached to rub them, but found his arms inoperable. They didn't feel asleep – more like puppet arms whose strings had been cut. Then he found his legs were also useless. Kortel fought the urge to panic as his eyes adjusted to the light.

"I should probably say it's good to see you again," the voice said. "But to be honest, the sight of you only brings back some very bad memories."

There was a high-pitched whirring, and Kortel thought he saw movement within the shadows. "Have we met?" he asked.

More whirring. "Oh yes." A cough, then a clearing of the throat. "Don't you remember?"

The whirring revved and two spiderlike arms emerged from the darkness, their sucker-pad feet catching the edge of Kortel's light. As they stepped, he could see the surface of their skin was a mesh composed of undulating metallic scales. A man appeared, his body integrated with a chair that was carried by four other legs – two on each side of the chair. He was older, maybe 70, his thin face expressionless. The chair seemed built of organic flex tubing, and the whole device looked like it could have crawled out of an Italian design annual. It whirred to a stop a few feet from Kortel.

"Still don't recognize me?" the man asked. His lips didn't move, yet his voice seemed to emanate from him.

Kortel's heart began to race. The whole scene felt like a twisted nightmare. "No," he said.

"Maybe I need to be closer – more in the light." The two front arms reached back and disengaged the chair with articulated fingers from inside their sucker pads. The chair and the man were brought forward, his knees stopping inches from Kortel's. "Is this better?" he asked.

Kortel tried to shake his head, but the muscles in his neck wouldn't respond. "I'm sorry," he said. "I still don't recognize you."

The man regarded Kortel with a sullen stare. "Come now, Jonathan. You should remember all the faces of the people you've killed...especially *this* one."

One of the man's eyebrows rose slightly before it sunk in. The lean face, the long nose, the thin lips. "My God," Kortel said. "Jeffrey?"

The edges of Jeffrey Trumble's lips turned up in a faint display of acknowledgement. The two front arms reversed their motion and locked the chair back into its original position. Trumble's face went back to hanging from his head.

You did quite the number on me. Trumble's disembodied voice was now inside Kortel's mind. Its tone was mournful and distant. *Clinically dead, the doctors said. But you know those chaps.... Occasionally they can be wrong.*

"How are you communicating with me?" Kortel asked.

Trumble's face remained blank. Tech to tech. *Unfortunately, I didn't retain much motor function, so normal speech is limited. But with you, I can communicate quite easily.*

"But how did you?–"

My body cooked for over a year in one of those ghastly German regeneration vats while the boys in the lab rebuilt part of my personality construct. I'd had the good sense to back myself up, but there were a few things I wanted to change. So while they worked on getting parts of my brain reconfigured, I spent my days at a spa in the south of France. A virtual purgatory, I'll admit, but it was a far cry from this wretched existence.

"How are you existing?"

Barely. I'm mostly integrated biotechnology. You, of all people, can relate to that concept. How do you like my chair? It's the latest from one of our R&D groups.

"Great if you want to scale an office tower."

It was designed for the military, but the lab boys made some modifications to accommodate my unique situation.

"Are you integrated?"

If you mean with the chair, yes. This is my life now, and I have you to thank for that.

"I recall that Takeda gave me no choice."

Cyril and I wanted nothing but the best for you. To think, I once thought of you as a son.

"I didn't need another father."

I think you did.

"Your policies killed my parents."

We let Hawaii happen to save millions of lives.

"At what cost?"

Someday you'll see that the husbandry of the world can't be left to the normals. If we did, they would eventually destroy it.

Kortel moved his eyes around the room. "I assume you're controlling me right now?"

A raucous laugh echoed inside Kortel's head. *Of course. We can't take any chances with you, Jonathan. You're way beyond us now. Tell me, has the partitioning begun?*

It took a minute for Kortel to register the question. "Do you mean the blue stuff?"

There was a pause, then a sound that resembled a laugh. *It would appear blue in a biomed scan.*

"Yeah, it has."

Right. Splendid. It took longer than we hoped, but what matters is that it's begun.

"What the hell will it do to me?" Kortel asked.

What it will do isn't important. What it will make you is.

"Okay, what will it make me?"

Another pause. *A god.*

Kortel figured if his body was off-line, maybe his mind wasn't, so he began to phase. His vision went to a swirl of color, followed by white.

"He's phasing," Nichols said from somewhere off to Kortel's right.

"Not to worry," Trumble replied, his voice suddenly outside of Kortel's head.

Kortel tried to create a grav wall around his immediate area and cut off Trumble's control.

"He's spiking," Nichols said, his voice rising.

A process that had become routine suddenly was a struggle.

Kortel tried to erect a wall, but something was blocking his ability to form the field.

Jonathan, Trumble whispered from deep inside Kortel's mind, *it's useless to phase. Please, stop before you hurt yourself.*

Figuring that whatever was controlling him was being produced from Trumble's technology, Kortel brought all of his telekinetic strength forward and focused on the chair. Instantly one of its front legs began deforming. The meshing of the skin merged together and melted to the floor, exposing the technical skeleton of the arm. The skeleton then began liquefying, and the device lurched. A back leg slid forward and steadied it.

"Jesus, Mary and Joseph," Nichols said. "He's altering matter!"

Trumble laughed. "Wonderful, isn't it?"

Suddenly, a thunderous jolt of hot pain crashed through Kortel's body. It started at the base of his neck and plowed into his abdomen.

Jonathan, please. Trumble's voice beckoned like it could have been one of Kortel's own thoughts. *Fighting is useless.*

Kortel ignored the warning and concentrated as hard as he could on the chair. He felt a drop of blood leave his nose and slide over his upper lip. *It's time to waste you,* he thought.

I don't think so, Trumble replied, and the pain crashed again.

I know a way. 20

SUDDENLY, Bixx realized she was picking at a hangnail on her thumb and couldn't remember when she had started. It was a bad habit, one she had picked up at the orphanage, and Rocket always scolded her just like the nuns had. Twenty minutes earlier, Aarons had ordered her, Rocket, Sanjiv, Kreet and Toffler out of bed and marched them over to the building where they had been the day before. He didn't say why he had gotten them up so early, just that Zvara wanted to talk with them. Bixx figured it had something to do with Toffler, because she caught the brunt of Aarons's s attention on the way over. Bixx couldn't make out what he had said to her, but she could tell it had upset Toffler. She had walked kind of slumped and with her head down.

Now they were all standing in the room with the one bulb. Rocket was on her right, the rest to her left. The only one from their group not present was the Brit, Marcus. Toffler looked gravely concerned, while Sanjiv just kept his attention focused on the tops of his shoes. Kreet, on the other hand, didn't seem too interested in what was going down. He just kept yawning and looking around.

Bixx glanced across the room at the stern faces of Zvara, Tarris and Richter. Tarris looked like he was about to climb over the table and kill the guy Aarons had brought in. The guy, Tony something, looked like he was about to shit in his pants.

"Go on," Aarons said. He slapped the back of Tony's head and almost knocked him out of his chair.

"It's like I said before." Tony looked from Aarons to Zvara. "It was a routine night. Totally by the book. We locked down the base and engaged the perimeter trip monitors."

"And you did not note anything unusual?" Zvara asked, his voice much deeper than the prior day.

Tony shook his head vigorously. "We had a couple of coyotes wander into Zone 4, but they just trotted through."

"Bullshit!" Tarris blurted.

Bixx flinched and drew blood from her hangnail. Rocket elbowed her, and she dropped her arms to her sides.

"Easy," Richter said, patting Tarris's shoulder. She was standing behind Zvara.

Tarris shrugged off her touch and pushed away from the table. "This is bullshit. Jonny's gone, and we don't know dick about where he is." He stood and began pacing behind Richter.

"Obviously, we have a mole," Zvara said. He motioned to Aarons. "Find this man and bring him to me. Then we will have our answer." He turned to Toffler. "And you have no idea where your assistant is?"

"No...sir," Toffler replied.

Zvara shook his head. "I assume you did a background check on this man Nichols?"

"Our HR department did. I didn't review their report."

Zvara waved the statement off. "No matter. This has been well thought out. I am sure his credentials were spotless."

The room fell into a desperate silence. Zvara rubbed the bridge of his nose.

"Sir?" Rocket said suddenly.

Zvara, Richter and Tarris looked over at once.

"Yes?" Zvara asked.

"I couldn't sleep last night, so I was looking out the window of our room, and..." Rocket hesitated.

"Go on," Zvara said, his voice gentler.

"I don't know if this means anything, but I watched this guard load what looked like recycle containers onto a truck."

"That's the week's trash pickup," Tony said. "It happens every Thursday night. It's totally routine. We contract it out to a local group."

"They think we're some kind of commune," Aarons said to Zvara. "It's the survivalist camp scenario we've been using for some time now. It's very effective in keeping the locals away."

Zvara sat up in his chair and leaned onto the table. "Did you see anything odd?" he asked.

Rocket thought for a moment.

"The containers were big," Bixx said, the words coming out almost as one.

"Yeah," Rocket said. "I used to work at Clone World, and theirs were half the size of these."

"We use the big ones to keep costs down," Tony said. He twisted to face Aarons. "That was the mandate from last month's–"

"Shut up," Aarons said and slapped the top of Tony's head again. The slight man spun back and grabbed the edge of the table.

Aarons turned his attention toward Bixx, his deep-set eyes taking her in with a kind of strange judgment. "Repeat what you just said," he ordered.

"Th-they were big."

"No! You said containers...plural, right?"

Aarons's look hardened, and Bixx froze. Her mind flashed on the headmaster of the orphanage, the night she had been caught showing off her budding telekinetic power to some of the other children. He had grabbed her by the hair and dragged her to his office. "You," he had said, slamming the door, "will not jeopardize the reputation of this institution. We've had your kind before. I know of people who will take you in.... You'll feel right at home with them."

"Hey, back off!" Rocket said to Aarons.

Aarons's attention locked onto Rocket. "Don't push me, son."

"There were three containers loaded last night," Bixx said.

Aarons's face scrunched into a question. He looked over to Zvara.

"Right," Richter said. "One for trash, one for Nichols and one for Jonathan."

"Mr. Aarons," Zvara said, his voice back to a deep timbre, "will you please bring me the man who loaded the trash last night?"

"That's Rodriguez." Tony said, his expression tightening with realization. "But he's in town seeing a...a doctor."

"Great," Tarris said, throwing his arms up. "We'll never see him again."

Zvara went back to rubbing the bridge of his nose.

* * *

Bixx stared into what the dining room whiteboard labeled Fiesta Casserole. It looked like something they had served at the orphanage, but darker and with green chunks of mystery vegetable that had a weird smell.

"What's a casserole?" she asked Rocket.

"Leftovers," he replied, his mouth full of the stuff. "All mixed together and given a fancy name." A little piece of the mystery vegetable landed next to Bixx's glass of tea.

"Say it," she said, "don't spit it."

"It's 'spray it,'" Rocket corrected. "Say it, don't *spray* it."

Bixx leaned into the plate and sniffed. "It looks like *kapustnyak*, but it doesn't smell like it." She picked up a larger piece of the mystery vegetable and examined it.

"It's a jalapeño," Rocket said. "They're sweet. Give it try."

Bixx took a bite and chewed. An acrid burning filled her

mouth and quickly spread into every corner of her throat. The sides of her tongue then began to sting. She spit the gnawed piece of jalapeño onto her plate. Rocket laughed.

"Vhat the hell is that!" Bixx exclaimed. She grabbed her tea and took a large gulp.

"A little treat from old Mexico," Rocket said.

Bixx pushed the plate away. "Disgusting! That's worse than *kapustnyak*."

Rocket scooped another helping, and Bixx hit him in the shoulder. His spoon dropped from his hand, plopping Fiesta Casserole into his drink.

"Come on," he said, and began extracting chunks out of his tea. "I was just playing with you."

Bixx wiped her mouth and started on her salad. "I made this," she said, pointing with her fork. "I know what's in it, and there's no halapeenos."

"Jalapeño. It's Spanish for 'kick your ass.'"

"Vhatever."

"May I join you?" Richter asked, stepping up behind Rocket.

"Sure," he said, gesturing at the seat next to him.

Richter settled into the chair and began neatly arranging her tableware and napkin. Bixx watched as she arranged everything on her tray just as if there was a kind of mathematical logic at work. Richter finished by folding her napkin in thirds and gently placing it on her lap. She wove her long fingers together and bowed her head.

Bixx had never found a place for religion in her life and was always curious about people who practiced their faith openly. Rocket kicked her under the table and mouthed, *You're staring*.

Richter had ordered the chicken and rice, which Bixx eyed with envy. She cut the breast into perfect cubes, then used them to plow the rice onto her fork. She demurely chewed each bite with a determination Bixx had never before seen. It was like Richter's life depended on her ability to process the food before ingesting. The whole ritual had Bixx fascinated. Rocket kicked her in the shin.

As everyone continued to eat in silence, Bixx tried to watch Richter. Rocket caught her and raised a threatening eyebrow.

More silence.

"Do you pray often?" Bixx asked, finally.

Rocket slammed his fork down. "I'm sorry, doctor, Bixx is a little–"

"It's okay." Richter addressed Bixx directly. "I usually don't pray before a meal. But lately I have been," she said as if the realization had just hit her. She wiped her mouth and refolded her napkin.

"Why?" Bixx asked.

The question seemed to stump Richter for a second, but then she smiled. "It comforts me."

"How?"

Richter placed her fork next to her plate. "There are a lot of things I can control in this world," she said, folding her hands like she was going to pray again. "For everything else, I turn to God."

"But you put that food on that plate, not him...or her," Bixx said.

"God gave me the brain and the ability to create a life that brings food to my table." She gestured at her plate. "So, in a way, He has put the food there."

Religion had always been such an abstract concept to Bixx, but Richter's analogy had a certain logic that made sense to her.

"What about our telekinetics?" Rocket asked. "Is that God-given, or is it just a mutation...part of some evolutional process?"

"Many scientists would probably say it's a mutation," Richter said. "I like to think of it as a gift."

"From God?" Bixx asked.

Richter nodded. "Yes...from God."

"Stuff I can't control," Bixx said, more to herself than Rocket or Richter.

"Do you pray?" Richter asked.

The question caught Bixx by surprise. "I, ah...don't know."

"What did you do before you went to bed at night, as a little girl?"

"I tucked the protein bar I took from dinner into the hole I had dug out in my mattress."

Rocket rolled his eyes. "Don't be so literal, Bixxy. She means did you pray before you went to bed. You know, on your knees, with your hands folded."

"*Nyet*. You had to be in bed before the alarm sounded. We never had time."

Richter leaned across the table and took Bixx's hand. The move startled Bixx, but for some reason, she didn't pull away.

"Bixx, dear," Richter said, "were you ever taught how to pray?"

Richter's hand was warm, and her long fingers came all the way past Bixx's wrist.

Just like her mother's had.

Bixx paused for a moment, thinking back through the layers of memories. An image of her mother – tall, lean, her long hair a mass of delicate shades of blonde – unfolded in her mind. She had only vague recollections of her parents, their details having been eroded with each passing year. A montage of history, viewed from Bixx's young eyes, sequenced through her mind.

"I don't know," she said in almost a whisper. She felt Richter's hand gently squeeze hers. The touch was...comforting.

"Maybe someone just needs to teach you," Richter said as she pulled her hand back.

The action melted the image, and Bixx looked over to Rocket. He had that look, just as he had the night before when he had professed his love. He had taken her other hand, and she hadn't even noticed.

They all returned to eating, but Bixx didn't have much of an appetite. The conversation had her thinking, and besides, some of the leaves in her salad had black edges, and the thought of eating them made her stomach turn. She glanced at Richter, who appeared deep in thought.

"Do you pray before you go to bed at night?" Bixx asked.

Richter's attention was focused somewhere over Bixx's

right shoulder. She didn't answer, but continued chewing.

"These days I seem to be praying a lot," she said finally.

"Why's that?" Rocket asked.

Richter went into her praying position, but instead of bowing her head, she rested her chin on her hands and stared forward.

"Doctor, is everything okay?" Bixx asked.

Richter closed her eyes. "The sun is becoming more active. There've been five massive flares just in the last three days."

"Is that why my netpad keeps dropping its connection?" Rocket asked.

"Most likely."

"Well, I'm sure it's not–"

"This is the start of the Tsunami cycle." Richter opened her eyes. "The readings are unmistakable."

"How long *is* the cycle?" Bixx asked.

Richter took in a long breath. "We don't know."

"Shit," Rocket said softly.

Richter looked painfully from Rocket to Bixx. "We have to find Jonathan. If we don't–" She bit off her words and went back to staring.

"I pray," Rocket suddenly interjected.

Richter chuckled and leaned back. "Then maybe God will hear you, because He sure doesn't seem to be hearing me."

Something in Richter's words clicked for Bixx. She pushed from the table and stood. "I'm not going to start yet," she declared.

"Oh, Bixx, honey," Richter said. "Praying isn't something you can just turn on or off."

"We have an old saying in my country. Praying is for the weak. If God gave me this brain, then He expects me to use it, right?"

"Well, yes...I suppose so."

"Then come on, I think I have a way to find Jonathan."

21 Not so black and white.

"WHAT do you think?" Tamara asked.

Kortel studied his wife's beautiful figure under the biofabric of the new dress. Its pattern slowly cycled from bright yellow roses to some kind of desert flower he had never heard of. Tamara knew all about it and had spent the better part of lunch explaining how important it had been to an Indian tribe called the Hopi. Kortel had only casually listened. All he knew was that the dress complemented Tamara's tall figure, hanging perfectly onto every curve. He watched intently as one of the Indian flowers delicately transformed into a rose across her left breast.

God, he loved her.

Tamara spun on the dressing room's platform, balancing on the ball of her foot like a ballerina. "I think this would be perfect to wear to little Jonathan's play, don't you?"

"I love you," Kortel said. "It'll be perfect."

Tamara's brow furrowed slightly. She trained her eyes on Kortel and smiled. "What did you say?"

"I said, 'I love it.'"

Her smile turned coy. "No, you said 'you,' not '*it*.'"

Kortel thought for a second. "I did?"

Tamara stepped down and walked over to Kortel, her eyes focused on him with a predatory hunger. She hiked the dress to her thighs, straddled him and settled on his lap. "Yes you did," she said, wrapping her arms around his neck.

"Okay...that's good, right?"

Tamara played with his hair, then her fingers traced the edge of his collar around to the front of his shirt. She began undoing his top button. Her eyes never wavered.

"Baby," Kortel said, suddenly embarrassed. "We're in public."

"I haven't heard you say you loved me for a long time."

Kortel thought back through their morning. He could have sworn he told her when she had stepped out of the shower. Hadn't he?

"I said I loved you this morning, when you were drying your hair."

Tamara started to undo the third button. "You never came back," she said, her eyes still locked on his.

"What do you mean?"

The tips of her fingers were now exploring the surface of his chest. "You never came back for me. You left me in

Chicago. Nicole was so heartbroken."

"But...I didn't. We're here, together."

Suddenly Tamara's eyes went black, and Kortel felt himself falling, his whole existence draining into the depths of her pupils. She leaned in. "I waited a long time for you to return." She reared back and raised her arm, her hand clenched so tight her knuckles were white. "It's time to take what's mine!"

"Wait, I can explain!–"

Tamara punched Kortel's chest, the force knocking the air out of his lungs and pressing him hard against the flimsy chair. Her fist sunk into his skin. Kortel tried to scream, but the shock and the lack of air only fueled his panic. The pain was crushing. Bright red blood crawled up Tamara's arm like a living thing as she dug for her prize.

"Got it," she said with a grotesque smile.

Kortel watched in horror as Tamara removed his heart from the gaping wound below his sternum.

"It's mine," she declared, cupping the throbbing lump of muscle as if she were about to devour it.

"Shit, easy, mate!" Kortel heard somewhere from the edge of his consciousness. He opened his eyes to a dim figure kneeling by his bed. Something was holding him down, the pressure heavy against his chest.

"Don't scream again," the voice said. "You're hurting my ears."

"Nichols?" Kortel asked, his throat raw and dry.

"Who'd you expect, Trumble?"

The pressure on him released, and the room came into focus. Marcus Nichols stood and stepped back.

"Was that your field holding me down?" Kortel asked.

Nichols folded his arms. "Yeah."

"Nice pressure for a normal."

"Former normal."

Kortel sat up. He felt like he'd been hit by an interzone freight hauler.

"How do you feel?" Nichols asked.

"Like shit."

"What kind of shit?"

"Hell, I don't know.... Dog shit?"

Nichols smirked. "No, you don't understand. Do you feel cold or warm? Is it a sharp pain or an overall body ache?"

"What are you getting at? I just feel bad, that's all."

"It's important," Nichols said. "Certain pains mean certain things."

Kortel leaned against the wall behind his bed and took in the room. It was about the size of his grad school apartment and tastefully furnished with dark wood antiques. They looked like the real thing, but how would he know? He couldn't tell the difference between a priceless heirloom and one of those cheap vat-grown ones from Korea.

"Dull," he said, rubbing his forehead.

"What kind of dull?"

"A dull, overall body ache, emanating from my sella turcica, down to my phalanges."

"Piss off."

"Hey, you asked."

"Mr. Nichols?" Trumble's voice beckoned omnisciently in the room.

"Yes, sir?"

"How's Jonathan feeling?"

"Like shit," Kortel said into the air. "And don't ask what kind."

Wouldn't think of it, Trumble replied inside Kortel's mind. *Are you hungry?*

"What time is it?"

6:30...p.m.

"Where are we?"

We're in a suburb of the City of Lights.

Kortel took a deep breath. The air was sweet, and the mere act of taking it in made the top of his head tingle. "There're worst places to wake up in," he said. "What's for dinner?"

Chicken Paillardes with mustard cream and tarragon.

"Is it bioprepped?"

Heavens, no.

"What's the dress, black tie?" Kortel was still in the same clothes from Zvara's base.

I think you'll like what's hanging in the armoire. It's the latest fashion from Beijing.

Kortel rubbed some sleep from his eyes. He glanced at Nichols. "You joining us?"

"For what?"

"Dinner."

"No, thanks. I have some work to finish up. I'll let you get ready." He pointed at a dark, narrow hallway to Kortel's left. "The lav's that way. Nice shower with lots of hot water. The rationing hasn't affected Mr. Trumble, I guess." He opened the doors of the armoire and gestured. "And for you, the latest in fashion." He turned to leave. The door was made of a rough-cut wood that looked like it could have been carved during the 18th century. It appeared not to have a lock and creaked heavily as Nichols opened it.

"Isn't there any security?" Kortel asked.

Nichols turned back. "I know you, Kortel. You won't cause trouble."

"How do you know that?"

"Because you're curious about what Trumble has to offer. You're no dumbass, but you always take the easy way.... It's your pattern." The door clicked behind Nichols and echoed across the marble floor.

* * *

Don't you like your dinner?

"I do, but my throat is sore, and it's hard to swallow." Kortel took another bite, chewed, and washed the Chicken Paillardes down with a rich Cabernet Sauvignon. Its dark plum and cherry flavors lingered through a long finish. He had tasted better, so he decided it was probably manufactured. The tarragon sauce burned his throat. He took another sip.

Trumble's expressionless gaze blanketed him from across the table while the chair tried to feed him another spoonful of mandarin-colored paste. One arm fed as another quickly wiped his mouth. The whole scene reminded Kortel of Tarris's mom feeding his kid brother.

What do you think of the wine?

Kortel buried his nose inside the glass and inhaled. "Brazilian," he said, inspecting the last of its legs.

The napkin arm stopped in midwipe. *And?*

"There's a really good private label wine factory in Rio that can knock off anything on the planet. I met one of their programmers at a conference once. Cocky son of a bitch, but he knew his wines. I told him I could spot one of his by how it smelled."

Bravo, Jonathan. And the chicken?

"Oh, it's all right. I wouldn't have used so much tarragon, but what do I know? I've been out of the game for a while."

The arm finished its wipe and disappeared under the table, while another raised a glass of the Cab to Trumble's lips. The straw in the glass swished around the rim, but the arm deftly maneuvered the glass so that the straw stopped at the perfect point for Trumble to take a sip.

My palate was somewhat damaged. I now like foods prepared with a little more taste.

Kortel continued eating in silence, keeping his attention focused on his plate. He could feel Trumble studying him like some kind of experiment. *Maybe I am,* he thought.

In a sense, you are. But arguably, one of the greatest ever! Trumble's voice resonated deep inside Kortel's mind.

More silence.

Is Armando still fretting over the sun?

Stunned, Kortel slowly lowered his fork. "How the hell do you know that?"

I have people everywhere. Just because I don't run the Agency anymore doesn't mean I'm out of touch with what's going on in the Tel world. There were many people who owed Cyril and me, and believe me, I'll spend the rest of my life cashing in on those debts. Is Dr. Richter still predicting the end of the world?

"Yes. She thinks it's just around the corner."

Well, depending on your view of time and the universe, a thousand years could be interpreted as just around the corner. There are some scientists who believe that her theories are total rubbish. What do you think?

"How would I know who's right? I'm just a chef."

You're more than a–

Kortel slammed his fist on the table. Instantly two of the chair's arms appeared, forming an "x" in front of Trumble's face.

"Enough of this shit," Kortel said. "What do you want?"

The arms slowly retracted.

What if Dr. Richter is correct?

"What? I thought you said it was a bunch of rubbish."

I'm like you. I leave the big questions to be answered by the scientists. What's important to me is the potential of it happening.

"I don't follow you."

Fear, Jonathan, can be very useful. I plan on leveraging the world's fear of the Tsunami, but I'm going to need your help. You see, Cyril and I also made many enemies when we were in charge, and there are debts to be paid. Because of your intervention, they can't be paid so easily now. I know all about Armando's concept to stop the Tsunami, and in theory, it could work. When we implanted you, we wanted to create the Infinite Tel. But we never imagined a scenario like this. If Dr. Richter's calculations are correct, you will have to fulfill your destiny.

"Wait a minute. You want to do what Zvara is going to do?"

If you mean linking powerful Tels together to create a gravitational wall to protect the earth, you're correct.

"And your ass is in a crack with who knows who and you want me to join you, so you can blackmail them to get you off the hook?"

Blackmail is an oversimplification.

"Man, these must be some big debts you owe."

They are.

"So, you really think Zvara's plan will work?"

In truth, I'm in the rubbish camp. I believe the sun is stable, but Dr. Richter's data is very compelling. The problem with Armando's plan is that he doesn't have the power to do it. But I do. For me, it's a win-win.

"Why don't you just kill the people you owe? The Agency's been doing that for years."

You just don't kill off these types of people, Jonathan. The repercussions of their deaths would cause even bigger problems...for the culture and me. And I don't want to die a second time. If Dr. Richter is correct, then you and I will serve mankind like no one ever has. Either way, I get what I want.

"Why would I even consider this? It was you and Cyril who

put all this tech into my head. I should waste you right here."

But you can't.

"I know, the great Jeffrey Trumble, master of all his domain. And now I've got this blue stuff." Kortel tapped the side of his head. "Mind telling me what it is?"

I would love to, but the technology you're referencing isn't part of ours. Why don't you ask your good friend Dr. Shoalburg? He should be able to answer that question.

"W-what do you mean by that? You talked before like it was a part of the original tech."

Trumble sighed. *You were always so naive. Cyril thought it was a weakness, but I felt it was one of your strengths. The world, Jonathan, is not all black and white.... You should know that by now. Never underestimate Armando Zvara. He is a man of means and will do anything to get what he wants.*

Kortel couldn't process what he just heard. He looked down and found his right hand twitching violently.

You see, Jonathan, life is complex. If you view it as something less, you only set yourself up for more pain. Trumble's eyes went to Kortel's hand.

Kortel desperately tried to massage the spasms. "You didn't answer my question," he said, rubbing. "Why should I go with you? What's in it for me?"

For the first time that evening, Jeffrey Trumble's face seemed to relax. There was a slight smile at the edge of his mouth. *It's not what, Jonathan.... It's who.*

Kortel sat motionless. His attention went to the dining

room door. The hallway that he took from his bedroom had been what, about 70 feet? It continued on for another 20 or so, but it dead-ended into a closed door. That was all he'd seen, except for that dark room he had woken up in the day before, and who knows where that was. He thought about making a break for it, but figured it would be a crapshoot. Besides, Trumble had control over his tech, and God knows what he'd do if Kortel tried to bolt. He looked back and found Trumble staring at him.

That was quite a dream you had earlier, or should I say nightmare?

Kortel felt the blood drain from his face. "How do you know what I dream?"

As your technology integrates, more of your body's functions become...oh, how can I put this? Manageable?

"Get out of my mind, or I'll–"

Or you'll what? You're not in control here, Jonathan. And if I were you, I'd listen to what I have to offer.

Kortel noticed his hand had stopped twitching. He leaned back in his chair. "Okay, fine. You're in control. So what did you mean before...it's not what, but who, or whatever? Dammit, just get to the point!"

The point, Jonathan, is that I can give you back what you thought was gone. Trumble paused. May I ask, do you think of her often?

"Think of who?" Then it struck Kortel. His dream. "Are you talking about Tamara?"

What if I told you I could restore parts of her memory – all of your moments together – without any trauma to her?

"You can't do that! It's impossible." Kortel was beginning

to feel dizzy. Maybe Trumble was playing with his tech. Or maybe it was the revelation that Zvara and Shoalburg had lied.

I'll have to call in one of those favors, but I'll need your help.

"It wouldn't be right.... You can't do that to her. She has a new life, and there's no place for me in it."

Life is too short, Jonathan. Isn't it about time you got something out of it?

Kortel grabbed the edge of the table; his fingers pulled at the white linen. The thought of having Tamara back in his life collided head-on with his rational self. "No," he said, "I won't let you."

A holojection suddenly appeared in the middle of the table. The image of Tamara, working at her desk in the art gallery, quivered above a shallow bowl of green apples. The holojection's depth seemed so real that Kortel for a microsecond actually felt he was inside the gallery. He watched in disbelief as Tamara stood and said hello to the camera.

"What the hell is this?"

Insurance, Jonathan. An old concept, to be sure, but one that works very well in this context. You remember James McCarris, don't you?

"Yes," Kortel said, cautiously.

I've employed James to keep an eye on Tamara...to make sure nothing bad happens to her. This is the feed from his optic nerve. Most of his brain functions are online. A slight laugh reverberated in Kortel's brain. *I called in one of the biggest favors owed to me to restore him.* There was another pause. *Look at her. Isn't she beautiful?*

Kortel was numb, and he knew it wasn't because of the technology. He watched Tamara show McCarris various works of art, gesturing and laughing as if they were old friends. Then they shook hands, and McCarris's eyes tracked Tamara through the open space of the gallery.

Why don't you go into the city for the weekend.... Get some clarity. I've arranged for you to stay at one of Paris's finest hotels. Eat, drink...get a massage. I know you'll make the right decision.

Tamara looked beautiful. Kortel couldn't take his eyes off of her, but as she stepped through a shaft of light, a shudder slashed through him. There, moving across her lean frame like a second skin, was the flowered dress he had seen in his dream.

Windows to the soul. 22

THE room in which Richter had dropped off Bixx wasn't like anything else on the base. Going through its doors was like stepping into another world, far away from New Mexico. Everything Bixx had seen up to this point was ancient, made of wood and retrofitted. Even the smell of the base was old; it reminded Bixx of her grandfather's farm, all musty and dry. But this room bore a faint technical edge, or at least what she pictured as such. Rocket had chosen to go back to their room – something about lunch not agreeing with him. Bixx had tried to get him to come, saying she needed his support, but he had just smiled and said, "You'll kick ass." Plus, he was in one of his moods, and she knew not to push it.

"Stay here for a second," Richter said. "Let me go talk to Shoalburg and see if they're ready." She briskly maneuvered through the maze of electronics towers until she disappeared around a large concrete column.

Bixx stood patiently near a row of lockers and surveyed the area. There were about a half-dozen lab techs busily going from workstation to workstation, their heads wrapped in the latest biointerface gear. The room was in the basement of the complex's centermost building. It had a raised floor, and the air was chilled, but not like a typical air-conditioned room. This was more like standing next to a refrigerator at a Grab and Go when some jerk had left the door open so that the cold air was rushing out. Bixx felt goose bumps raise on her arms, and she glanced down at her chest. She hadn't been blessed with her mother's shape, so she never worried about going braless, unless she was headed to someplace cold.

"Come on," Richter said, marching up. Her eyes went to Bixx's T-shirt. "Oh, honey, you're freezing in that skimpy thing. Here, put this on." She grabbed a sweater off a hook that was holding about dozen others. "They keep these around so people don't freeze to death."

The room was barely lit by the ambient light from the electronics, so Bixx kept close, following Richter around the concrete column like a shadow. They made their way through more computer stacks until they emerged into an open area that was brighter, though still cast in a green glow. Shoalburg was hunched at a small console, his interface cables tethered from his eye sockets like a techno umbilical. Zvara was sitting on a metal table at the edge of the light, tucked mostly in the shadows, while he pored over a netpad. Tarris was leaning against another console, moving a toothpick through its paces with all the determination of a surgeon.

Bixx stepped around Richter and instantly felt the stares of Tarris and Zvara. Shoalburg turned, and his interface cables slapped against the counter. An awkward silence settled around them.

Zvara finally said, "Dr. Richter says you have a way to find Jonathan." His tired eyes landed on Bixx with a palpable desperation.

"I-I think I do, sir," she said, the words coming out with more of her Russian accent than usual.

Richter nudged her. "Tell them what you told me."

Bixx hesitated.

Zvara sucked in a deep breath. "Would you like some water?"

"No, sir. Thank you."

"Bixx has a special way of negotiating the Net," Richter offered.

Zvara's brow furrowed.

Richter placed a hand on Bixx's shoulder. "Go ahead," she whispered.

Bixx proceeded to tell them why she and the others had come to New Mexico in the first place: how she had discovered James McCarris's cerebral Net feed and hacked its security skin. She told them how she had merged with his personality construct and discovered his hatred for Kortel, as well as his plan for revenge.

Everyone remained quiet when she finished. Shoalburg hadn't moved, and Tarris's toothpick was locked between his teeth.

"How long have you had this talent?" Zvara asked.

"Since the orphanage."

"And you really think that you can find Jonathan by tapping back into McCarris's stream?"

Bixx pulled the sweater tight across her chest and nodded.

Zvara folded his arms and thoughtfully tapped his netpad against his chin. He looked at Tarris. "What do you think?"

The toothpick disappeared, then reappeared at the opposite corner of Tarris's mouth. "We got dick right now." He pulled the toothpick from his lips and flicked it into the darkness. "I vote for letting her try. What the hell do we have to lose?"

"Carter?"

Shoalburg twisted in his chair and faced Zvara. His chrome interface connectors caught the light and flashed into Bixx's eyes. The effect was eerie, considering they were nestled where his eyes should have been.

"Her file says she displays an extraordinary amount of awareness when it comes to navigation, with elevated levels of primary and secondary tracing." He shrugged. "I agree with Tarris. We've nothing to lose."

"My *file*?" Bixx demanded.

Zvara set his netpad down and stood. His imposing figure caught the edge of the light and bathed him in a greenish hue. He focused on Bixx, and she felt goose bumps on her arm again. He walked up and put his hands in his pockets.

"There is no need for you to be upset," he said. "I like to know everything about whomever I am dealing with. And from what I have read, you are an extraordinary young girl."

Bixx felt herself blush. "Thank you, sir."

"Come," Zvara said, gesturing to the console where Tarris leaned. "I think you will like our equipment."

Tarris pushed away from the console and pulled a chair out all in the same movement, which was amazing to Bixx, given his disability. His motor movement was at times more fluid than that of a normal person, and she wondered if he had programmed the tech in his legs to be more graceful. Maybe he had downloaded the matrix of some famous ballet dancer or sports star. Was that even possible?

"Here you go," Tarris said, patting the chair's biofabric.

Bixx settled in and felt the chair mold to the contour of her body.

Shoalburg scooted across the area and bumped against the arm of her chair. Up close, his implants appeared the consistency of mercury. He looked at her as if he could see her, which she figured he could, but only in the context of the Net, and probably in a manner only he could process. He handed her a tiny wafer that seemed made from the same material as his implants.

"This is a new prototype interface I've been working on," he said proudly. "It'll enhance your connection."

Bixx turned the piece of tech over in her palm and thought she saw it quiver slightly. She looked from Richter to Zvara and back to Shoalburg, who was staring at her like a bug.

"Does it work like the regular ones?" she asked.

"Basically," Shoalburg said. "Just place it on your forehead and relax. It packs more of a hit than what you're used to."

Bixx raised the wafer to her forehead.

"Oh, and try and keep your tongue in the back of your mouth. One of our lab boys bit his the other day, and it bled for an hour."

The wafer felt like it was heating up between Bixx's fingers. She took a deep breath, moved her tongue back and closed her eyes.

The threshold jump was almost instantaneous. Bixx squirmed in her chair. The Net exploded onto her visual field with a profound intensity. She thought she heard herself gasp.

Are you okay? Shoalburg's voice was soft and somewhat reassuring. It penetrated the Net's vast white noise with total clarity.

"Yeah...I guess. This is amazing. The spatial acuity is beyond anything I've ever seen."

Shoalburg laughed. *I thought you'd like it. I'm going to back out of your field's parameters, but I'll be monitoring your travel. Just think of me as another conscience.*

Bixx nodded, and the action almost made her sick. It usually wasn't that important to remain still when in the Net, because the duality wasn't that harsh – at least not for her. But Shoalburg's prototype was a billion times more real, and Bixx quickly learned that even the slightest movement could send her into a kind of dizziness shock. She felt something metal touch the side of her ankle. Again, the nausea.

Here's a bucket, in case you need to throw up.

Bixx almost nodded okay, but caught herself.

Oh, I forgot to mention: with my prototype, there's another threshold jump. Good luck.

"But–"

The second jump happened even faster than the first one. The suddenness startled Bixx, and she gripped the arms of the chair as if they would actually help her control the freefall. The Net shifted before her. She couldn't tell how; she just knew that it did. It now possessed such dimensional perfection, Bixx thought that if she reached out, she'd actually be able to touch one of the data streams.

Then something happened.

Usually when jacked, there was a sense of your "outer self." It would hover at the edge of your conscience, reminding you that the Net was just an illusion – a trick played on your cerebral pathways. But without warning, that presence, with all of its reassuring comfort, simply had dropped away.

To Bixx, it felt as if she were losing part of her essence, as if the fabric of her being was shredding and her soul might ooze out the tear. The metal bucket, the cool plastic of the chair's arms, even the seat's biofabric, which any other time she would have been a little squeamish about, vanished. Bixx found herself floating among the zettaflops of information without the lifeline she had taken for granted. A primal sense of panic began to rise in her, but she quickly engaged the breathing sequences she had been taught in her virt classes. The feeling subsided.

"Amazing," she whispered.

Bixx started emptying her mind and preparing to hunt for McCarris's data stream. Dr. Lee, her Advanced Virt professor at the Agency, had singled her out to teach her the art of *Listening with the Heart*. He had called her porous, but she never understood what he meant until years later. "You must listen for the chi," he had instructed. "Every person – every thing – has a life force. That chi is present in the Net. You must empty your mind and open your heart, even if the one you seek wants to harm you. Remember, you must show forgiveness before you can *listen*."

Bixx drifted effortlessly as she "listened" for the data flow she had felt previously. Soon, she caught the drone, then sensed its presence. She opened her eyes and saw McCarris's stream. Its distinctive signature had been imprinted onto her psyche so that she had no problem distinguishing it from other flows. Remembering her original encounter with McCarris's stream, Bixx performed another series of breathing exercises to relieve her fear. She closed her eyes, focused on the core of the drone and let go.

Bixx waited for the impact, but it never came. She opened her eyes to the river of data that was McCarris's life, but this time, there were no torrents of emotion. Instead, the streaks of informational light were displayed as an undulating mass of electric color. The other time she had entered McCarris's stream, Bixx's matrix became a "part" of it, but now she felt more like an observer. Gone was the feeling of chaos. Whether it was Shoalburg's interface or just her abilities, Bixx instinctively knew where to focus to find McCarris's chi. She pictured his gray-blue eyes and opened her mind.

Instantly the Net fell away, replaced by an oddly pedestrian scene. Bixx took a second to adjust, because the feeling of reality was so accurate that it scared her. It felt as if she were actually standing in a gallery opening, with people talking and laughing and milling about with fine-stemmed glasses of white wine. As she studied the scene, the depth of field and proportional range was astounding. People looked at her like she actually existed within their space. Suddenly, a hand came into her field of vision, but the sensation was that of her own hand. She glanced at its features and recoiled. It was a man's hand. Bixx instantly realized what had happened, but the shock was nonetheless frightening.

She was looking out the windows of McCarris's soul.

The initial jolt seemed to subside rather quickly, and Bixx began feeling comfortable with the arrangement. She wondered if Shoalburg's interface was making the situation more palatable for her brain to handle, because she was surprised at her lack of panic, and even more surprised at her curious desire to hang out and see what would happen.

It took a few moments to adjust to being a man. First, there was McCarris's height. He was at least a foot and a half taller than Bixx, and looking down at people was a bit disarming. Then there was the sheer bulk of his body, not to mention the obvious anatomical differences. Once, in a severely drunken state with two of her girlfriends, she had mused about what it would be like to have a penis, and now that she was in a situation to find out, she was completely repulsed by the idea. Studying the scene, Bixx had the feeling that if she let herself go, she might merge with McCarris's construct. A bald older man approached and smiled. He was about McCarris's height, barrel-chested and had a peculiar brown spot on his forehead.

"Are you enjoying the show?" he asked, his smile full of

perfectly manufactured teeth.

"Yes, I am," McCarris answered. The sound of his voice had a slight reverberation, like feedback she had heard in old-time music vids.

"I'm Ryan Pudder, owner of the gallery."

The men chatted for a moment before Pudder moved on to another guest. McCarris shifted his attention to his left and began walking through the space. Bixx braced for a wave of nausea, but the movement felt queerly comfortable...almost too comfortable. His attention went from painting to painting. They were hideous works that looked to Bixx like someone had wiped his ass on the canvas. Thankfully, McCarris only lingered for a few seconds at each piece. Bixx felt someone tapping her shoulder. McCarris turned, and a pretty woman with short blonde hair was standing there with drinks in her hands.

"Mr. McCarris, I'm so glad you made it. You can't browse the gallery without a little libation, now can you?" The woman handed McCarris a glass of wine.

"Thank you," McCarris said, and immediately took a sip.

Bixx instantly felt the wine's coolness pass down her virtual throat, and she wondered if she could get drunk in this techno-schizophrenia.

"I wouldn't have missed this for the world," McCarris said. His Southern accent was more distinct now. He took another sip, and his attention went to the woman's breasts. She was wearing a low-cut flowered dress, and one of the weirdly shaped flowers changed into a rose. His gaze went back to her face. She had the prettiest blue eyes Bixx had ever seen – bright and full of life. She smiled and cocked her head, and Bixx felt something flush through McCarris's body. She became aware of his penis and fought back a yelp.

"See anything you like?" the woman asked.

McCarris leaned into the woman, and Bixx could smell her perfume. It was floral and complemented her appearance well.

"My real opinion?" McCarris asked.

The woman shyly nodded and smiled, then looked around to see if anyone was within earshot. She took another sip from her glass.

"I think it looks like a monkey did these," McCarris whispered.

The woman giggled into her wine. "Shhh," she said, wiping her chin with a small cocktail napkin. "The artist is right over there." She motioned discreetly to a tall Middle-Eastern man holding court in front of a particularly atrocious work.

McCarris and the woman laughed, and Bixx felt that flushing again. Their laughter waned, and both stared at each other for a moment.

"Say," McCarris said, "would you like to get some dinner after this?"

The woman smiled and glanced away. When she looked back, her eyes locked on McCarris, and Bixx felt something pass through his nervous body. It was a strange feeling: passionate, but darkly aggressive.

"Why, Mr. McCarris, are you asking me on a date?"

"Ms. Connor, we Southern boys don't call it a date. We

call it a walk. And if there were a row of magnolias, I'd walk you among them."

"Well, you won't find any magnolia trees in Chicago, Mr. McCarris. But you can drive me to a nice restaurant."

"Consider it done."

The name Connor was so familiar to Bixx, but she couldn't place it. Pudder came up to Connor's side and whispered in her ear. Her face grew serious, and then she smiled at McCarris.

"Will you excuse me for a moment? My presence has been requested by the *artiste*." She rolled her eyes.

"Sure. I'll catch up with you later."

Connor smiled and tilted her head.

McCarris looked around and walked over to a secluded corner of the gallery. He pulled out a netpad, and Bixx intently noted the coordinates he tapped in. The NetCom logo pixeled up; the face of Marcus Nichols appeared, and a cold shiver cut through Bixx. She hoped McCarris hadn't felt it.

"How's it going?" Nichols asked.

"Swimmingly," McCarris replied.

"You gonna get some tonight?"

"Possibly."

Nichols smirked. "You're supposed to get close, not marry the bitch."

"Don't worry. I'm a professional. Tonight's for sport."

"Right. Report back in the morning."

"Make it the afternoon."

"Whatever." Nichols's image cut out.

"I've got good news," a voice said into Bixx's ear.

McCarris quickly pocketed the netpad and turned to find Connor standing there, her drink almost empty. "H-hey you," he said. "What happened to monkey boy?"

Connor glanced over her shoulder. "His assholiness is too busy pontificating about how great he is." She downed the rest of her wine and placed the empty glass on a serving cart.

"So what's the good news?" McCarris asked.

"Ryan's letting me leave early tonight. He says I deserve it.... After this week," Connor gave a nod to the artist, "that's an understatement." She wrapped her arm around McCarris's. "So, Southern boy, where are you taking me?"

"I know of a great little biofood place. Do you like bio?"

"Depends. What'd you have in mind?"

"It's called *Kortel's*. I've been there once, and it was excellent."

"*Tres chic*, Mr. McCarris. Isn't that the place where the owner just disappeared one day?"

Bixx felt a sudden rush of anger course through McCarris. The muscles of his neck, chest and arms tightened. "I read that he was killed. Some kind of tragic death."

"Oh, how terrible." Connor patted McCarris's arm, and the anger ebbed. "Let's go," she said, looking up with those beautiful eyes, "before monkey boy beckons, and I'm stuck here all night."

Strange that he would he take her to Kortel's old restaurant. And why did the name Connor nag at Bixx? She racked her brain, trying to remember the rumors she'd heard. Hadn't he fallen in love with some kind of high-end hooker once? Tammy? Tamara... Tamara *Connor*?

As McCarris and Connor strolled toward the gallery's entrance, several guests stopped them to chat. Bixx decided it was a good time to back out of the limbo-state of piggybacking with McCarris, so she emptied her mind and pictured the Net outside of his stream. Again, like a cerebral magic trick, she found herself back in the Net, looking down at McCarris's flow.

Bixx had a great head for figures and immediately pictured the coordinate numbers McCarris had entered into his netpad. Nothing happened at first, and she began wondering if her ability was degrading, possibly because of limbic short-circuiting with Shoalburg's tech. But then the Net threw her a lateral, shifting everything into a hyper-blur that almost hurt physically.

When it finished, Bixx was staring at five delicate sans serif brass numbers attached to a richly lacquered wood door. The grain had been stained a dark glossy cherry so that the finish had an almost liquid appearance. The numbers, 22176, were washed in a spot of soft light. Above them, embedded in the door, was the unblinking eye of a vid lens, the kind used in ultra-high-end hotels. A man's fist came into view and rapped hard on the door, just below the numbers. Bixx flinched and thought she felt the tops of her knuckles tingle. A moment went by before the door slowly opened on Jonathan Kortel. He had a towel around his waist and looked as if he had just stepped out of a shower. Bixx almost peed her virtual pants.

"You told me you'd be ready," said the voice of Marcus

Nichols. Bixx knew she was inside Nichols now, but how? Did he have the kind of tech to connect into?

"I fell asleep," Kortel replied. He turned, and Bixx watched him walk into a hotel suite that was bigger than most homes and lighted like a Japanese art vid. A bank of tall windows stretched the length of the cavernous space, and she could see the Paris skyline beyond. Its millions of lights blinked lazily through the thermals of a hot night.

Nichols said, "Jeffrey doesn't like to be kept waiting."

Kortel shot him a stern look and cinched the towel tighter. Bixx had only met him once, and he had definitely not been half naked. She was surprised at how ripped his body was and had barely begun to imagine what might be under the towel when Kortel turned and started drying his hair with it. Nichols's attention immediately went to the New Eiffel Tower, which was performing its famous light show. Bixx tried to will him to look back, but Nichols kept watching the Tower.

"Hurry it up," he said. Nichols's attention went back to where Kortel had been standing, but he had already gone down the hallway.

Damn.

"Ease up," Kortel yelled from somewhere deep in the suite. "You all need me a lot more than I need you." Bixx figured the bathroom was huge, because she could barely hear Kortel's voice.

"Asshole thinks he's so fucking powerful," Nichols said to himself. Bixx could feel anger building in him, but it had an odd edge to it that felt like jealousy. Several tense minutes of silence went by. Nichols was clearly growing pissed. Bixx could almost taste his rage. More time passed, and he glanced at his watch.

"God*damn* it," he said under his breath. Nichols quickly stood and stormed toward the hallway. His vision had clearly narrowed; only the center was in focus now. The hallway was long and lined with large monochromes of sliced fruit that, at this scale, looked like studies of gothic medical experiments. Nichols entered the bathroom and swept his attention from side to side.

"Kortel, where the fuck *are* you?" He searched the huge room, from the toilet area to the shower – which itself was nearly the size of Bixx and Rocket's apartment – to another large space that she guessed was for the super rich to have someone dress them, because it contained a little platform and three large mirrors. "Kortel?!" Nichols screamed again. Bixx felt adrenaline racing, but she couldn't distinguish whose it was.

"What the hell?" he said, looking wildly from side to side. Bixx could feel his rage mixing with panic.

Suddenly the door in front of Nichols blew open, sending its latticework splintering in all directions. Kortel was standing inside what looked like a linen closet, dressed in workout pants and running shoes. His head was cocked down, though he was looking forward under his brow. His hair had been combed, but his chest was still slick with moisture.

Bixx felt her throat begin to close as a pressure – like two giant hands – pushed Nichols back up the hallway. He tried to speak, but all that came out was gurgling as he frantically grabbed at his throat. Bixx felt herself floating backward and immediately realized that Nichols was horizontal as he sailed above the deep pile carpet of the hallway.

"I can bend time, you dumbass. What did you think I'd do?... Just let you push me around?"

Nichols gurgled an answer, which Bixx couldn't decipher. She figured it was probably some archaic Cockney expletive. They were now back in the main room, and Nichols's attention went to the skyline for a second.

"You can tell Trumble to–" Kortel grabbed his chest, and the pressure at Nichols's throat relaxed. Bixx felt a stabbing pain across her back as Nichols crashed onto a glass coffee table. His vision had shifted, and the room was cast in shades of deep red now, although Bixx knew this was his optic nerve changing, not the light in the room. A heat began rising in Nichols's body as he slowly got himself to his feet. Kortel was on his knees, clutching his chest.

Nichols wiped blood from his nose. "Oh, I've been fucking waiting for this day," he said. "Get up, you piece of shit, and learn a lesson." Bixx could feel his muscles tighten as the heat increased.

It must be his tech engaging, she thought. *But how's he able to control Kortel?*

Kortel looked up like a wounded animal. He suddenly flew backward, slamming hard against a finely tailored cloth wall. He clutched wildly at the fabric, which tore and fell on top of him as he landed in a heap on the hardwood.

Nichols scrambled around a couch to see where he had landed, but when he looked down, Kortel wasn't there. Suddenly Nichols flew backward across the main room. He landed, twisted over a bar, and smashed into a row of liquor bottles and glasses. The whole scene remarkably resembled the night he had slammed Bixx against the mirror in that club's bathroom, but, thank God, without the full intensity. She felt she was sharing in Nichols's pain, but from a distance.

Nichols struggled to see over the bar, and when he stood, Bixx almost screamed at what she saw. Kortel was flying through the room, flat-out, his hands stretched in front of him like some comic vid character. She could feel Nichols's astonishment, and for a second, he froze.

Kortel flew right up and grabbed Nichols's throat, his thumbs digging into the esophagus. Only the whites of his eyes were showing, and Bixx, for the first time, felt fear run through Nichols's nervous system.

The grav pressure around Nichols's head was tremendous, and Bixx could feel his tech trying to counter it.

"Either I die, or you do," Nichols managed.

Bixx desperately tried to figure out how she could help, as Nichols's tech punched back at Kortel's telekinetic strength.

Nichols now had his hands at Kortel's throat, and the two Tels were locked together. Kortel slowly floated backward, dragging Nichols across the bar and into the room. He lifted the Brit off the floor and carried him up to the suite's tall ceiling. Nichols squirmed in his grip. Kortel released his hold, but Bixx could still feel the pressure at Nichols's throat.

He's formed a tight grav wave around him, Bixx thought.

Kortel spread his arms. Nichols began to lose oxygen.

Suddenly, though, Bixx felt the heat of Nichols's tech build again, and both men slowly lowered onto the remains of the coffee table. The glass crunched under their feet.

"Give it up, Kortel." Nichols's voice was hoarse. "Your time has passed."

Bixx watched in horror as Kortel began to shake, slowly at first, then more violently.

"This is what you did to my father, you bastard," Nichols said. "How does it feel?"

Kortel had become almost a blur, and he had risen off the floor about a foot. Bixx started to freak. She knew she had to do something – and fast. She cleared her mind and thought of Nichols's tech. She knew what bioimplants looked like and pictured them in Nichols's brain, fused within the gray matter. She focused intently on the thought of them dying, turning black, and flushing out of his system.

Nichols screamed and grabbed his head.

Kortel collapsed to his hands and knees and looked up. His eyes rolled forward and narrowed.

Bixx could feel Nichols trying to engage his tech, so she concentrated on it dying. She knew she had to keep the pressure on, or he might get the best of Kortel again.

"I am so *fucking* tired of you," Kortel said, blood pouring from his nose.

Panic was crashing in waves through Nichols. "W-What are you going to do?"

Kortel struggled to his feet and leveled his gaze. "What I

should have done to your father."

"NO!"

Bixx felt an intense grav field build around Nichols, but she kept her focus on his tech. The air around his body began to distort as the grav field grew. Kortel stepped back and casually raised his hand. Nichols rose off the broken glass, his legs and arms flailing.

Bixx sensed her connection with the Net was beginning to deteriorate, and she started to panic. The feeling was like being a kid again, hiding inside her parents' cramped and muffled laundry closet. But the thought of being trapped in Nichols's chi was infinitely more frightening.

"Time for you to go," Kortel said.

"Where?" Nichols asked, the sweat pouring from his armpits.

"Hell."

Kortel waved his hand, and the next thing Bixx felt was crashing backwards through one of the suite's large windows. She could feel the night wind hit Nichols's face, and through his eyes saw the lights of the *Arc de Triomphe*. They screamed in unison as his body began to flip and his feet arched over his back. While they fell, Bixx felt shards from the window tear flesh from his back and arms. He flipped through a spray of glass and blood and began tumbling forward again. The 22-story distance compressed at an unholy rate. Nichols instinctually put his hands out in a futile attempt to stop himself from hitting the pavement. Bixx felt a throbbing down her left arm. She knew his heart was beginning to fail. Complete and primordial fear tore through

Bixx as the top of a green cafe umbrella rose toward them.

"Mother," Nichols said to himself.

A waiter looked up. His mouth formed an "O" as a tray of drinks slipped from his hand. The red star logo on top of the umbrella filled Bixx's vision.

Bixx opened her eyes to the faces of Zvara, Tarris and Shoalburg, who had replaced his eyes in his head. She was hyperventilating and covered with sweat. Zvara truly looked scared, and Tarris seemed pissed. Shoalburg had no expression – just the cool demeanor of a scientist.

"Oh my God! Oh my God!" Bixx yelled between gulps of air.

"Dear, it's all right," Bixx heard to her left. She turned to see Richter kneeling next to her chair.

Tear trails streaked Richter's face. She spread her arms. "Come here," she said, forcing a smile.

Bixx hesitated. She had been without a mother for so long that the thought of someone pretending made her guard go up. But something shifted in Bixx, and she dropped to her knees and fell into Richter's arms.

"It's all right," Richter whispered. She began rocking. "You didn't die."

Bixx began sobbing. Whether it was the near-death experience or the cumulative effect of every hell she had faced in her life, everything came out in a mournful cry into Richter's shoulder.

"Shhh," Richter said, patting Bixx's head.

While Bixx cried, fractured images flashed through her mind: Connor's eyes, Kortel's bloodied face...the waiter's shock.

"We lost your connection when you entered McCarris's stream," Zvara said.

"Then I regained the connection as you and Nichols went out the window," Shoalburg continued. "I-I'm sorry it took so long to get you out. I would have never let it go that far."

Bixx pulled away from Richter's embrace and turned to Shoalburg, her face awash in mucus and tears. She bunched the sleeve of the sweater and wiped her eyes. "Thanks for getting me out when you did. I...I don't know what would have happened if you hadn't."

Shoalburg exchanged tentative glances with Zvara and Richter. He smiled feebly. "Probably, ah...nothing. It's hard to say."

Zvara knelt to the right of Bixx's chair and placed his hand on hers. The gesture was oddly comforting. "When you are ready," he said gently, "you will need to tell us what happened in there."

Tarris flicked another toothpick into the darkness. "At least we know where Jonathan is, and that he's safe."

Bixx stood and faced him. "He's not safe," she said, wiping her checks with the other sleeve. "There's a guy named Jeffrey after him, and James McCarris is working for him."

"Jeffrey *Trumble?*" Zvara asked, his voice full of concern and unbelief.

The image of Connor hanging on McCarris's arm flashed

across Bixx's mind. She remembered his comments about Kortel, and the hatred she felt from him.

Zvara slowly stood, the compassion wiped from his face. "Olga," he said gravely, "I think now is a good time to tell us what happened."

Trompe l'oeil. 23

KORTEL looked at his hands. They were shaking, and he couldn't decide if it was because his tech was free of Trumble's control or because he was scared.

Scared, he thought. *Damn scared.*

The humid night air filled the suite. When the HVAC engaged, Kortel glanced at the open window, or rather, the opening where the window had been, because all that was left was a metal frame bent toward the skyline – probably caused by the distortion wave from his grav field. He had maintained it on Nichols the entire time, and since Kortel hadn't kept a line of sight, it probably drove Nichols's body into the pavement. Kortel didn't want to think about what that might look like.

"Jesus," he said under his breath. But wasn't that the point, that he had kept his field on Nichols *all the way down*? Kortel wanted him to die. Horribly.

The sing-songy wail of a police gunship began dominating the congested street noise. Kortel knew it would only be a matter of minutes before Nichols's dive would be pixeled across every major news portal in Paris. He backed away from the window and headed to the bathroom, where he began gathering what little he had collected in the two days he had been in Trumble's grip: that Beijing fashion statement, a comb, some soap, three biobars and the top to a workout suit, compliments of the hotel's spa.

What the hell am I doing? Kortel threw the comb and soap into a corner, zipped on the workout top and pocketed the biobars. The suit's fabric compensated for the humid air when he ran back into the suite's living room.

The gunship's siren drew closer.

Kortel took a last glance out the window. He remembered the look on Nichols's face and something shot down his nerves. Turning to leave, there was a reflection of light in the remains of the coffee table. It was the screen on Nichols's netpad.

Thank you, God.

As Kortel lifted the pad out of the shards, two 60-million candlepower beams began sweeping the buildings across the street. At the down blast of the gunship's stabilizer engines, Kortel sprinted out of the suite. He ran the length of the hallway, passed the turbolifts and entered the stairwell. The *Napoléon* was an older hotel. Its fire stairs spiraled down an open center. Kortel looked down the 22-story drop and quickly calculated the distance. He climbed onto the railing, formed a grav wave corridor, and jumped.

The space between the stairs was so narrow that Kortel kept his arms tucked close to his sides. He had done a similar stunt once before, but that involved ascending 70 stories of the center of a very wide elevator shaft. Just before reaching the bottom, he increased the field and slowed his fall. The soles of the spa's cross-trainers shifted to their sports tread as he gently settled onto the concrete.

Kortel cracked opened the first floor exit door and found he was at the back of the lobby, close to a set of broad palms. He thought about pulling the suit's hood over his head, but figured that would draw attention. Given that a guest had just sailed out of the 22nd floor of one of Paris's finer hotels, he was struck at how calm the lobby was.

A manager type scurried about, and three policemen huddled next to a table with the biggest floral arrangement Kortel had ever seen. They seemed to be taking the whole event rather casually, as if this kind of thing happened all the time in Paris. The front of the hotel was walled with floor-to-ceiling windows, and he could see that the police were beginning to shut the street down. A large crime scene truck pulled to the curb.

Kortel folded the suit's hood back into its compartment and began walking casually across the lobby. He chose a path well around the police and hugged the wall opposite the registration desk. When he approached the hotel's entrance, the doorman tipped his hat and began pulling on one of the ornate doorknobs.

"Arrêter, s'il vous plaît!"

The doorman stopped in mid-pull and gave a sideways

glance. Kortel turned slowly.

An officer, dressed in the traditional uniform of the *Police Nationale*, had stepped from the huddle and was gesturing sternly with his white-gloved hand. He wore a pair of police Net glasses, but they looked like they could have come from a boutique on the *Champs Elysées*.

"You are American?" he asked, walking toward Kortel.

"Yes, I am." Kortel had slipped into partial phase and was seriously considering sending a grav wave through the entire lobby. His vision was speckled with the swirling colors of the phase jump.

"Your name, please."

"Jonathan Kortel."

"You are a guest of the *Napoléon*?"

"A guest of a guest."

The officer eyed him. "Do you always jog at 2:30 in the morning, Mr. Kortel?" He flipped open his netpad, clicked through some files and muttered something in French.

"Only when I can't sleep."

"Jet lag?" the officer said helpfully, still working something on his pad. He suddenly looked up and stared forward, and Kortel sensed that information was being fed to him from his couture eyewear.

"Oui, monsieur!" The officer's attention shifted to Kortel. "Enjoy your run. And please be careful. The streets of Paris can be troublesome this time of night." He saluted crisply and walked off through the lobby.

Kortel stood down his phase.

The doorman smiled this time, and Kortel quickly walked to the hotel's cabstand. Another doorman, dressed in a tight-fitting black suit, consulted his netpad while he waved Kortel over.

"Where are you going?" he asked in a thick French accent.

Kortel froze. He had been so focused on getting out of the hotel that he hadn't considered his utter lack of credit or identification.

"A cab, *oui*?"

Suddenly, Nichols's netpad hummed inside one of the front pockets of the workout suit. Kortel removed the pad and flipped it open.

The doorman smiled tersely and walked away.

Tarris Finn grinned from the tiny screen. "*Bonjour*, dickhead!"

"How the hell?"

"Don't ask. It's way too complicated."

"But I just–"

"Threw Nichols out the window – we know. Now shut up and listen. We've got to get you out of there."

"Yeah, but the hotel's probably got me on–"

"No, they don't. We just hacked in, and you're off their grid. Did that Paris cop hassle you much?"

"Ah...he was about to, but he got called away."

Tarris smiled. "You're welcome."

Kortel felt the tension release from his shoulders. "Thanks. I owe you."

Tarris waved him off. "That's the least of your concerns.

You've got to get back here right now."

"There's something I have to take care of first."

This statement sent Tarris into a little anxiety dance. "Man, the shit is hitting the stellar fan back here. Richter thinks the flare could come within the next two weeks. We need you–"

"I *have* to go to Chicago."

"We know all about McCarris stalking Tamara. What's Trumble blackmailing you for?"

Kortel didn't even want to know how Tarris had that information. "Some bullshit."

Tarris shook his head. "Man, that guy's a cockroach. I thought you took him out."

"He's connected in ways you wouldn't believe."

"Yeah, well, soon there won't be anything left to be connected with!"

"Tarris, just get me to Chicago. I promise I'll get back to New Mexico in time."

Tarris rolled his eyes. "I can't believe I'm negotiating for the survival of the planet."

"Tarris!" A distortion field formed off to Kortel's left and silently crushed in the side of a service van. "Look, Trumble knows all about the Tsunami. He doesn't think Richter's correct, but he's not taking any chances. He wants to do the same thing as Zvara, but on his own terms."

"And he knows he can't pull it off without you, so he's going to leverage Tamara."

Kortel nodded. "That's why I have to get to Chicago."

"Hold on." Tarris set his netpad down, and the screen shifted to a static image of black piping and bundles of zip-tied holocable. Kortel could barely hear him talking with Zvara. It sounded like they were getting into it.

A siren cut the air, and another crime scene truck sped past the cabstand. It skidded to a halt, and Kortel watched six personnel in orange HAZMAT gear jump out and begin unloading equipment. The screen shifted again, and Tarris's image reappeared. He looked worried. "Our time frame is critical, so we've got an idea," he said. "We can assume Trumble knows about Nichols's death and that he's contacted McCarris already. They probably think you're on your way to Chicago right now.... In fact, we'll make it look like you are."

"But–"

"Jonny, we don't have time! We have a way of getting to McCarris faster than you, so let us take care of him."

"How can you do that?"

"I can't get into it right now; just trust me."

That would be hard for Kortel. "I can't just...do nothing!"

"You won't." Tarris's voice was grave. "You're going to take out Trumble."

The words hit Kortel hard. Killing in self-defense was one thing, but murder was something he didn't want to consider. He stared past the screen at a *Napoléon* logo etched in the driveway's flagstone. Someone had ground a cigarette butt into the accent mark.

"Hey," Tarris said, "you with me on this?"

Kortel reluctantly nodded.

"That's my Jonny. Now, go to the hotel's trans counter. There'll be a rental waiting for you in your name. When you're done, contact us, and we'll get you back to New Mexico."

"How will I–"

Tarris's expression went critical. "You're the most powerful Tel ever. Just *make* it happen. If you don't, he will."

Kortel studied his friend's face and thought of Tamara. "I'm trusting you, Tarris."

Several disruption lines cut through the signal's picture, and Tarris reappeared. "I'm not going to let anything happen to her, I promise. Now get going. We don't have much time."

The image went to static.

* * *

"What would you like to hear, Mr. Kortel?"

Kortel thought for a moment. "Davis, Miles."

Haunting riffs from a concert early in Davis's career filled the cabin. It was a remixed version from his hard-bop period and was so clean that it could have been recorded yesterday.

Thanks to Tarris and Shoalburg, Kortel was navigating through a northern Paris suburb in a fancy rental. They had somehow managed to hack the bioencryption wall of Nichols's netpad to make it available for Kortel's use. They also had infused one of Kortel's old Net accounts with enough Euro Credit to last him a year. The vehicle was high-tech, even by Euro standards, and Nichols's pad had no problem porting with its navigation system. Kortel prayed that Nichols's last trip had been from Trumble's so that all he would have to do is retrace the route from the pad.

It was almost 5 in the morning, and the sky was beginning to fill with predawn light. Kortel intently studied the road, but his memory of the trip to the hotel was sketchy, at best.

The rental began speaking: "Mr. Kortel, you will be leaving the National French Interway System in one minute. Please prepare to take control of the vehicle."

Kortel gripped the steering toggle and began piloting. The nav system instructed him where to go and kept reminding him of inane things like the great savings he could expect if he would just take the time and apply for a credit rating. He fiddled with a couple of the control pads and tried to override the voiceover before he finally gave up and settled into guiding the rental through the narrow French streets.

"Mr. Kortel, please take a right at the next intersection. And did you know, you'll be eligible for a free upgrade in 53 kilometers?"

"Blow me."

"I'm sorry, please repeat the command."

Kortel slowed and turned as instructed. He was now on a dirt road, skirting a crumbling, vine-covered wall that looked like it could have been built before World War II. He drove for about a mile when the rental chirped again.

"Mr. Kortel, the next left will be the driveway entrance of the original departure point. If you're ending your trip with us, *avoir un grand jour*! Please leave your *Citroen Organique II* where it can be easily collected. *Bonjour*!"

Kortel debated whether he should park a few blocks away and be covert about the whole thing. But sneaking up on a guy like Trumble was absurd, and Kortel figured he had already been scanned and analyzed by the home's security system. It probably had produced a 10-point scenario on how to take him out seconds after recognizing Nichols wasn't piloting the rental.

"What the hell," he said, and angled the rental up to a large wooden gate that looked older than the wall. Kortel waited as the netpad dialogued with the vehicle's systems. After a moment, the gate slowly drew back, and he pulled forward into a small courtyard. The rental's hydraulics compensated for the loose gravel as he parked near a large poplar tree.

The house appeared harmless enough, much like all the other quaint homes in the town. Kortel removed the netpad and scanned the area for anything living. Nichols's pad was a basic corporate unit capable of complex tasks, though probably not powerful enough to penetrate fiber-reinforced walls. Kortel realized that even if he had an InterVision model, Trumble's place was probably so webbed up it wouldn't have mattered. Surprisingly, the pad revealed more detail than Kortel expected. He stepped from the rental and ran another sweep, but still caught no signs of anything living, human or otherwise.

The home's garage door was up. Kortel went and checked it out. It was bigger than it looked from the courtyard – able to hold four CityCars and maybe a couple of EuroPeds, if they were mounted under the cabinets. It looked like it had been swept recently, and all the shelves were empty. There was a solid door on the far wall. Kortel considered unlocking it, but decided not to chance it.

He returned to the courtyard and approached the back door. It had four panes of old rippled glass and no visible security devices. Kortel scanned again, with the same results. He wondered if the home's security was feeding disinformation to the netpad, making the place *appear* empty.

Pressing his face against the glass, Kortel could only make out blurred shapes. He passed the pad down the right side of the door. On the second pass, it clicked open, and he cautiously entered. Slipping into partial phase, he made his way through an empty mudroom and into a large modern kitchen. He stopped and scanned again. Still nothing.

On his previous "visit," most of his time had been spent in rooms beneath the main house, and he hadn't seen much of the first floor, except for the night Nichols had taken him to the hotel. They had gone out the front, so he had never seen the back of the house.

Kortel inspected the counters and found everything had been thoroughly cleaned. As he walked around a large butcher-block island, he began to consider that the readings were correct. He referenced the pad and saw that the hallway on the other side of the kitchen led to the front of the house. Following it, he came to a foyer that felt vaguely familiar. He tried to recall the night he went to the *Napoléon*, but all he could remember were fractured, meaningless images. Since it had been just two days ago, Kortel concluded that Nichols had probably jerked with his memory.

The only thing that made any sense was a distant image of an ornate wooden door. If only he could remember.

"Damnit!"

In the room to his right, sitting in the middle of a large dining table, a lavish fruit bowl exploded. Hundreds of brightly colored plaster fragments sprayed about. One particularly large chunk from an orange smashed against one of the two doors in the room, causing it to quiver slightly. Perhaps it was a trick of the morning light, but Kortel figured it was more likely fatigue. He hadn't slept and was beginning to get that jittery feeling he used to get in Chicago after he had partied all night. He watched the door quiver again and realized it wasn't the light or his fatigue. Then the images aligned in his mind, and he remembered emerging from the basement into a large room with a fireplace and a table. A dining room. Nichols had led him through this room into the foyer.

Kortel approached the strange door. He ran his fingers across its surface and discovered it was actually an image – a kind of holographic *trompe l'oeil*, though extremely sophisticated in its production. He stepped back and focused a narrow grav wave directly at its center. The door's image began to degrade, then it went to static and vanished. Behind it was a reinforced metal door and frame. Kortel increased the field, and the whole thing crumpled like foil.

Now it all came rushing back. He descended the narrow stairs and began searching the corridors of the basement. Everywhere he looked had been scrubbed cleaned; even the bed where he had slept had been stripped and redressed. Kortel checked the armoire and found the rest of the Beijing casual wear.

Kortel stepped back into the main corridor and scanned again, but nothing registered. He stormed upstairs and searched the rest of the house, but found only the same meticulous cleaning effort in every room.

Kortel went back to the courtyard and climbed into the rental. He engaged its organics, ported the netpad and hit recall. Static filled the onboard com screen.

"Come on, Tarris. Connect."

He tried four more times, but was always greeted with pixilated snow. Maybe Tarris and Shoalburg's hacking had been compromised. He should have at least gotten a TransLink logo or a Network Error icon. Static meant the whole system had gone down, satellites and all. Or it was the netpad. He thought about testing it by calling the Pudder Gallery to warn Tamara, but what the hell would that accomplish?

Suddenly the netpad flashed an incoming tag: Unknown. He thought about letting it pass to vidmail, but he had nothing to lose now. He pulled the pad from the port and flipped it open. Trumble's stern face pixeled up.

"Jonathan." His lips didn't move. "You are truly amazing. Cyril felt that you would burn out someday, and we'd have to institutionalize you. But here you are, defying my technology and killing with reckless abandon. Tell me, when you threw my son out the window, was he still alive?"

Stunned, Kortel remembered the look on Nichols's face.

"Yes," he said finally.

Trumble's eyes closed for a second, then slowly opened. "Marcus was discovered in Liverpool as an infant. Cyril begged me to take him in. He said it would strengthen our relationship." He paused. "Marcus never got beyond a Level 2, so we implanted him, much like we did you. He achieved a modest gain, but the boy was never satisfied. Then he became unruly. I guess the military did that to him. It was only in the last year that we came back together. He helped with my recovery. I will miss him."

"Look, Jeffrey. I'm sorry about what–"

"I know that you're headed to Chicago. What do you hope to accomplish? I've already instructed James to kill that whore of yours. Shall we call it an eye for an eye?"

Something pressed against Kortel's heart. "I thought we had a deal."

A small laugh answered him. "Deal's off."

Kortel felt nauseous. His throat was dry, and he tried to swallow. "Okay, Jeffrey. Let's–"

"I've never landed from the north before. You get such a lovely view of Lake Michigan."

The back of Kortel's neck prickled. "What are you doing *there?*"

"Just making sure my order is carried out. Tamara is a very beautiful woman, and I know how young men think."

At that moment, a part of Kortel gave way. Out near the liminal point of his rational self, the factors that governed reason and control reverted, exposing something mammalian. Raw.

"I don't know how you're jamming my technology," Trumble said, "but when I break through, I'll introduce you to hell."

A heat was building inside Kortel. It coursed through his body on a wave of primal anger. Every nerve was firing off a message of limitless strength. He could feel his technology metastasizing, and for the first time he embraced it.

"If she dies," he said. "You die."

Trumble's eyes narrowed. "I look forward to that. Again."

"WHAT is *she* doing here?" Tarris asked.

Bixx looked at Rocket, who looked at Kreet.

"Ms. Toffler is here to document the proceedings," Kreet said, trying to sound important but failing miserably. Ever since teaming with Toffler, he had been running an attitude, and with Nichols gone, he had grown downright rude. He now addressed everyone as "people" and kept demanding that they act natural. They were creating a docu-drama, and he was the line producer, but the way Bixx saw it, the only thing he was producing was a lot of resentment.

Bixx watched Toffler angle close to Tarris. She was wearing the vid gear Nichols had carried in the chrome cases. She seemed to be going for one of those reaction shots she talked about incessantly. Bixx never understood all the terms Toffler used but figured she knew what she was doing. Toffler had spent the last couple of days creating what she called "master takes" and establishing shots. She told Bixx this was going to be her legacy piece, whatever that meant. Now she was practically sticking the fiber lens of the vid gear up Tarris's nose.

"Lady," he said, his voice threatening, "if you don't get that equipment out of my face, I'm going to cram it up your–"

"We're set to go, everyone!" Shoalburg announced.

"Excellent," Zvara said. He turned to Bixx. "Are you ready?"

Toffler angled into Bixx, who could feel the heat from the vid gear's lights on the side of her face.

"Ms. Toffler," Zvara said, "I have allowed you to document this because the world should know the real story behind stopping the Tsunami. But must you do this...what is it called?"

"Back story," Toffler said.

"Yes. Must you do this back story now?"

Toffler's eyes went to Zvara. "You told me you wanted to present the Tel culture in the best light. I think you said, 'Show the world we're not a threat.' The best way to do that is to document your struggle. It's compassion I'm going for. Real, raw, in-your-face material."

"No shit," Tarris said.

"I realize that," Zvara said, walking around Bixx. He placed his hands on her shoulders; their weight surprised her. "But what we are about to do here," he said, "is not what I had in mind."

Toffler clicked off the lights, peeled the vid gear from her head, and drew right up to Zvara's personal space. "If I can work this correctly," she said conspiratorially, "I can promise you an audience share in the billions. Everyone, and I mean everyone, will see this production. When I'm through editing, Jonathan Kortel will look like the second coming."

Zvara leaned into Toffler until she stepped back. "My dear woman," he said, offering a slight smile, "he might *be*."

Toffler grinned. "Even better. Religion is hot right now, and the world could use something new to worship."

"If we don't do this soon," Shoalburg said, "he might end up a martyr."

"All right, Ms. Toffler," Zvara said. "Continue, but be mindful that there are lives at stake."

"Don't worry," she said, grabbing the vid gear. "After five years in the China Wars, I think I can handle this."

Rocket knelt and took Bixx's hand. Zvara thought he might have to persuade her to go back in, but Bixx didn't need any convincing. Time was against them, and she was the only one who could find McCarris's stream. Still, having Rocket there made her feel safe.

"I'll be right over there," he said and pointed to Shoalburg's console. "All you have to do is find his stream. Once Shoalburg's synced, you can back out. Nobody's expecting you to do the dirty work, okay?"

Bixx's stomach was doing flips. The thought of reentering McCarris's body was tough enough, but doing it so that Shoalburg could cut his Net feed was making her physically ill. "You're not going to kill him, right?" she asked.

Rocket squeezed her hand. "No, baby, they're just going to shut off some of his base functions. Kind of like putting him in a coma." He placed Shoalburg's interface unit in her palm.

Bixx felt Zvara lean next to her ear. "It is time," he said, and patted her shoulder.

"Good," Kreet said. "Now remember, people, act natural."

"Kreet," Toffler said sternly, "would you please go back to my room and monitor the uplink."

"But–"

"Now!"

Kreet mumbled something and walked out of the lab.

"Is Kreet short for cretin?" Tarris asked.

Shoalburg laughed under his breath.

Bixx eyed the interface and raised it to her forehead.

"On my mark," Shoalburg said. "Three, two, one."

The interface's tentacles grabbed Bixx's head, and the room fell away. It had been just a few hours since she'd been yanked out of Nichols, and in that time Shoalburg said he had customized the unit for her. The phase jumps came instantly, and before Bixx could prep, the Net exploded onto her visual field.

You okay? Shoalburg asked inside her mind.

Of course not, Bixx thought. *You're going to kill him.*

We're not going to kill him, unless we absolutely have to.

Bixx felt herself gasp. *Y-you can hear my thoughts?*

See is more accurate. And for the last time, we're not going to kill him. I've made some adjustments to the interface unit, and we shouldn't lose communication like we did before.

Shouldn't?

Okay, won't. Now listen – the last incept we have for McCarris was at the restaurant, but we don't have anything after that. Something is interfering with our ability to track him. He took a Net call during dinner at Kortel's. The feed was untraceable, so I'm betting it was Trumble. I just...

What?

I just hope we're not too late. Now go do whatever it is you do. I'll tell you when to back out. Good luck.

Bixx felt Shoalburg's presence fade into the white noise. She tried to focus on McCarris's chi, but the images of falling with Nichols were still ricocheting about her mind.

Get it together.

Bixx closed her eyes and did a quick breathing exercise. It was hard to forgive someone like McCarris, but she had to if she was going to connect again. She tried to think of him as a victim of circumstance – a pawn. Almost immediately, she heard the distinctive droning of McCarris's stream, then the cerebral shift came, and her cognitive sense slipped away.

Bixx slowly opened her eyes and felt the surreal duality of being with McCarris again. He was in what looked like a small living room, and the lighting was low. The furniture was trendy; the kind Bixx had seen in vidzines for people who cared about style. From this point of view, she couldn't see anything that indicated whether he was at Tamara's apartment or some boutique hotel.

Okay, Dr. Shoalburg, she thought, *I've got you in.*

A moment went by.

Doctor?

Hold on. Shoalburg's presence felt distant, like an old memory. *I'm having trouble getting synced. Stay connected until I can get this worked out.*

Bixx's stomach began to flip again.

McCarris raised a drink to his mouth. She felt the burn of whiskey down her throat. Sensations were stronger this time.

"Come on out," McCarris said. "I won't bite."

"Just a second." It was Tamara. She sounded like she was in another room.

McCarris took another gulp; a cube of ice slid past his lips. He crunched down, and Bixx's teeth stung.

Tamara appeared at of one of the two doorways in the room, which drew McCarris's attention. She had changed out of the flowered dress – or maybe it had changed. The pattern was different. It was darker and made up of small black birds, and the "v" of the neck was much lower. Bixx noted that it looked higher off Tamara's knees than before.

"*Hello* there," McCarris said. "Aren't you a picture?" Bixx felt him getting excited.

Tamara smiled. "This feels much better."

"Here." McCarris picked up another drink off a small side table, but this one appeared to be vodka or gin. "I hope you like the way I made it."

Tamara took the glass and drank. Her eyebrows went up. "Oh, I usually like a little tonic with my vodka." She took another sip. "If I didn't know better, I'd say you're trying to get me drunk, Mr. McCarris."

"Who, me? I'm a gentleman. I would never take advantage of a lady." McCarris gestured to the couch, and they sat.

"Well, thank you for such a lovely dinner," Tamara said, settling in. "I haven't been to a restaurant like that in a long time."

McCarris faced her and rested his arm on the top of the couch. "Really?" he said. He swirled the ice in his drink. "I'm surprised a beautiful lady like yourself doesn't get taken to wonderful places all the time." He took a sip. "And you're welcome. It was my pleasure."

Tamara leaned in, and McCarris's attention went to her cleavage.

Pig.

"I'm afraid I don't have time for much dating. Between the gallery and Nicole, my life is pretty full."

McCarris passed a finger down the side of her face and guided a stray lock of hair away from her eye. "Maybe that's going to change," he said tenderly.

Tamara leaned into his gesture and looked up with those incredibly clear blue eyes. "I thought you weren't going to be in Chicago for very long."

"I'm thinking of changing my plans," he said, leaning in.

Tamara glanced away. "I'm sorry; I haven't done this in a long time." She looked back with a hint of sadness in her eyes.

Bixx was going crazy. It was like watching a bad slasher vid where the whole audience knew the girl was going to get it.

With their lips almost touching, McCarris gently took her chin with his fingers. "I told you before," he whispered, "I don't bite."

Bixx had kissed a girl once, on a dare and full of *Stolichnaya*. But as McCarris and Tamara's lips touched, she felt a disturbing aggression building behind his emotion. It was foreign, and she felt him succumbing to it.

Where the hell is Shoalburg?

Bixx couldn't take it anymore. As McCarris and Tamara kissed, she thought about jacking with his Net feed, but that was way out of her league. Then an idea hit her.

She screamed.

"Oh, shit," McCarris said, almost biting Tamara's lip.

Her eyes went big. "Are you all right?"

McCarris's vision blurred. "I-I don't know." He rubbed his temples for a second, then shook it off. "Now then," he said, and put his arm around Tamara, "where were we?"

"Are you sure you're okay?"

McCarris smiled. "Very."

When McCarris and Tamara began kissing, Bixx felt like screaming again. But something out near the edge of her mind stopped her. It was a dynamic presence that seemed to be closing on her parameters.

Finally. Dr. Shoalburg, is that you?

Suddenly Tamara and McCarris morphed, and Bixx was standing in a low mist of infinite whiteness.

"Vhat the hell?" She looked around, but there were no edges and distance was hard to judge. The mist seemed to extend forever. A rush of adrenaline crashed through her nerves. "Doctor, I need your help!"

An older man formed in front of her. He was tall and thin and dressed like he could have stepped out of one of the fashion vids always playing at the Nitz Salon on 23rd. His suit undulated between an aluminumlike herringbone and mossy green tweed. In the latter state, it seemed to absorb light.

"Who are you?" he asked. His voice was human, but with an electronic edge that sounded a bit like rushing waters.

Bixx didn't know if she should answer.

"I asked you a question." Now the man sounded like an avalanche, thundering and apocalyptic. He had a faint accent that Bixx couldn't place. She recoiled and covered her ears.

"Shut up!" she yelled.

Suddenly the man appeared hundreds of feet tall. His form took on the angular characteristics of an office tower. He looked down through the clouds of white mist. "Well?" he boomed.

Bixx had dealt with hackers before, and the giant routine was so last-century. She shifted her parameter settings and was instantly face to face with the asshole. "This is a secured link," she said, modulating her voice to sound menacing. "Who the hell are you?"

The man's surprise shifted, and his eyes filled with a kind of liquid fire. "Tell Armando he's wasting his time."

Instantly, Bixx found herself floating in the Net with McCarris's stream off to her right.

"Shoalburg, where are you?"

There was no reply.

What was it he had said? The call had come from Trumble?

Bixx put it together and knew she had to get back into McCarris. She tried several times, but couldn't connect. She began to panic.

Shoalburg's voice came through without warning. *Bixx, can you hear me?*

"Yes, yes! I can."

Why aren't you connected to McCarris?

"I got pulled. I think by Trumble."

Oh my God. Have you tried to reconnect?

"Of course, but I can't. Something's blocking me."

Let me try and help–

Shoalburg's presence vanished.

"A-are you there?"

... this might work. Here... His voice crackled, then vanished.

"What? What might work?" Bixx felt a surge of energy. It struck at the base of her skull and needled through her nervous system. Suddenly, she was back in McCarris. The room was darker, and he and Tamara were still kissing, but now there was an intense passion about them.

The edge of McCarris's hand brushed against one of Tamara's breasts. He began kissing her neck. She moaned softly.

Aren't you a little young to be a voyeur?

It was Trumble.

Could two streams merge with another? Bixx's brain was spinning. *Get out of here!* she demanded.

There was an odd sound that resembled a laugh. *You're the trespasser. How did you hack into this proprietary wetware?*

Poshol k chortu! Bixx thought.

Again the laugh. *Young lady, I already live in hell.*

Tamara moaned loudly as McCarris gently bit one of her nipples through the fabric. The pattern of birds had migrated to the back of the dress, and the area where McCarris was kissing had become much darker.

They seem to be enjoying each other. Trumble's voice echoed in Bixx's mind. *It's a shame it all has to end.*

Not if I can help it, she thought.

I doubt you can.

McCarris's hand slid between Tamara's legs. Bixx could feel the soft cotton of her panties on his fingertips. His other hand had moved to the side of her neck; his thumb gently stroked the underline of her jaw. Her breathing grew deeper. Then there was a change in McCarris's feed. Something was coming down his cerebral stream and corrupting his parameters. Bixx could sense that his passion was being replaced with something dark and evil.

Both hands went to Tamara's throat. His thumbs dug in. She began to struggle, but he had shifted so that one of his knees was pressing against her stomach. She tried to cry out, but couldn't.

"Carter," Bixx said. "Please, please connect in!"

He can't help you now.

The more Tamara fought, the deeper McCarris dug his fingers. One of her legs thrashed and sent her drink careening off the coffee table. She was beating him about the face, but the insurgent data had numbed his ability to feel pain.

Trumble laughed.

Bixx screamed again, louder and harder than she ever had

before. It came from somewhere deep and instinctual. A high-pitched, inhuman cry that seemed to carry all of her fear.

McCarris yelled and grabbed his head. Tamara connected her elbow square on his jaw and sent him tumbling backward. He landed on his side, and Bixx felt something small and hard in his pocket.

...out of there. I'm trying to get synced.... It was Shoalburg.

McCarris struggled to his feet and backed away.

Bixx screamed once more.

McCarris doubled over, knocking a small lamp to the floor and casting the room into harsh shadows. He reached into his pocket. Bixx felt his fingers wrapping around the butt of a handheld Light-Force. His index finger passed over the ID point, and the weapon whined with its charge-up.

"Carter!" Bixx yelled. "Do something!"

...can't connect. Can you try and...

Tamara had slid off the couch. She was on hands and knees, struggling to catch her breath. McCarris took aim. In the upper corner of his vision, the Light-Force's site monitor aligned with her left eye.

"Mommy?" Tamara's daughter appeared in the other doorway, rubbing her eyes. McCarris moved his aim, and Bixx watched in horror as the little girl's forehead appeared in the sight monitor.

"Nicole!" Tamara said, her voice hoarse and deep with fear.

McCarris swung back.

Tamara's eyes darted from her child to the weapon. They were filled with terror. "Who are you?" she begged. "What do you want?"

McCarris didn't answer, and Bixx could still feel Trumble's presence controlling him. McCarris pivoted the Light-Force toward Nicole.

"NO!" Tamara screamed. "Please...no." She was crying now and pleading, her arms stretched toward McCarris.

Bixx could feel him struggle against the insurgent data.

"I-I'm sorry," he said painfully, as if he couldn't believe what he was about to do.

The insurgent data flooded McCarris's neural network, the last of his original programming transformed. He clicked off the safety.

At the sound, Bixx was overcome with a defining sense of purpose. "No," she whispered. "I won't let you."

McCarris flinched.

Suddenly, Bixx's spatial parameters returned and she was now physically one with McCarris. She felt the warm metal of the Light-Force in her hand and began turning it on him. In the sight monitor, his chest angled into view. He struggled with her, but Bixx didn't back down. She opened her mind and focused all of her will on McCarris's chi...

and pulled the trigger.

You better be worth it. 25

KORTEL drew the plastic curtain aside and entered the small area that had been set up for Bixx. The flight back from Paris had been delayed due to an atmospheric disturbance, and nobody at the Air France counter would give him a straight answer about it. The jump jet from New York was equally screwed up, arriving in Albuquerque 20 minutes behind schedule, which was unheard of. Now, he was looking down at the latest victim in a struggle that seemed to never end.

Bixx wasn't like the rest of her friends. She possessed a toughness Kortel had seen in many Russian Tel girls, a "screw it" attitude that got them through the chauvinistic Russian system. But now, lying there jacked into a mountain of Shoalburg's tech, Bixx looked more frail than he had ever seen her. A weird-looking interface hugged her head like it was about to crawl down her throat, and her chest was so crowded with medoptic cables that it was hard to tell whether she was a boy or a girl. The blunt pain of tired anger filled Kortel, and he began thinking of terrible new ways to kill Trumble.

Zvara glanced at him, his dark eyes more sunken than usual.

Shoalburg noticed Kortel over the top of his medpad and gave a slight nod. "When did you get in, Jonny?" he asked.

"Late last night. My flight was delayed." Kortel motioned at Bixx. "Armando filled me in on most of what happened. How's she doing?"

Shoalburg shrugged and set the pad down. "To be honest? Not good." His voice was heavy with frustration.

"She keeps calling out 'Anari,' " Zvara said.

The name sent a shiver through Kortel.

Zvara picked up on it. "Do you know this person?"

"Yeah. It was Tamara's best friend from the club. But Bixx couldn't have known her."

"Tell us about this Anari."

"She was a waitress. James was supposed to have erased her, but he didn't. He had a thing for her. They saw each other for over a year before I found out...." Although it had been years, the memory of McCarris convulsing in Kortel's telekinetic grip filled his mind afresh. He asked Shoalburg, "How did she end up like this?"

"Trumble was doing a damn good job of walling me up." Shoalburg looked down at Bixx. "She was amazing. I don't know how she did it, but she was able to affect McCarris's ability to process

Trumble's downfeed. She has an incredibly intuitive gift that seems to be magnified by the Net. I could tell she was trying to stop McCarris, but Trumble's feed was too complex, so I jacked the connection and let her merge with McCarris's neural net."

"God, Carter. That's pretty radical."

"We were out of options." Shoalburg looked tentatively at Zvara.

"What?" Kortel asked.

"My interface–"

"Oh, Carter."

"What? It's been thoroughly tested. In trials, we never had any problems."

"But you did here, right?"

Shoalburg reluctantly nodded. "When Bixx merged, it didn't keep the streams separated. The peripheral interface VRMs didn't align with the local NNEs...."

"Just get to the point."

"I don't *know* the point."

"What do you mean?"

"When their streams merged, Bixx and McCarris became...one. I don't know how. It just happened, and Bixx took advantage of it. She turned the Light-Force on herself, I-I mean McCarris."

"She didn't–"

"No! I pulled her before the discharge."

"Wait a minute. How could the Light-Force discharge if you pulled her?"

Shoalburg and Zvara exchanged looks again.

The truth suddenly hit Kortel. "*James* pulled the trigger?"

"Yes," Shoalburg said.

Another shiver. "Jesus," he said to himself.

The area filled with an awkward silence. Kortel leaned down and inspected the interface.

"Why is she still connected?" he asked.

"I pulled her pretty abruptly," Shoalburg said. "We think that some traces of McCarris's neural net came with her. I'm not sure what will happen if I disengage it."

"God, Carter, what *do* you know?"

"We're in unknown territory here, Jonny. I've never worked with someone like Bixx. She's different. I didn't know you could even merge two personality constructs."

A small headache was building in the back of Kortel's head.

"Anari!" Bixx called out.

The area grew quiet again.

"What *is* that?" Kortel asked.

"It's not a what," Shoalburg said. "It's McCarris, or what's left of him."

"How long will she be like this?" Kortel asked, rubbing the back of his neck.

"It's hard to say...."

Just then, the plastic curtain pulled back, and Rocket was standing there. From the look of him, Kortel figured he hadn't slept for days. His mop of curls was flattened to one side, his eyes red and swollen. They shifted away from Kortel almost as soon as they took him in.

"Any change?" Rocket asked, walking over to Shoalburg. He dragged a metal stool next to the bed and sat.

"No," Zvara said.

Rocket stroked Bixx's forehead and whispered something into her ear.

Shoalburg grabbed the medpad off a side table. "Actually, there has been *some* improvement. Her theta waves are showing more activity, but it's her delta waves that concern me."

"Why's that?" Rocket asked.

"They're cycling erratically. Normally brainwaves run in 90-minute increments, but hers are all over the place. Something's going on in her head that I can't access through the Web or the interface."

Rocket looked up through his thick curls. "What if she never wakes up?"

"That would be unlikely. The real question is: what will she be like when she does?"

One of the monitors in Shoalburg's equipment chimed, and a holoimage of Richter appeared.

"Armando?" she asked, her arms folded tightly across her chest.

Zvara stepped over to the monitor. "Yes, doctor?"

Richter moved closer; her image loomed in the holoparameters. "It's the sun," she said gravely.

Zvara glanced first at Shoalburg, then Kortel. "It has begun."

Shoalburg quickly began reviewing some of the monitors hooked to Bixx.

Kortel started to follow Zvara out through the curtain, but

a hand grabbed his shoulder and spun him around. It was Rocket. He started to speak, but stopped and glared. Kortel could feel the hatred radiating off of him.

Shoalburg pulled Rocket back. "Easy, there," he said.

Rocket shrugged off his grip. "Fuck off."

"Hey, it's not his fault. Bixx knew the risks."

"How could she, Carter? You didn't even know them."

Zvara came up to Kortel's side. "Rocket, please. There are bigger issues at stake right now."

"Shut up, old man." Tears were welling at the corners of Rocket's eyes. "She could die for what? A *theory*? You don't even know if the sun will go Tsunami."

"Rocket–"

"No! You used her to get what you wanted." He passed his glare across Kortel and Shoalburg. "You're all *guilty*!"

Zvara stepped closer. "That's enough!"

Rocket froze. Kortel couldn't sense whether it had been voluntary or a result of Zvara's power.

"No one forced Bixx to go back in," Zvara said, his voice deep with authority. "She understood what was at stake…and didn't let her emotions get in the way."

Damn, Kortel thought. *Two contractions.*

Zvara stepped up to Rocket and took his shoulders. "Rocket, I need your strength now." His tone was softer. "This won't succeed without our best. You know Bixx would want you to do this."

Rocket broke from Zvara's hold and got in Kortel's face. "*You*," he said, tears running down his cheeks, "better be worth it."

The bastard. 26

BIXX opened her eyes.

I'm alive.

She was on her back, staring through thick darkness at an old wooden ceiling. Some exposed ductwork was catching light, but she couldn't tell the source. She moved her hands to her stomach and discovered she was still in the same clothes. Maybe Shoalburg had taken her to an infirmary somewhere.

Bixx stretched. Her bare feet touched something cold and metallic. She recoiled, and her knees tangled in thin, crisp sheets that smelled vaguely of industrial cleaner. She sat up and bunched the sheets around her in a futile attempt at comfort. The room was cavernous and held hundreds of empty beds. The ceiling was taller than she had first thought, and there was a chill in the air.

"Hello?" she called out. *What's going on? Where is everybody?* "Dr. Shoalburg? Rocket?"

She swung her legs over the side of the bed and peered at the floor. It was soiled by years of dirt and traffic, and she wondered if the tiny octagonal tiles were as cold as the bed frame. Her attention went to the dresser that separated her area from the next bed.

"Oh my God," she said.

There, hanging precariously off the edge of the dresser, was her Bible from the orphanage. It was open, and Bixx could see the bookmark ribbon she had painted as a little girl. Its fluorescent yellow and pink flowers glowed faintly. Instinctually, she reached for it.

"Happy to see it again?" a voice asked from the dark.

Bixx yelped and slipped from the bed. As she fell, her hand hit the Bible and knocked it from the dresser. The sound of it hitting the floor echoed throughout the room. She snatched it up and backed herself into the corner created by the edge of the dresser and the bed frame.

"Who said that?" she asked, searching for details in the blackness. Her Bible smelled of old memories. Bixx held it close to her chest.

There was no answer.

Bixx peeked over the mattress, but the room was too large and dark for her to make out anything beyond the footboard.

"I asked if you were happy to see it again...your Bible."

A shadow shifted, and she caught the edge of a man's silhouette. He was standing in the aisle that separated her bed's row from the next.

Bixx hugged her knees. "Who are you?"

There was a laugh. "I don't think you could say that I am a who anymore – more like a what. Or maybe, a was."

The voice was familiar, but tinged with a techno quality. The inflection sounded whimsical, and Bixx took a wild guess.

"Mr. McCarris?" she called out.

"In the digital."

Bixx's heart was racing. "How is that possible? I thought I–"

"Killed me? Just the body, I suppose." The form moved toward her bed and passed through a shaft of light. Bixx caught a thin vertical slice of McCarris's face. "Kind of liberating in a disembodied sort of way." He raised his hands and inspected them. "Weirdest sensation I've ever felt. It's like having a lucid dream. I guess I should thank you."

"Why?"

"Because now I don't have to deal with my body. Being continuously jacked was no party. Sure, it had its advantages, but for the most part, it was a pain in the ass." He leaned against the footboard. "By the way, that was a brilliant move."

"Thanks," Bixx said, "but I don't think I did anything. I must have been pulled before I . . ." McCarris's comment suddenly registered. "Wait a second. If I was pulled, then...did *you* fire the Light-Force?"

He looked away. "I was tired of dealing," he said.

Bixx's stomach tightened. "If you're dead, then am I?"

"No, you're still connected. This is the Net." McCarris gestured at the room. "It's synced with your brain. I guess it's creating this illusion from your memories."

Bixx felt the weight of her situation pressing down. She slowly stood and crawled back onto the bed. "Am I dying?" she asked, looking at her hands.

"Not from what I can sense. You're in some sort of coma, but I don't have any idea how you entered my consciousness, or vice versa."

Suddenly, Bixx's spatial reference changed; she was in the chaos of the Net, but before she could focus, another shift occurred, and she was back on the bed. She shrieked.

"You okay?" McCarris asked.

She didn't know what to say.

"Did you just *jump?*"

"Yes. I was back in the Net, but now I'm here again."

"That figures. I've been doing it, too. But for me, it's more like jumping into your memories." He folded his arms. "You've had a tough life."

Bixx's Russian heritage went up like the wall around Chernobyl. "No tougher than anyone else's."

"Not from what I've seen."

"Where are we?" she asked, changing the subject.

"Inside your head."

"No, I mean, what is *this?*" She shook the Bible at McCarris.

"You tell me. This is your memory."

Bixx stood on the bed and surveyed the room. "This looks like the orphanage were I was raised. But it feels different."

"Probably because it is."

"What do you mean?" She sat and crossed her legs.

"From what I can gather, our streams have merged. I'm guessing that your mind has retreated to a place that represents safety to you. Your bed at the orphanage, for example. But dreams are full of metaphors. They're usually not exact. Kind of like when you have damaged data, and the program fills in the gaps. Your mind is doing the same thing, so it's not going to feel exact. Does that make sense?"

"Sort of. But how are you existing?"

"On the Agency mainframe…in the Net…who knows? Probably all of it, in some form."

"Do you know how long you'll be like this?"

Silence.

"Mr. McCarris?"

"I don't know." He walked into the middle of the aisle and motioned for her to follow. "Come on."

"Where?"

"Let's find out why we're here. Or actually, why you've put us here."

Bixx began to slide off the bed but stopped, remembering what a monster McCarris had been to Tamara.

"What's the matter," he asked. "You afraid?"

"No, it's just that you're a...I don't know."

McCarris walked up to the side of the bed, and Bixx could see his face in the dim light. His cheeks and neck had a light speckling of acne scars, which Bixx thought was odd, considering he could have had it all removed at any DermaBox. "I think the word you're looking for is asshole," he offered.

"I was thinking *govnyuk*."

"And what's that?"

"Shithead."

McCarris nodded. "I can't say I blame you. But if you were really connected to me, you would know I didn't want to kill her. My programming was being altered."

Bixx flashed on the moment back in Chicago when McCarris was about to pull the trigger on Tamara's child. He had said something about being sorry, and she remembered feeling his struggle against the rush of Trumble's data.

"I can feel you remembering." He leaned in, his breath nonexistent. "I can see what you see."

Bixx studied his blue eyes. There was a faint pixeled edge in the makeup of his image – a rasterization of the detail. She wondered what sort of data was coursing behind his face now that he was nothing more than a logarithmic flow of ones and zeros.

"Then you know what I think of you," she said.

McCarris forced a smile. "I'm the one who should be scared." He straightened. "By the way, how did you hack Trumble's feed? That was the most encrypted stream I've ever seen."

Bixx shrugged. "I don't know. I felt the boost from Dr. Shoalburg, and then I just did it."

"Did what?"

"Listened. I can't describe it. It's like leaving my body. I open my mind and listen for the essence of someone. Their chi."

McCarris's face went blank. Bixx couldn't tell whether he wasn't getting it or something had disrupted his feed.

"Interesting," he said finally.

* * *

"Anything look familiar?" McCarris asked while they walked.

Bixx was intently studying the room, hoping that another jump would happen and she'd wake up from this psychotic nightmare, when she saw the light source that had illuminated McCarris's face. It was one of the round glass exit signs on the other side of the room.

"Some things do, and others, I don't remember so well." She stopped and pointed. "Like that sign. That never worked when I was here. But now it does. Weird."

"That's one word for it," McCarris said. He twisted to see what was behind them. "Was this place always so empty?"

Bixx turned in his direction, but the room dropped off into darkness so that she couldn't see the other side. "No. There were usually a couple hundred of us here. All crammed together. I remember..."

"What?"

"The smell." She winced. "It was awful. And they never did anything about it. We could only shower every third day."

McCarris made a clicking sound, like Bixx's grandfather had when he called his favorite horse. "And you could only shower for three minutes."

The whole thought of McCarris being inside her mind creeped Bixx out. Since his essence was a stream of continuously changing data packs, she wondered what would become of him. They started walking toward the exit sign.

"Do you think you have a soul?" she asked, turning down another aisle.

"I must," he said, sounding more like he was convincing himself. "How else could I exist?"

"Technology," Bixx offered. "Maybe controlled by the Agency's AI. How would you know? You would mistake its programmed promptings as your own will, your own thoughts. Can you feel your blood moving?"

McCarris pondered this. "Can you?"

"Yes."

"That's because you're still flesh *and* blood. I'm...." He hesitated.

"See?" she said. "That's my point. What are you now?"

McCarris didn't answer, and Bixx really couldn't blame him. As they approached the exit sign, she noticed it was casting an uneven light. Only certain things were highlighted by it, and she couldn't figure out if there was any pattern to it. Maybe there was a glitch in the programming.

McCarris's pace slowed, and he began looking around. Suddenly, he stuck his hand out and stopped her. This was the first time his form had made contact with hers, and she could feel the pressure of his hand against her shoulder. She could also sense his chi. It was warm, and there was an undercurrent of power that

Bixx took for his connection to the Net.

"Hold up," he said, still glancing about.

"What do you see?" she asked.

McCarris whirled his face around, and Bixx noticed that the color of his eyes was deeper and had a liquid texture that was frighteningly real. For a second, her spatial dynamics wavered. Then she jumped and found herself in a kitchen. It was old, like her grandmother's, and a little boy was cowering in a corner. A man was standing over him, his belt drawn. The boy was terrified and crying.

Suddenly, the dynamics jumped again, and she was back in the orphanage.

"What just happened?" McCarris asked.

Bixx shivered; her tongue had a bitter metallic taste. "Ah, nothing...I mean, your eyes. They're kind of like water."

"Really?" McCarris studied her. "Hey, you just jumped, didn't you?"

"Yes, how can you tell?"

"Because your stream changed. Patterns merged, then separated. It was hard to look at. Where'd you go?"

"Nowhere."

"Bull. Tell me."

"I was in a kitchen, and there was a little boy with a man standing over him. The boy looked frightened."

"Did the man have dark hair?"

"Yes."

"Was he holding a belt?"

Bixx nodded.

McCarris shook his head. "Welcome to *my* childhood."

Bixx couldn't think of anything to say. His memory resonated with her; there had been many abused children at the orphanage who had told her their stories. "I'm sorry," she said after an awkward pause.

McCarris waved her off. "The Agency was the best thing that ever happened to me. My ol' man didn't understand our gift. He was an SP."

"What's that?"

"Sinless Perfectionist. The Church of the One-Way Ticket. There's only one way to God," McCarris emphasized this by pointing at the ceiling, "and in Daddy's eyes, that was to beat the living tar out of me after a night of drugging."

Bixx desperately wanted to change the subject. "Why do you keep looking around?" she asked.

"Because I see this differently than you. Since you're still alive, this all looks real, right?"

"Yes."

"To me, this is all code and shapes and colors. It's incredibly complex, but I recognize certain flow patterns. I used to do a little programming when I was younger, and this looks like a kind of imaging matrix. But this," he pointed at the exit door, "is different."

"Why?"

McCarris hesitated. "Because it's military."

The word sent another shiver through her, and Bixx began to feel cold. She folded her arms and hugged her Bible. "Military?" she asked. "What do you mean?"

McCarris walked up to the door and ran his hand across it. There was nothing special about the actual exit, from what Bixx could remember. Like the other furniture in the room, it was heavily stained, and its surface looked wet from years of repeated refinishing. McCarris's fingers seemed to meld with the wood, and Bixx couldn't tell if it was a trick from the light. He leaned in and raised his other hand.

"What do you see?" she asked.

He didn't acknowledge her.

Finally, McCarris removed his hands and slowly turned. The look on his face was serious, like he was processing the data and didn't like what he saw.

"How well do you remember your time here?" he asked.

The question seemed odd. "Pretty well," Bixx said. "Why?"

More of the concerned look. "All of this," he said, raising his arms to the room, "is a sophisticated layering program. I've seen this before in the wetware that was developed by one of our SBUs for the DoD."

"Your SB what's for the who?"

"Single business units. Real companies that our culture operates behind. Carter worked for one. Where do you think all the new implant stuff comes from? The Department of Defense has contracts with several of our companies. Back in the '80s, there was one that developed wetware that could mask a soldier's trauma. They used it in the China wars, and it made us a bundle."

"But I lived in Russia."

"I know. This is a bastard version of it. In some ways, it's better." McCarris craned to look at the ceiling. "Yeah. Not a bad rip-off. Amazing architecture."

Bixx was getting frustrated. "I don't get it. What's the military have to do with my memories?"

McCarris stepped closer and regarded her with care. "Whatever's behind that door is definitely not civilian. Part of what you remember of the orphanage *is* real. I can see that in the data. But this…" He stopped himself.

"What?" Bixx urged. "You saw something, didn't you?"

McCarris thrust his hands into his pockets and looked at his feet. "It's a masking program, used to block out severe trauma." He looked up. "Something's being hidden from you, and it's got a military signature. Do you have any periods of blackouts, lack of memory, stuff like that?"

Nausea was building inside Bixx. She found it hard to focus on the question. McCarris must have sensed it, because he took her shoulder.

"Are you all right?" he asked.

She wasn't, but she nodded anyway.

"Look, I've seen this kind of data before. Whatever's behind that door is very black – secret ops stuff. You've got a hell of an ability, and I wouldn't put it past the Russians to experiment on their young, especially the gifted ones."

Bixx fought to keep from puking. "You mean the Russian Command knows about the Tels?"

"Absolutely. We've been in partnership with governments for years."

Bixx's legs seemed to have transformed into something elastic, pliable. She found it hard to stand and leaned against a table.

"They did something to you, Bixx. Now, whether it was to enhance your gift or jack you for some agenda, that's hard to say."

"What do you mean...*agenda*?"

McCarris shrugged. "Could be a million things. Net projecting. Transcription coding. Even SIW."

"What's SIW?"

"Subversive Internet Warfare."

Bixx edged herself along the table and sat in a large chair. Her stomach was in knots. "Could you find out?" she asked. "You know, go in and see what they did?"

McCarris considered her request while his attention stayed focused on the door. "I guess I could try. What's the worst that could happen?" He laughed, but his demeanor shifted. "Weird thing is, I don't see any tech in you. Either what they did was totally organic, or the masking is hiding it." He shuddered, then started for the door.

"James?" Bixx called out.

McCarris turned.

"Thanks."

He smiled. "I've got a lot of bad karma to correct. It's the least I can do." He made that clicking sound and continued toward the exit. "Besides," he called back over his shoulder, "what else have I got to do, right?"

When McCarris reached the door, he positioned his legs

like he was going to push on it. Then he gently placed his fingertips against the center panel and leaned in.

Suddenly, a bright light exploded from the point of contact. He screamed and stumbled backward.

Bixx launched from the chair and ran toward him.

McCarris held up his hand. “Don’t!” he said.

She stopped about 10 feet from him. He was doubled over, and his form was degrading.

“What can I do?” she asked, feeling a strange compassion for him.

McCarris’s image was now about 50 percent of its original quality. He examined his hands and arms. “The bastard,” he said to himself.

“Who?” Bixx asked.

McCarris glanced up, his expression twisted in pain. “Trumble,” he gasped, and then vanished.

27 Weird.

TRAILING Shoalburg down the narrow hallway, Kortel pondered the irony that the father of nano implants hadn't indulged in the cosmetic side of the technology. With bioaug basically a global religion, people didn't bother with diet or exercise; they just "restructured." Not that Shoalburg was fat, but he was, as Kortel's uncle used to say, carrying more than his fair share.

"Maybe we *should* fry," Kortel mumbled.

Shoalburg turned. "What's that?"

"Nothing."

"Gotta stay focused."

"Right."

They all cut hard lefts down another hallway. Zvara was leading and hadn't said a word since they'd left Bixx's med station. Behind him were Rocket and Shoalburg with Toffler bringing up the rear. She had appeared after they entered Richter's building, and Kortel could feel the heat of her vid lights on the back of his neck.

He leaned forward to Shoalburg's ear and whispered, "Why does Zvara allow her so much access?"

"Don't worry about that," Shoalburg said over his shoulder. "After we pull this off, you'll be famous."

Kortel didn't want to be famous. He didn't really want to be anything. If he had a magic wand, he would have waved it and wished for the way things had been when his biggest concern was whether the hostess would show for the night run at his restaurant. The thought of trudging through a sooty blanket of icy Chicago snow to the Wacker Street maglev sounded pretty appealing right now.

They approached two tall doors made of composite metal. They were windowless and looked out of place amid all the old wood and plaster.

Zvara swiped a pass card through an optical reader, and the doors clicked. He looked back at Kortel as if he had felt his gaze.

"This compound was a weapons lab during the China Wars," he said. "The technology is old, but it still works. Dr. Richter believes in security." Zvara raised a hand, and the door opened. It was odd to see him use his power so casually. Kortel almost said something, but then Zvara glanced over his shoulder, and it hit Kortel that this was it. Ever since he had arrived, they had been training him to use his ability on a colossal scale. Now the time had arrived, the nexus, where history from here on out would probably be referred to as post-Tsunami.

Kortel followed Zvara through rows of computer stacks similar to the ones in Shoalburg's lab. Unlike his intelligent chaos, however, Richter's maze evinced a distinct order. She was German, and Kortel had never met one who wasn't an organizational freak. The group came to a control bay that had a dozen lab techs huddled around a large holojection of the sun. Its surface was so stunning that Kortel imagined he felt heat coming from it. Richter was at the center of the huddle, her interface idly perched on top of her head.

She and Zvara didn't say anything; they just exchanged looks that said the shit had hit the galactic fan.

Shoalburg cleared his throat. "How bad?"

Richter regarded him as one who had asked the dumbest question in the history of their short-lived species before she resumed studying the holoimage.

"What is our time frame?" Zvara asked.

"We don't know," she said, pulling the interface into position. Its tentacles wrapped around her head, and she recoiled. The room became strangely quiet.

"Doctor–"

"Watch this," Richter blurted. She pointed to the projected sun and looked at them one by one as if she were making eye contact. A small flare erupted from the holoimage and engulfed her hand.

Shoalburg seemed unimpressed.

Then another flare, this one enormous, arched from the surface. It passed through Richter, Zvara, Kortel and Shoalburg. Rocket actually jumped out of its way. It fractured and disappeared just beyond a stack of Net processors.

"My God," Shoalburg said.

"Don't you see?" The interface was hugging Richter's head like a trained sea creature. "This is only the preliminary stage."

"How long until we all die?" Rocket asked Kortel. His voice was calm, but there was anger in his eyes.

Everyone turned.

Zvara intervened. "Doctor, please. What is the time frame?"

Richter faced him. "It could be any time," she said. "An hour? A day? We need to act."

"Does anyone not understand what you need to do?" Zvara asked to the room.

The techs remained silent.

"They understand, Armando," Richter said for them.

"Ready, Jonny?" Shoalburg's eyes moved across Kortel, and for the first time since he could remember, they seemed unfamiliar, even alien.

"Sure," Kortel said. "Let's get on with it."

Zvara motioned to seven chairs stocked with electronics and bioptic cable. They looked like dentist rigs Kortel had seen in one of Tarris's father's old medical catalogs. Tech guys were already sitting in three of them.

"I am sorry there was no time for all of you to train together," Zvara said. "Please, introduce yourselves."

One of the techs, an Asian, bowed slightly in his chair. His skin was deathly white, and his eyes were dark lines of concentration.

"Even in the face of disaster," another said through a thick beard, "there's always time for decorum." He had a distinct accent that sounded South African. He raised a hand, and Kortel shook it. "Ah, the famous Mr. Kortel. Thought I'd never see the day that I'd be working with you. My name's Bundles, Aubrey Bundles."

"Good to meet you." As Kortel settled into one of the chairs, Toffler stepped in for a close-up. He raised his hand, and she slid back, slamming against a computer stack. "Sorry," he said, "not now."

The move didn't faze Toffler. She sidestepped away for another angle.

The third tech leaned around Bundles and smiled. He had the Eastern Euro look Kortel had seen in Russia. His greeting was toothy, and his thick cheeks went almost to his eyes when he grinned.

"Isato is from Tokyo," Bundles said. "And Petrov here is from somewhere north of the Circle. Near the Kara Sea, I think."

"And you?" Kortel asked.

"Johannesburg."

"These are some of the best I could find," Shoalburg said, removing his eyes. His placed them on the tray next to his chair and slipped in his neural connectors.

Zvara was now in the farthest chair. He leaned forward and looked at Kortel. "Are you clear on what to do?"

The only thing clear to Kortel was that if this worked, he'd start believing in God again. Training with Zvara and Shoalburg had been one thing, but until he had looked into the faces now around him, it hadn't sunk in that he'd have to link with such a diverse group of Tels. The whole idea of a joined phase with more than 100 other telepaths was crazy enough. But the plan was based on a theory – a very loose, Shoalburgian theory – of doing it jacked and using the global network of the worldwide Web to create a grav phase so massive that it would strengthen the earth's gravitational field and deflect the Tsunami flare. Shoalburg calculated that linking through 3,000 or so satellites alone would do the job, but Zvara insisted upon using every jump point, relay node, and any other digital portal to ensure maximum coverage. When Shoalburg explained the theoretical physics of the concept, Kortel hadn't believed him. But when Zvara launched himself into the metaphysical passion of it all, Kortel realized that the whole New Mexico complex had been developed for one thing: to train him to be what Richter called a lens. He was to be the focal point through which all of their combined telekinetic power would be channeled. It would be a one-time shot: either he'd do it, or the planet would be destroyed...or maybe just part of it would; Richter didn't really know for sure. The flare might even miss the earth altogether, but who could say? Regardless, Kortel was now hours, maybe minutes, from stopping it. And how the hell was he going to do that...*exactly*? Even with all of the training, Kortel knew that when it came to the real thing, he'd have to improvise. He had asked Zvara, but all he could do was orate about Kortel's duty to mankind. Richter had been more fire and brimstone, opining that God would lead him, whatever that meant. Tarris's spin was a little more to Kortel's liking. He said to go in and let it fucking rip, which sounded like something he would have said years ago, when he was high on Jack. But there was still the "it" factor in Tarris's version, and Kortel was damned if he knew what it was. Bixx, though, seemed to have the best take on Kortel's dilemma. Listen to your heart, she had told him. It won't fail you.

Suddenly, one of Richter's computers chimed, and Kortel thought the holoimage of the sun had changed color slightly. A tech rushed over to the console, while the others scurried to their stations. Richter remained fixed on the holoimage.

"What is the situation now?" Zvara asked her.

Richter, still facing the sun, raised her hand. "Hold on," she said. Then her posture slumped and Kortel knew the answer.

A lab tech hurried to Kortel's chair and swung a diagnostic unit into place over his head. Similar techs did the same with the others.

Rocket was on Kortel's right. "Is it okay to be scared shitless?" he asked.

Shoalburg glanced over. "Way ahead of you."

A figure approached Kortel from the lab's darkness. "You better not be," Tarris said.

Kortel looked into the face of his old friend and smiled. "See you when this is over."

Tarris laughed and patted Kortel's shoulder. "My money's on you. Vegas has you at 2 to 1."

"That's optimistic."

Tarris leaned in. "It's realistic. Now get in there and stop this killer flare before it ruins my evening."

"Remember," Shoalburg said, "we're linking with over a hundred others. Don't go into phase until we're all connected. This trans-portal won't be like the one you had in training. It'll be more, ah, personal."

"Personal?" Bundles asked.

"Kick in ass," the Asian declared.

"On my mark," Zvara said.

Kortel heard the vacuum release of seven interface canisters being opened.

"Three."

His tech dangled the white disc inches above his face.

"Two."

It quivered imperceptibly, and he could almost feel it prepping.

"One."

"Shit," Kortel said when the interface's tentacles grabbed his head.

As his vision returned, Kortel felt the spatial nausea Shoalburg had warned about. Even though he had done hundreds of simulations, none of them compared to this. Every one of his senses was firing at what seemed a billion times the norm, and he was suddenly grateful for the comfort he received from the simple awareness of his body.

Kortel felt like he was standing on a tiled floor inside a large space. He flashed on the Hawaii memorial and how dark it became once the doors had closed. This was similar, but somehow bigger. When his eyes began to adjust, he could make out shapes and color. Gradually, the area took form, and he saw patches of detail in the faint light. He stepped forward, and his boot caught the edge of a table, possibly a chair.

Weird. This didn't look or feel anything like the simulations. Shoalburg had said it would be different, and Kortel was having trouble understanding why he would have simmed an old gymnasium for the trans-portal. And what gave with all the beds?

Seeing a ghost. 28

THE hair on the back of Bixx's neck bristled. McCarris's form had simply vanished. No pixel flux. Not even a hint of what Rocket called "data death." She glanced about. The room that had been her home for so many years suddenly felt strange. She had to remind herself that it was nothing more than photons and neural stimulation, that she was lying in a bed somewhere, that it was probably a sunny New Mexico day. At any moment, Shoalburg or Richter would bring her out of her coma. She began walking toward the bed where she had awoken, hoping she could fall back to sleep and not deal with this bullshit anymore. Maybe she'd wake up in Rocket's arms. Better yet, maybe none of this had ever happened.

Bixx sensed a ripple in the downfeed. A bright flash appeared on the other side of the room. She dropped to her knees and crawled behind the closest bed. The light died. Even though it was merely a simulation, she had to act as if it were real. Bixx was a pro at sim apps and figured this one was no exception. It would probably demand that she move through the space as if she were actually in the orphanage. Memory readers were tricky programs and could really mess with your emotions if you let them. Bixx waited, but nothing happened. Then she heard a table being bumped and a man swearing.

A figure slowly moved up the farthest aisle from hers. Bixx thought about making a break for it but didn't know if the app extended beyond the main room. If she wasn't careful, she could find herself opening a door to nowhere. The figure stopped and turned in her direction. Bixx hunkered down, barely able to see over the footboard. The man began cutting through the rows of beds that separated his aisle from hers. When he got within four beds, Bixx decided to take a chance. She sprang from her position and ran down the aisle toward the back of the room.

"Hey, wait!" she heard behind her. The voice sounded familiar, but she couldn't really tell.

Bixx skidded to a stop almost at the exact spot where McCarris had vanished. She looked back and saw the figure running toward her. His stride was athletic and smooth, and he was closing fast. She searched for the stairwell door that would take her to the ground floor. It should have been to her left, against the wall, but it wasn't there.

"Bixx, it's me!"

The sound of her name stopped her. She looked back and recognized Jonathan Kortel.

"What are you doing in the trans-portal?" he asked, trotting to a stop.

"The what?"

"The trans-portal. I don't know if you realize it or not, but you're in a med station. Shoalburg says you're in some kind of Net coma – something to do with your beta waves. He has you jacked into God knows what."

"McCarris said I was in a coma–"

"What? McCarris was *here*?"

"Yes. He said my mind created this sim of my old orphanage."

"I thought he was dead."

"It wasn't *him*. It was his residual personality data. I'd heard that if people died while jacked, their personality constructs might live on. Since McCarris's was already backed up, it makes sense. It's pretty cool, really. So what are you doing here?"

Kortel regarded her, his expression grave. "The Tsunami cycle has started."

The words invaded Bixx like a virus, needling through the fabric of her construct.

"Richter thinks it might start within a day," Kortel said, his voice edged with doubt.

"But you don't think so?"

"I don't know.... I can't imagine something like the Tsunami would sneak past the entire scientific community. Richter can't be the only one who's figured it out."

"Maybe she isn't," Bixx said. "What if the governments are keeping it a secret, you know, so the world doesn't freak out and get all crazy? And what if Richter's right?"

Kortel leaned in. "Then we better not screw this up."

Suddenly, Bixx sensed a tremendous surge in her feed. For an instant, she felt the duality of being in the med station and the Net. She gasped.

"You okay?" Kortel asked.

"I...I don't know. I could feel myself for a second...my real self."

"Maybe the drugs Shoalburg's been giving you are starting to work."

The surge happened again, and Kortel reacted. It drew his attention to the door below the exit sign.

"You felt it, didn't you?" Bixx asked.

"Yes." Kortel walked up to the door and ran his fingers over its surface. "I've seen this kind of programming before."

"It's military."

Kortel nodded, still examining the wood. "What's it doing embedded in your construct? Is it coming from your brain?"

"McCarris thought the Russian military might have tested on me when I was a kid, then used what he called a–"

"Layering program. I knew I'd seen this before." Kortel bent forward and examined the doorknob.

"Where?"

"In Russia," he said, straightening. "A couple of Tels I stayed with thought they'd been jacked with, too."

"McCarris thought they could have been prepping me to be some kind of weapon," Bixx said.

"Maybe. Anything's possible." Kortel began walking toward her. "I've given up trying to figure it all out. We Tels don't seem to have much say in our lives."

The comment sounded odd to Bixx, considering Kortel's power. "I'm nowhere close to your level," she said.

He gave her a knowing grin. "You're special, Bixx. I've seen what you can do. You're hyper-smart and have a gift for nav'ing the Net that most info jocks would die for. McCarris is probably right. The question is: What did they prep you for?"

At that moment, two waves of distortion cascaded through the large room. One wave rippled across the roof; the other traveled across the floor. It passed under their feet, causing their forms to waver below their knees.

"What the hell is that?" Kortel asked.

Bixx followed the upper wave as it moved down the back wall. The exit sign liquefied as it passed, then assumed its original shape. The door remained unaffected as the wave washed around it.

"Digital inversion," she said, and watched the two waves meet in the center of the wall and dissipate.

"Doesn't that mean–"

Just then, a blinding light consumed the room. Bixx covered her eyes, but her action was futile. The light penetrated her construct's reality parameters and blinded her.

"Shit!" she heard Kortel yell.

"Hold still!" she said.

"What is this?"

"A digital logarithmic spatial inversion code."

"A *what?*"

"An upgrade."

"You're kidding, right?"

The light withdrew as quickly as it had appeared, and Bixx's eyes instantly adjusted.

"Can you see?" she asked.

Kortel rubbed his eyes. "Yeah," he said, blinking. "But shouldn't I be blind for a couple of seconds?"

"Normally, yes. But I think this new code has rewritten the construct's parameters."

Both Bixx and Kortel were facing the back wall. The room's physical appearance hadn't changed: the wood and paint looked the same, and even the exit sign was still cracked. But something about the door didn't feel right.

"Does the door look different to you?" Bixx asked.

Kortel approached it, motioning for her to stay back. He got halfway and stopped.

"What do you see?" she asked.

"It's opened now, just a crack." He beckoned Bixx forward, but his attention went past her.

Instinctually, Bixx looked over her shoulder, but what she saw didn't register. The room, which had been disturbingly empty, was now filled with children. On top of each bed was a child sitting cross-legged. There were rows and rows of them, all roughly between the ages of 12 and 16.

"Okay," Kortel whispered. "Did you create this?"

"No!" Bixx shook her head. "I have no idea what this is. And why are you whispering?"

"Because." He pointed. "It looks like they're meditating."

Strangely, they did look like they were meditating. "So what do we do?" Bixx asked.

"I don't know. Our time's running out, and I'm supposed to be in a trans-portal, linking with a hundred Tels."

"Maybe the key to getting you into that portal is these kids." Bixx grabbed Kortel's arm. "Come on."

As they walked up the closest aisle, Bixx saw that Kortel was right. Each child's eyes were closed, and all of them were sitting in the lotus position.

"They don't seem to notice us," Kortel whispered.

"Or are choosing not to," Bixx replied.

"Is it me, or did the room get larger?"

Bixx studied the space. "I think it did."

"So how many beds are there?"

"When I was here, this room could hold up to 200, but I can't tell now."

They turned down the next aisle, and Bixx took in the faces of the children. There was a mixture of races and nationalities, and there seemed to be no pattern to their positioning in the room. They were dressed like they had just walked in off the street, and a small medpad hung at the foot of each bed. Kortel stopped and lifted one off its hook. The child, a slight Indian girl with long black hair and delicate features, didn't stir.

"Who is she?" Bixx asked.

"I can't pronounce her name. Tanvi-something. It says she's from New Delhi." He replaced the medpad, and they continued walking.

Halfway up the third aisle, Kortel pointed. "Look, an empty bed!"

They rushed over, and Kortel removed the medpad from the footboard.

"Well?" Bixx asked.

Kortel handed the medpad to Bixx and walked away.

She read the name. *Kortel, Jonathan.*

"What does this mean?" she asked.

"How would I know?" He faced her. "You created this, right?"

"Not this. I'm not sure what's going on."

Kortel came back and took the medpad from her. He scanned its files and shook his head. "Everything's here. Right down to my blood type and genetic profile." He tossed it on the bed, and immediately its image merged into the folds of the sheets. He stepped back. "What the hell?" He turned to the room. "Hey, kids! Wake up!"

None of the children moved.

"Maybe this *is* the trans-portal," Bixx offered.

"No," Kortel said, his attention focused on the Indian girl. "I know Carter, and this isn't it." He walked around the bed and reached for the girl's shoulder.

"Don't!" Bixx said.

He stopped in mid-reach. "Why?"

"Because."

Kortel rolled his eyes and continued.

"NO!" Bixx yelled. A distortion exploded in front of the girl, sending Kortel flying backward down the aisle. He landed on his back and slid to rest against the leg of a bed.

"See," he called out. "I said you were special."

Bixx couldn't believe what she had done. "I'm so sorry. I didn't mean to do that."

Kortel got to his feet and dusted himself off. He approached, but kept his distance. "I guess I'll have to be more careful around you. How did you do that, anyway?"

I...I don't know exactly. I just do it."

"You just *do* it?"

Bixx nodded.

Kortel raised an eyebrow. "Let's find your bed."

"It's over there, in the last row. I woke up in it...before McCarris appeared."

Kortel's attention lingered where Bixx was pointing.

"What are you thinking?" she asked.

"I've got to connect before it's too late."

"How?"

"I'm not sure. But if I had to guess, I'd say this bed is the key."

"Don't climb on until I get to mine." Bixx turned and sprinted toward her bed. The thought of jacking with the greatest of her kind was, well, unbelievable. It was a Net junkie's wet dream, and Bixx almost fell as she scrambled toward her bed.

"You need to concentrate on getting better."

"Do I look like I feel bad?" Bixx said, sliding past her bed.

"What do you think happened to McCarris's residual data?" Kortel's figure was barely visible in the darkness. Bixx could only make out his silhouette. He had climbed onto his bed and was looking back at her.

"I don't know," she said, crawling over the footboard. The bed was now made; the sheets felt cool and crisp against her hands.

"Did he say anything before he crashed?"

Bixx glanced at the two children on either side of her and crossed her legs to match theirs. The image of McCarris – his face flushed with shock, Trumble's name on his lips – flashed across her mind.

"He used Trumble's name," she said, hoping this wouldn't stop Kortel from jacking.

The silence was crushing.

"Great," Kortel said.

KORTEL assumed the lotus position. He drew a deep breath and let his exhale linger. Surprisingly, he didn't feel nervous. In fact, he didn't feel anything. He had been through so much lately that this seemed a fitting end to a very weird ride. And if they did pull this off, he'd march straight back to Chicago and reconnect with Tamara. He checked his position relative to the boy next to him. The boy's legs were in full lotus, but Kortel's left foot was still tucked under his right knee. Ever since a biobike accident with a girl from Skokie, he had lost a lot of his flexibility.

"Screw it," he said under his breath.

He surveyed the room and wondered if this would work. Even if he did connect with the portal, what if Carter was wrong? What if he couldn't figure out what to do? What had Bixx told him, to listen with his heart?

He took another breath and closed his eyes.

Nothing.

"Hey, Bixx," he said, turning. "Is it taking–"

The shift hit him with such force that he thought his organs would explode through his skin. It took all of his will not to scream. The orphanage scenario began degrading, though not like the usual app flux. This was bizarre – similar to what he thought Riders experienced when they peaked on Jack. Tarris had tried to explain it once but had never found the words.

All the detail generated from the orphanage's matrix melted into itself, leaving the digi-frame exposed. And for a brief, astonishing second, Kortel saw the skeleton of the military program. In its raw form, it was an undulating pillar of crystalline black energy. It shuddered through Kortel's construct, and he fought the reflex to vomit. His visual range narrowed into a brilliant circle of white, and suddenly he was being transported through the chaos of the Net, falling through an endless black void, his arms and legs splayed. He landed on his stomach, and his face dug into something warm and gritty. The sound of waves crashing against a beach echoed at the edge of his awareness. He couldn't open his eyes.

"It's about damn time!" he heard. The voice was faint from a distance and sounded familiar.

Kortel coughed and spit and felt a thin layer of sand clinging to his face. He struggled to his hands and knees, and spit again. The rays of a high sun were burning the back of his neck, and there was a faint smell of bougainvillea and dead fish. A strong breeze tugged at the collar of his jacket, and he heard the sound of feet pounding against wet sand.

"Where have you been?"

"Carter?" Kortel asked, tasting bits of sand under his tongue. He opened his eyes to the sting of sunshine and watched Shoalburg's shadow grow around him.

"Get up; we're at the critical point."

Shoalburg's hands were at Kortel's shoulders, and then he was standing, wobbly, on a brilliant white beach. To his right was a row of people, 50 probably, dressed like they had been yanked out of their everyday lives and dropped into paradise. To his left was the same. He thought he saw the guy from Johannesburg.

"What the hell is going on?" he asked, brushing the crusted sand from his lapel. "Why the face plant after the shift?"

Shoalburg eyed him sternly. "This is your construct – your portal. It's not like the simulations we ran, but the protocols are the same, and they're set to your neural mapping."

"Then, where are you?"

"I'm in *my* portal."

"And all these people?"

"In theirs."

"But–"

"Jonathan! Richter says the Tsunami cycle is entering its final phase. You have to get connected and synced with the others. Come on."

Shoalburg pulled Kortel into position between an elderly black man and a teen-age Asian girl. The man looked like a mid-level exec, and his suit's pattern shifted as he made room. He took Kortel's hand and laced his fingers in a firm grip. The girl was dressed like she came straight from the mall. She smiled politely from under a hood of black bangs and took his other hand. If Zvara had been successful, Kortel was now holding hands with a hundred of the most powerful Tels on the planet. He watched a wave roll in, its transparent arc catching the sun like green crystal.

Shoalburg stepped in front of Kortel, and his androidian eyes studied him. "Are you ready to play God?" he asked.

"Where am I, Carter?"

"You're in a lab."

"No, where's this beach supposed to be?"

A knowing grin formed at the edges of Shoalburg's mouth. "Turn around, Jonny."

Kortel complied and saw a set of old steps at an opening in the undergrowth. He immediately knew they led to the path that had connected his parents' home to the beach. Something shivered through Kortel, and the businessman squeezed his hand.

"Why here?" Kortel asked, his attention focused on the chipped whitewash of the top step.

"Because…"

Shoalburg's voice had changed, and Kortel sensed a shift in the construct. He turned back to find his father standing in front of him.

"This is *your* safe place, son," his father said. His hand went to Kortel's chin, cupping it with profound care. "Look at you...your mother would be so proud."

Kortel figured that the matrix's core had read his brain's emotional cues and conjured up a reasonably accurate image of his father. Anyway, how the hell would he know what his father really looked like? The last time he had seen his father, Kortel had been a child. He could barely remember his life on Hawaii, much less the details of his father's face. But rather than reassuring Kortel, the sight of his father standing there in his khaki shorts and lab coat made Kortel edgy, nervous. He knew this was an illusion and slapped the hand away.

His father didn't react.

Kortel got in the image's face. "Get the hell out of here!"

The businessman pulled him back.

"Who are you talking to?" Shoalburg called. He was leaning away from the line on Kortel's right, about 20 people down.

Kortel was suddenly confused. He looked into his father's eyes, and something fell away from his heart. Then the image slowly dispersed, and Kortel was staring at the ocean again. The waves were now only half their original strength and lapped the beach in a steady, hypnotic rhythm.

"We're connecting now," he heard Shoalburg yell.

About 50 feet from the beach, Kortel noticed a figure emerging from the surf. It was a man, and as he came closer, Kortel saw that he was dressed in a dapper gray suit, complete with a bowler and an umbrella hanging from his right forearm. It seemed he was walking up a set of sunken stairs, but strangely, he remained perfectly dry. When the identity of the man registered with Kortel, a spike of adrenaline coursed through his body.

"Trumble?" he whispered.

Jeffrey Trumble tipped his hat and kept walking.

Kortel let go of the people and tried to run, but his feet had merged with the sand. He glanced at the businessman, but he had already slipped into phase. The girl looked the same, along with all the others.

Trumble was making his way up the beach. He cavalierly poked the umbrella into the sand with every other step.

"Hello, Jonathan," he said as he approached. This was a younger Trumble, somewhere in his mid-40s. He was trim and proper, with a jaunty step. He removed the bowler.

"What the hell do you want?" Kortel demanded. The wind had picked up, and the collar of his jacket was slapping his cheek.

Trumble casually looked down both sides of the beach, then leveled his gaze at Kortel. The classic British demeanor had been replaced by something darker, more sinister. "Surely you didn't think I would miss your big moment in history," he said.

"I have to connect with the group."

"That can wait."

"You don't understand; the Tsunami–"

"I know all about it. We have a few moments."

"No, we don't!" Kortel sensed a flux in the Hawaii construct and thought he saw the waves jitter.

Trumble eyed him.

"What?" Kortel asked.

"I was just thinking of the first time I met you. Cyril thought of you as a son, you know, but I couldn't get past your arrogance." Trumble looked away. The wind blew his hair across his forehead. "He always wanted a child."

"Jeffrey, look...I can't–"

"Do you miss them much?"

"Who?"

"Your parents."

Kortel hesitated. "Yes, very much."

Trumble's attention focused on something down the beach. "And I miss Cyril...*very* much."

A gust of hot wind blew between them, and Kortel's lapel slapped his cheek again. "So, what now?" he asked and glanced at his feet, or what was left of them.

Trumble returned the bowler to his head, cocked it slightly, and passed his fingers down its brim. He smiled softly and placed his hands on Kortel's shoulders.

"You," he said, with a wink, "get to see your parents again."

The comment didn't hit immediately, but the punch of raw energy to Kortel's chest did. The waves jittered again. He tried to speak, but those parameters seemed to have been altered. Trumble's hands squeezed tighter, and it felt like his fingers were digging to bone.

"You can't," Kortel said, barely finding the strength to get the words out. "The Tsunami!" He tried to grab Trumble, but his arms wouldn't move. Pain surged through his neural system and exploded inside his head. His legs buckled, but he didn't fall. The ocean and beach, even the sky were shifting, or maybe his vision was just collapsing. Trumble's eyes rolled back, and his grip tightened. A new wave of pain crashed through Kortel's body. He screamed.

The sun, whose warmth had comforted just moments before, now burned the flesh from his body.

"Jeffery, please," Kortel managed between gasps. "We have to save–"

The fabric of the idyllic Hawaiian matrix jumped, and Kortel felt himself back in Richter's lab. The horizon morphed into the underside of the interfacer. There was a strange smell in the air, like something burning. He screamed again, and the Hawaiian matrix returned. A pain shot up his right arm; a crushing pressure weighed upon his chest.

I'm dying, he thought as his mind raced through images from his life. Tamara's face flashed, and tears came to his eyes.

Part of Trumble's form had become a hideous collage of fractal swirls that Kortel had studied in his grade school computer class. But these were unbelievably more complex, and he couldn't look at them without feeling like he might fall into their centers.

Out of the corner of his eye, Kortel saw two figures standing at the edge of the surf – a man and a woman – and even though they were far away, he knew they were his parents. They stood motionless, the waves lapping their ankles. The rational side of Kortel knew they weren't real, that they were part of Trumble's deathblow, designed to send him over the edge. But another part of Kortel ached to join them, and he felt himself starting to let go.

Another surge of excruciating energy carved through Kortel's being. He could feel his heart failing. "The hell with it," he murmured.

Then, somewhere off to his left, there came a detached, murderous wail. Although he tried to look, his head wouldn't move. The pitch of the scream rose, and a figure entered the edge of Kortel's vision.

Bixx was charging up the beach.

She slammed into Trumble and drove her hands into the center of the largest swirl. Trumble didn't acknowledge her at first, but when she yelled something in Russian, his patterns coalesced back into the 40-something man. His eyes rolled forward and locked onto Bixx.

"Die, you fucker!" she screamed, and she jumped and wrapped her legs around Trumble's waist.

A look of astonishment came over Trumble, and Kortel felt his heart begin beating again.

THE energy coming from Trumble's avatar was beyond anything Bixx had ever experienced. She had sensed it before he had emerged from the ocean and didn't understand why no one had come to Kortel's defense. As they struggled, the fabric of her construct began to weaken.

Trumble removed one of his hands from Kortel and wrapped it around her neck. Bixx thought they had lost Kortel, but this move seemed to bring him back.

"You are very foolish," Trumble said, struggling to get the words out.

Bixx ignored him and tried to open her mind. If she could tap his core, she might be able to disrupt his feed and give Kortel an opening to link with the others. She channeled her energy toward Trumble's heart and squeezed his throat with all of her will.

Trumble's image wavered. "It won't work," he managed.

A tremendous force lacerated Bixx's construct. The duality she had previously felt returned. She could feel herself in the med station. Hands were holding her down, and a distant voice told her to remain calm. She sensed her eyes opening, and the ceiling of the med station appeared through the Hawaiian matrix. An unbearable pain coursed through her.

Shoalburg, she heard. It was Richter, cutting through the chaos of the Net. *What's happening? Why isn't Jonathan connected?*

I can't tell, Shoalburg replied. *Something–*

Static replaced the voices. A flash of ball lightning exploded in Bixx's vision, and she was back on the beach.

It's starting, Richter said. More static.

Kortel had his hands at Trumble's throat.

Trumble let go of Kortel and placed his other hand against Bixx's chest. Hot pain surged through her body. She could see Trumble's matrix in its raw form. It was like viewing all of his life at once, and the sight of it was almost overwhelming.

My God, she heard Richter say. *It's bigger than we thought.*

Bixx summoned all of her strength and unleashed it on Trumble. Her scream brought Kortel's attention around.

Trumble's image blurred.

"Let go and connect!" she yelled at Kortel.

He hesitated.

"Do it. *Now*!"

Kortel released Trumble and grabbed the hands of the businessman and girl.

Trumble watched him, then threw his attention at Bixx. His eyes filled with rage.

Bixx focused all of her power at the core of his construct and imagined it exploding. *"Paashol v'chorte!"* she yelled.

Trumble cried out and splintered into a million spiraling fragments of pixilated color. Another flash, and his form blew apart.

Bixx fell. Her elbow caught the brunt of it, but her face plowed into the sand. A gull squawked high above her. She tried to raise her head, but her construct was damaged. Her physical senses were off; the sand felt more like syrup without the sweet smell. A gust of wind passed over her back, and she tasted mint on her tongue. A deep ache throbbed through her body.

"Jonathan?"

Another gull squawked.

Bixx forced her head to turn. She tried to look at Kortel, but the sun was blinding.

"Jonathan?!"

The wind blew, and the minty taste returned.

Bixx struggled to her feet and searched the beach, but the people – and Kortel – were gone.

"Where are you?!" she yelled.

An odd shadow caught her attention, and she forced herself to look up.

"Oh my God," Bixx said. The line of people hovered hand in hand 30 feet above the beach. Kortel was floating another 20 feet or so above them. His arms were spread, and he was looking to the sky. Bixx thought of the Tsunami.

Suddenly, a flash of light obliterated everything, which reminded Bixx of the history vids that described what people saw at the detonation of an atomic bomb. A silent force slammed her to the sand.

It seemed like an eternity before Bixx's eyes would focus.... When she could, she saw bands of threatening clouds moving in slow time-lapse across the sky, and the wind whipping the palms and forming little tornadoes along the beach. She tried to wipe her face to no avail; the wind kept pelting her with gusts of fine sand.

"Jonathan?" she called out, shielding her eyes.

The people were still floating, but Kortel was gone. Their forms, glowing bright against the darkening sky, rippled for a moment before they dispersed into the wind. She heard a moan. Kortel was sprawled on the beach about 60 feet away. A rumble of distant thunder echoed off the ocean.

Panic cut through Bixx's pain as she ran to his side. "Oh, God, no," she said, dropping to her knees.

Kortel was on his back. His eyes were searching the sky. He looked desperate, like he had lost something he couldn't find among the clouds. There was another clap of thunder.

Bixx slipped her hand under Kortel's neck and gently raised his head. His eyes rolled, then focused, but he didn't seem to recognize her. His form wavered, and his digital framework showed beneath his skin. Bixx knew something was terribly wrong, but she didn't know what to do. Drops of rain began pelting the sand around them.

"Jonathan," she said. "I think your core is degrading. You have to disconnect now, before it's too late."

Kortel coughed, and his eyes went to Bixx. He smiled. "Hey," he said, his voice static and hoarse, "did we stop it?"

Bixx didn't know how to answer. Since their forms were still intact, she figured they must have stopped the Tsunami. Then again, they could be residual data themselves. "Yes," she said after some hesitation, "we did." The rain began to fall harder.

He nodded and coughed. His eyes went to the sky and began searching again.

Bixx gently brushed the sand from his forehead. Kortel took her hand. Another rumble of thunder came off the ocean.

"I'm going to miss that sound," he whispered, and his form vanished.

31 You believed in me.

THE jump jet smelled of stale air and Australian leather. It banked gracefully through a thin layer of clouds while Bixx studied the sun's reflection on the ocean. From this altitude, it looked like a blanket of diamonds thrown over a narrow stretch of the Pacific. She felt a hand at her arm.

"What are you looking at?" Richter asked. She was leaning on the armrest and peering out the window.

Bixx didn't answer.

"Beautiful, isn't it?"

"What is?" Bixx asked.

Richter leaned in to get a better view, and Bixx caught a hint of her perfume. It was clean and delicate and reminded her of something her mother had once worn.

"The ocean," Richter said, "when sunlight falls on it."

Seven months had passed since the Tsunami. Toffler's documentary had aired two weeks earlier and was still embroiled in a wave of media controversy. Much of the scientific community had dismissed Richter's work as fringe science. They argued that the earth's magnetosphere had been strengthened not by some secret cult of genetic mutants, but by a convergency of natural causes. All that Bixx could grasp was that it had something to do with the earth's core shifting, but the finer details eluded her. There had been a small group of influential academics who had predicted the flare, however, and they hailed Richter's achievement as nothing short of genius. Some media rumors even had Richter in the running for the Gates Prize, but she had laughed those off as being generated by her university's PR machine.

Toffler's promotional blitz had put her on all the big talk shows. She had defended her work as genuine and declared that the Tels would soon become a part of everyday life.

"Hey, Bixx," Tarris said, "where'd you go?"

Bixx pulled her attention from the view and turned to her friends. Zvara was seated in one of the chairs that faced the cabin and was deep in his netpad. Shoalburg was across the aisle from Richter, and Tarris was in the seat next to Zvara. He was facing Bixx and hugging Kortel's urn. Since they had left New Mexico, the only time she had seen him without it had been at the LAX security checkpoint, where he had been forced to turn it over for inspection. That fiasco had delayed their takeoff for more than 20 minutes.

"Everywhere," she replied. "Nowhere."

Tarris nodded and resumed staring out the window. His fingers played with the raised edge of the urn's keypad.

The leadership of the five world Agencies had viewed Toffler's documentary with great trepidation. They had acquiesced to its airing only after Zvara's relentless lobbying. They predicted the world would most likely lump their kind in the same category as aliens and relegate them to the tabloid media. Currently, the world was still reeling from the concept of the Tels, and since the broadcast, Bixx hadn't seen an info show that didn't have some panel discussing their possible existence. Conservative religious leaders claimed the idea was an affront to God, while many scientists believed the concept was ridiculous, reciting the accepted wisdom that the human brain was incapable of altering gravity. On one show, a Sinless Perfectionist almost strangled an MIT professor. Bixx and Rocket had laughed their guts out watching the show's security try and tackle the 400-pound woman. Tarris had even heard of a group in Nebraska that was already worshipping the Tels. They called themselves Kortelians and claimed that they had seen Kortel's image in a field of corn. Bixx had never heard of such a thing, but Rocket assured her that farmers had been seeing things in crops for centuries. Not a few corporations had jumped at the marketing potential. Action figures and virtual games were beginning to enter the Asian marketplace, and a friend of Rocket's had sent him a black net Bixx doll. Bixx had been shocked at the size of its breasts, but Rocket loved it and ordered a dozen. Because of the conspicuous timing, Bixx suspected Toffler had a hand in the merchandising push, but Toffler denied having anything to do with it. She had gone on about "intellectual property" and said her company had unleashed an army of lawyers to shut down any pirating. Sanjiv was pissed that there was no figure in his likeness. Nor was there a Kreet doll, but that had been okay, because he had disappeared after the Tsunami, and nobody really cared what he thought, anyway.

Bixx felt the craft begin to slow and sensed it was descending.

Shoalburg had brought her out of her coma a day after the Tsunami passed. She had asked about Kortel several times, but Shoalburg always dodged the question, saying he had to check on one thing or another. It had been Tarris who finally told her. He had come to her bedside and explained what had happened, or at least, what they knew about it.

Shoalburg's concept had worked. Kortel had channeled the combined grav force of the hundred most powerful Tels through every available satellite and had created a protective field that deflected the flare around the earth. The tech in Kortel's brain, his "soulware," as he called it, had merged with the blue mass that had puzzled Richter and Shoalburg. The combined tech had acted like a conduit for the grav wave. Richter was still processing the data, but Tarris figured the amount of energy must have been enormous. He had choked up when he described how Kortel, at the height of the phase, had burst into flames. It had taken four of Richter's lab techs with extinguishers to put him out. Toffler said she had captured it on vid, but had vacillated whether to keep it in the documentary or not. She finally decided not to air it out of respect for Kortel's memory. Bixx suspected that Zvara might have *persuaded* her into the decision, but she could never get him to admit it. There was also an awful rumor going around that the footage of Kortel dying had made it onto the black net, but Rocket had searched and never found it.

"Mr. Zvara," the pilot said over the intercom, "we'll be at the drop point in 10 minutes."

Zvara looked up from the netpad and glanced out his window. "We must be near the edge of the Hawaiian Zone." There was sadness in his voice, and Bixx thought he had aged considerably over the last seven months.

"We are being allowed only 15 minutes," Zvara said, his thoughts clearly somewhere over the water.

"How did you get permission to come out here?" Richter asked.

"There was a law enacted after the Event that allowed relatives access to certain areas near the Zone for services. I spoke with the department that handles this and convinced them we were as close to family as Jonathan had."

"Would everyone please fasten their seat belts," the pilot announced. "We'll be starting our vertical descent in just a few minutes."

"Tarris," Shoalburg said, "how did it go down with the lawyers?"

When the plane began banking, light angled through the cabin. It passed across Tarris's face.

"Pretty straightforward," he said. "Jonny's AI at his loft in Chicago had his will on file. He donated the bulk of his estate to the Hawaii Victim's Fund. The rest got split up."

The engines roared, and the jet's forward momentum came

to a halt. It started to descend, and Bixx watched the ocean's glittering surface rise beneath them.

"One minute till hover point," the pilot blurted.

"I'm sorry Rocket couldn't make it," Richter said.

Bixx forced a smile. "It's okay. He falls apart at stuff like this."

The truth was that Rocket hadn't gotten past the idea that Zvara had used Bixx. Bixx had defended Zvara, saying he had to do what he thought was best. She figured her life was a small price to pay. Rocket said that was all bullshit, which brought about the worst argument they ever had. But in a way, this trip had been good for Bixx. She was using the time to reflect on the direction she and Rocket were headed. She caught Tarris staring.

"What are you going to do with that?" he asked, pointing to the miniature urn that hung around her neck. It contained a small amount of Kortel's ashes. Bixx had told Zvara she had one for each of her parents and wanted one of Kortel. He hadn't questioned her request.

"I'm working on a special place for it," she said.

Zvara looked up and grinned, and Bixx couldn't remember if she'd ever seen him smile before.

"There'll be a little bump as we level off into our hovering position," the pilot said, his drawl a little more pronounced. "Once we're there, I'll open the door. Remember, we have 15 minutes before the military will scramble some interceptors. And be careful. The winds out here can be tricky."

The jet rocked slightly and came to a halt. The door between Tarris and Bixx hissed, then slid into the roof of the fuselage. The Pacific looked surprising calm as it rolled 20 feet below them. The wind scattered napkins into every corner of the cabin. Bixx could barely hear the jet's engines and was amazed at how they could be muffled so well.

The sound of the ocean filled the cabin, and everyone stared at the opening.

"Tarris?" Zvara gestured at the door. "Please."

Tarris looked mournfully around the cabin, then at the urn. He entered the security code on the panel, and its top clicked. He raised the armrest and slid over in his seat.

The wind had died. The sun was beginning to set. It was a beautiful scene, and Bixx couldn't help but wonder if Kortel was smiling down on them.

Tarris knelt at the opening. "Jonny..." He tried to continue, but started crying. Zvara put a hand at his shoulder.

Richter took one of Bixx's arms.

"You were a brother to me," Tarris said finally. "I'll always love you." He lowered the urn to the edge of the door and tipped it. Kortel's ashes blew under the jet and over the Pacific. Everyone was dabbing at tears except Bixx. She wanted to cry, but the need had been purged back in New Mexico on a small mesa near the compound.

Tarris wiped his eyes with the sleeve of his shirt and returned to his seat. Zvara approached the opening and fell on his hands and knees. He bent over until his forehead touched the floor, and it struck Bixx that she'd never known what religion he was, if any. This looked like ans Islamic ritual, but she wasn't sure. Besides, it didn't matter.

This was how Zvara wanted to pray, and that's what was important. His face was expressionless as he settled back into his seat. Shoalburg angled toward the opening and sank to one knee. He was quiet for a moment before he crossed himself. Zvara motioned for Richter, but she waved him off with a tearful smile.

"Three minutes to liftoff," the pilot announced.

"Bixx," Zvara said. "It is your turn."

Bixx unbuckled her seatbelt and went to her knees in front of the opening. A storm was building beyond the horizon, and brilliant rays of orange and pale purple arched through the clouds. Her thoughts went to what Kortel had said to her in the virt world of the orphanage. He had told her she was special, that she had a gift.

"You believed in me," she whispered to the ocean.

* * *

The hum of the maglev deepened, and Bixx looked up from her netpad.

"Next stop, LaSalle Street Station," a soft female voice announced. "Please stand clear of the sliding doors."

Bixx resumed reading about the mayoral race in the local press. She didn't care much for politics, and coming from Russia, had learned that politics was more about power than about helping the people. The article detailed the pros and cons of the challenger. It seemed she was a descendant of a famous mayor named Daley. Usually, Bixx would have clicked to the sports section, but this woman had vowed to fight organized crime, and any God-fearing Russian had to give it up for a woman who would go against the Mafia.

"Welcome to the LaSalle Street Station. Thank you for using the Chicago Transit Authority."

The maglev slowed to a stop, and the doors slid open. It was late in the afternoon, and Bixx followed the stream of commuters who made their way to the exits. She stepped onto the platform and waded into a current of business types who, according to her Chicago Guide, descended into this nine-block stretch of LaSalle every evening to decompress. She had read on the plane that this area had become home to the elite of the city's art crowd. Trendy galleries, haute cafes and couturier boutiques lined the crowded street. The guide's GPS indicated that the Pudder Gallery was two blocks north, on the left side. Bixx's coat had already sensed the cold winter wind, and its collar and cuffs had tightened to the point of pain. She was usually okay with apparel that thought for itself, but this rental seemed to have a mind of its own.

"Relax," she instructed. "Ten percent of current pressure."

The collar gave slightly, but the cuffs remained too tight. Her fingers tingled.

"Loosen the sleeves, or you're going in the trash."

The coat's waistband tightened around Bixx's hips.

"Pizdets!" she exclaimed, and pressed the emergency off button. The coat relaxed, and Bixx began feeling her fingers again.

She made her way up the street, stopping only to check out a pair of boots she knew she couldn't afford and to buy a

Hydro Bite, which, depending how hard you shook it, could be drank or eaten. Bixx liked to eat them, and as she waited for the vending kiosk to prep her Bite, dozens of adverts demanded she buy everything from a space station condo to diapers that would eat a baby's waste. Two of the verts got into a fight about which had grabbed Bixx's attention first, when suddenly the BioDiaper advert morphed into the face of Jonathan Kortel. The image was so bizarre that Bixx didn't register it at first. She almost dropped the Bite when Kortel's smiling image said, "thank you," and called her by name.

That's impossible, she thought. She had seen Kortel's construct degrade with her own eyes, and there was no way that any part of his personality matrix could have survived. Yet...his image lingered.

"Hey, lady," a man said behind her. "Some of us want to eat in this century!"

"Back off, asshole!" Bixx said, turning into the face of a middle-aged corporate suit.

The guy stepped back, clearly concerned by the crazy bitch's attitude.

The BioDiaper advert had returned, and Bixx took her receipt. She slowly backed away from the kiosk, wondering.

"Are you okay?" the suit asked.

"Yeah," Bixx said, trying to wrap her head around what she had just seen.

"Damn Riders," the suit muttered as he slid his chip-card into the kiosk.

While Bixx walked away, she ran through Kortel's final moments on the beach. After two blocks, she finally shrugged the apparition off to exhaustion. After all, her flight had been in a holding pattern for over an hour, and the cab to the hotel had been a ride from hell.

It was 4:45, and the guide said the Pudder Gallery would close at 5. Bixx crossed the street, barely dodging a CitiCab that had an unusual amount of urban art attached to it.

The gallery's window had been converted into some kind of art installation. It looked like an enormous shadow box, and a crowd huddled in front it. Bixx caught the side of a woman's naked figure inside the box as she hurried through the building's weapons detector.

The interior of the gallery looked almost exactly like it had when she had been merged with McCarris. The sight of it was unsettling, and she stood for a moment remembering. The painting McCarris had commented on remained hanging on a far wall, which sent a chill through her.

"May I help you?"

Bixx turned and found herself face to face with Tamara Connor.

"Oh," she said.

Tamara smiled. "I'm sorry, did I startle you?"

"No, I just...never mind."

"Is it still cold outside?"

"Ah, yes...it is."

"Well then, we'll be closing in 10 minutes. If you want

to look at the work, take your time. I'll be here for another half hour, at least. If you need anything, my name is Nicole."

She offered her hand, and Bixx shook it. Tamara was taller than Bixx expected and more attractive. She had looked pretty through McCarris's eyes, but in person, there was an innocence that hadn't translated. And her eyes were so blue they could have come from one of the mannequins in the shoe boutique four blocks back on LaSalle.

"Thanks," Bixx said, not really knowing how she would proceed.

Tamara smiled and disappeared behind a desk at the back of the gallery.

Bixx wandered the space and took in the various pieces. She rounded a large iron column and came upon a triptych of small paintings. They were hung in an alcove with a single spot illuminating each canvas. In the center of each painting was an amorphous figure depicted in aggressive strokes of dark colors. The figure looked like a man and seemed to be turning, so that by the third painting he was looking at the viewer. Bixx figured these were the ones Tarris had told her about. She had discussed her trip with him, sort of fishing for his approval. He had been unusually polite, saying that if this was what she needed to do, who was he to stop her? She stood silently in front of the third painting, captivated by its raw emotion.

After 30 minutes, Bixx was the only person left. She did a quick breathing exercise and approached Tamara's desk.

"Excuse me," she said.

Tamara looked up, and those blue eyes searched Bixx.

"I..." She hesitated.

Tamara's expression hardened slightly.

"I have to confess," Bixx said, her heart racing. "I'm not here for the work. I mean, it's pretty and all, but I don't know anything about art."

"You don't need to know much about art to enjoy it," Tamara responded.

"I know." Bixx glanced at the front door.

"Is there something wrong?"

Bixx caught herself trembling. "Look, I came to tell you something."

Tamara's eyes widened, and she nervously folded her computer and tucked it between two art history vid pads standing on her desk. One of them started to topple. "If you're from Family Services," she said, catching the pad, "you'll have to speak with my lawyer."

"Oh no!" Bixx said. "It's nothing like that."

Tamara relaxed and leaned back in her chair. "Who are you?"

"My friends call me Bixx."

"Really. Am I a friend?"

This struck Bixx as odd. She could feel the leftover emotion from Kortel's funeral rising. "Yeah," she replied, her voice cracking, "you could say that."

"Are you okay?"

Bixx nodded. "Could I sit down?"

Tamara motioned to one of the chairs in front of her desk.

Bixx sat and glanced over her shoulder at the triptych. "I've come here to tell you about the man in the paintings. The ones over there."

Tamara's eyes went to the triptych, and Bixx could tell she'd struck a nerve. "Really?" she said, folding her arms. "Tell me what you know."

"You're the artist, and you painted them from your dreams."

Tamara slowly unfolded her arms.

"Don't freak out," Bixx said.

"I'm not," Tamara said. "Quite the contrary; tell me more."

"You love the man in the paintings, but you don't know why, right? It's like you've been together before, but you have no memory of that time."

Tamara's eyes darted between the paintings and Bixx. Her face went pale.

"It all feels real, like you lived it once?"

Tamara cautiously nodded, her mouth open.

"Do the dreams happen every night, like a loop stuck in your head?"

"Yes," Tamara said, just above a whisper. "Almost every night. My therapist says it's my repressed anger toward my father."

Bixx shook her head. "But you don't believe that, do you, Tamara?"

"How do you know my real name?"

"I know a lot about you." Bixx twisted in the chair and pointed at the triptych. "Because I knew that man once. And he knew you."

Tamara's lower lip quivered as she stared at the paintings. Her eyes went to Bixx. "You said 'knew' him, past tense."

"Yeah," Bixx said, her emotions rising. "He died...several months ago." She started playing with the urn that hung from her neck.

Tamara's attention went to it. "That's an interesting piece."

Bixx reached back and unclasped the necklace. She held the urn for a second before placing it in the middle of the desk. "I lost my parents when I was a kid. I keep some of their ashes in something like this." Bixx touched the barrel-shaped pendant. "I think you should have this particular one."

Tamara stared at the urn and dabbed at the corners of her eyes. "Why am I crying?" she asked. "I didn't even know him."

"Actually," Bixx said, "you did."

Tamara picked up the urn and cupped it reverently in her hands. "What was his name?"

"Jonathan Kortel."

Her face was blank at first, but it quickly changed into a look of shocked recognition. "Oh my God, not the man from that documentary?"

Bixx nodded.

"He lived here, in Chicago. His restaurant is just a few blocks from the..."

Tamara looked at the paintings again, and Bixx could tell she was putting the pieces together. "Are you saying I'm the blonde woman?... The one they talked about?"

Bixx gave a faint smile.

Tamara shook her head. "I watched it, but I didn't believe it. I thought it was one of those shows that looks real, but isn't." Tamara glanced at Bixx warily. "And you're one of those...?"

"We're called Tels," Bixx said. "And yes, you're the one they called 'His Love.' They didn't use your name in the documentary because it would have made things hard for you."

Bixx couldn't read Tamara's expression. Either she was in shock or couldn't grasp the seriousness of her situation. "Listen," she said, "eventually some reporter is going to figure it all out and come looking for you. It's better that you hear the truth from someone you can trust and not from a stupid newscast."

"Why don't I remember any of it? I remember that time period, but not *him*."

"Well, you do…in a way. Your dreams are fragments of the memories. It's kind of hard to explain."

Tamara turned the urn over in her hands, and Bixx saw a shift in her. A look of acceptance had settled behind her eyes, and their crystalline blue seemed brighter.

"Tell me about him," she said. "Tell me everything you can remember."

A warm feeling of peace moved through Bixx. "Sure, I'd love to."

ACKNOWLEDGEMENTS

I would like to thank the following for their assistance, inspiration and patience: Bryan Pudder, Tim Evans, Patrick Florer, Lisa Glasgow, Brian Moreland, Pat O'Connell, Rick Silvestre and Max Wright...you all were there for me when I needed you.

For the Russian transcriptions: Edward Topal and his book *Dermo*, and *www.insultmonger.com* (for expert translations of Russian cursing and its many levels). For future trends in technology: *www.socialtechnologies.com* and its wealth of future forecasts and models of global trends. And to NASA News and the Langley Research Center Web site for its white papers on the future of commercial aviation.

Special thanks to my editor and friend, Jay Johnson, for his faith in the *Tels* series.

And to Trish, with love.

Dallas, 2006

ABOUT THE AUTHOR

Born and raised outside of Chicago, Illinois, this is Mr. Black's third work of science fiction. Today, he lives and works in Dallas, Texas, where he manages his own graphic design firm and feeds his passion for tennis. He is currently working on a new book of near-future fiction.

SECOND PLACE ForeWord Magazine's Book of the Year
FINALIST for Science Fiction Independent Publishers Book Awards.

"It's a HIGHLY ORIGINAL novel set in the near future and IT MOVES AT LIGHTNING SPEED....The ENSUING ACTION IS BIZARRE enough to read like something straight out of *The X-Files.*" ~ *Steve Powers, Dallas Morning News*

soulware

PAUL BLACK

BOOK TWO IN THE TELS TRILOGY

THE WORLD IS NOT WHAT IT SEEMS. For Jonathan Kortel, his life has changed forever. He has a telekinetic gift that is faster than light, and he's now part of a secret new group of humans. They're called the Tels, and they live in the shadows of a future where the Biolution and its flood of technology have changed all the rules.

Having been thrust into a world he cannot control, Jonathan begins a quest to uncover what's really going on in the Tel world. Because he soon realizes that he's not only their star pupil; he's their most important experiment.

Here continues the journey of Jonathan Kortel, author Paul Black's fascinating future character, introduced in his award-winning 2003 novel *The Tels. Soulware* picks up where *The Tels* left off, following Jonathan as he discovers his true destiny. Deeply intriguing and powerfully suspenseful, Paul Black has created a vision of the future that is haunting and disturbingly real.

Available at all online retailers including **Amazon.com** and **BN.com**.